Gwendolyn & Eddie

MICHAEL O.L. SEABAUGH

VIRGINIA BEACH
CAPE CHARLES

who has landed in the middle of their marriage. Seabaugh masterfully describes the charm of Southern horse country culture while slowly unveiling the dangerous faults that lurk beneath it."

—MARIANNE PARTRIDGE-POETT, editor-in-chief of the *Santa Barbara Independent*, first female editor-in-chief of the *Village Voice*

"*Gwendolyn & Eddie* will make you laugh and deeply feel. Michael Seabaugh is a master of balancing levity and seriousness. Through complex characters, readers get a glimpse into what it's like to be caged—and what it's like to find your wildness. A beautiful book that unpacks the 'conventional' marriage of the times, the defiance of those conventions, and the struggle to live a life you deserve. Seabaugh made this reader believe men really can understand women—and maybe even monkeys. A captivating, enthralling, and provocative work."

—MIRANDA FAYE DILLON, award-winning author of *The Unshatterables*

"In this richly detailed novel, for most of her life a woman remains loyal to a monkey she didn't want and a husband she shouldn't have chosen. Among a reader's many rewards will be learning to which of them she extends a final courtesy."

—LEONARD H. ORR, author of *Entitled*

"As an author, Seabaugh's skill with the pen radiates across every chapter, making *Gwendolyn & Eddie* a must-read for 2025. With a beautiful cover to match, there is little to find fault with when it comes to this charming story of a woman and an excitable monkey. It is a novel packed full of bold and colorful personalities, and the unexpected antics that come with it."

—*AEB REVIEWS*

Gwendolyn & Eddie
by Michael O.L. Seabaugh

© Copyright 2025 Michael O.L. Seabaugh

ISBN 979-8-88824-521-7

All rights reserved. No part of this publication may be reproduced, stored in a retrieval system, or transmitted in any form or by any means—electronic, mechanical, photocopy, recording, or any other—except for brief quotations in printed reviews, without the prior written permission of the author.

This is a work of fiction. All the characters in this book are fictitious, and any resemblance to actual persons, living or dead, is purely coincidental. The names, incidents, dialogue, and opinions expressed are products of the author's imagination and are not to be construed as real.

Published by

◀ köehlerbooks™

3705 Shore Drive
Virginia Beach, VA 23455
800-435-4811
www.koehlerbooks.com

For Patricia

1957

1

Bless Your Heart

Gwendolyn breathed in the familiar earthy aroma of the Mississippi River that mingled bracingly with the bright bergamot scent of her Earl Grey tea. She cherished these quiet moments on her rooftop landing, which offered a splendid view of the river's graceful curve to the south. Known as a widow's walk, this picturesque perch, encircled by a wrought-iron railing, added a special charm to her Edwardian wedding cake of a house. It was predawn in June, the air still cool and gentle before the oppressive humidity of the day would descend, demanding her attention to the cherished labors of mothering and wifery. She smiled at the whimsical thought that she might resemble the Victorian wives who once stood here, pacing with worry and anticipation for their riverboat captain husbands' return. It was a peculiar notion, considering her husband was a doctor, not a riverboat captain, and very much alive—perhaps a little too alive at times. Her life, she reminded herself, was a dream come true.

The shrill ring of the phone downstairs shattered her reverie. Glancing at her Cartier Tank watch—a wedding anniversary gift that she never took off—she noted that it was almost 5 a.m. This could only mean one thing, she thought as she hurried down to the kitchen. Reaching for the phone, she tried to calm her breathing.

She was, after all, not one of those nineteenth century aspiring widows who had once paced her rooftop.

"Good morning. Dr. Bollinger's residence."

"Isn't this your house, too?" came a familiar voice from the other end.

"Yes, Dixie. What has he done this time?"

"What are you talking about, darlin'? I'm calling to see if you can fill in as a fourth for bridge next week."

"At five in the morning?"

Dixie roared her famously loud and quasi-endearing laugh, a cross between a foghorn and a wild animal's mating call. "Come on, Gwennie. Of course, it's about Paul Stanley." She said his name as everyone did, like it was one word: *Paulstanley*.

Gwendolyn approached with caution. "Yes?"

"As I am sure you know, he was here for poker night, or as I call it, the Small Dick Society."

"I'm well aware you call it that. What *has* he done?"

"Well, there is good news and there is bad news. Which do you want first?"

"Dixie, it's now five-o-five in the morning. I really don't care."

Another booming, semidisturbing laugh erupted that made Gwendolyn wonder if Dixie had been up all night drinking with the men. As soon as the question occurred to her, she dismissed it for the silly thought it was. Of course, Dixie had been.

"Okay, Gwennie, well enough. I don't sleep anymore as a matter of principle, but I suppose that's unique to me. So, here goes. The good news is your husband is drunk, but he's being driven home. Well, I suppose that qualifies as mixed news."

"Dixie, please, what is the bad news?"

"He's bringing home a drunk monkey."

Silence. Then, "Go on."

"He won him in the poker game from Busby, who got him, you will remember, as a pet for our Betty, who, as you also know, is off to college. She never really took to him, and now he's yours. One less thing for me to worry about."

Gwendolyn expelled a big sigh. "Well, at least tell me his name."

"We just called him Monkey. Name him what you like."

Dixie was married to Paul Stanley's cousin Busby, another one of the many Bollinger doctors. She was one of Gwendolyn's best friends despite the always-startling laugh. Women in Southeast Missouri didn't normally guffaw. But Dixie, as her name suggested, was not from around there, but somewhere more . . . well . . . Deep South. Gwendolyn wouldn't recall much more of the conversation with Dixie, so discombobulated by the news that she was about to acquire a monkey—and just her fate, probably an alcoholic monkey at that.

Paul Stanley arrived home, and a monkey indeed accompanied him on a leash. Gwendolyn, after thirteen years of marriage and well accustomed to dealing with Paul Stanley's follies, had never encountered one quite like this. She opened the back door and found her husband with his eyes at half-mast and with that askew smile she once considered charming, and at certain disarmed moments, still did.

This was not one of them.

The monkey was a scrawny little creature, jumping from one corner of her visual frame to another, screeching in the most disturbing way. All Gwendolyn could do was take the leash from her sheepish husband and let him pass by her and stumble his way up the stairs.

She stood there with a leashed monkey as the summer dawn began its primitive stirrings. Then what ensued was the strangest moment, as if time stood absolutely still.

Eddie the Monkey, and Gwendolyn the Wife, looked into each other's eyes.

Gwendolyn realized she had just named the monkey Eddie, a name with which she had no history. This gave her pause. Then a memory emerged of something Paul Stanley had said to her when he was jokingly replying to her question of why he insisted on shortening her name to the more obscure iteration of *Wendy*: "You name it, you tame it."

Eddie started a frightening cacophony of movement and sound. This monkey dance almost made her smile. This display of animalistic fireworks didn't particularly cow Gwendolyn, who was raising three high-spirited children and one unruly husband. She gave a sharp yank on the leash, as she would a dog in training, and took Eddie down to the unfinished basement. When she let him off the leash, he leaped from one exposed pipe to another, dominating the space as he might have if he had been in a jungle. It occurred to Gwendolyn that he could be trying to intimidate her with this ferocious display of territorial virility, but she dismissed this thought when she realized that he was a monkey, and a drunk one at that. She brought him down a large bowl of clean water, a dog bed, and made a mental note that she would need to do some research later that morning to find out what to feed such a creature.

But for now, she knew one thing for certain: This monkey named Eddie needed to sober up. And she needed to get on with what this day would require of her.

She set about fulfilling her tasks. Three children needed rousing, grooming, and feeding. She reminded herself as she encountered their usual grumpy protests that she and Paul Stanley had produced the perfect family. Gilda, ten, Oliver, six, and her baby Franny, five; each unique in their personalities, but all three blessed with good looks and smarts.

As soon as she marshaled the children into their tasks for the morning and answered the inevitable call from the hospital about Dr. Bollinger's whereabouts, she knew she would inevitably have to open the basement door and confront God knows what behind it.

The basement was as still as her heart was not. She took a few steps down the stairs, trying to adjust to the gloom. The eerie quiet unsettled her. What was she expecting? A raging King Kong to come crashing out of the darkness as if in a Hollywood horror movie?

She walked around a corner, and there she saw him. His front paws curled up in front of him like a prayer, his long, sinuous tail wrapped around his body like an embrace. He peered at her sideways, whimpering what seemed to her to be a sad song. Except for her children, Gwendolyn never gave in to moments of sentimentality; it was a human indulgence that she had needed to forsake some time ago. But she couldn't help herself in that moment as she saw the scared little creature in the corner of her basement, so far away from a jungle, no trees to fly through or anything that looked like home. She realized that this little beast was now utterly her responsibility. His very survival was up to her.

The thought could not linger. "I'll be right back," she said as she turned to walk up the stairs to the kitchen. She paused in the doorway as she noticed that Eddie's whimpering had evolved into cooing.

In the kitchen, she panicked. *What does a monkey eat anyway? Bugs? Lettuce? Canned tuna? Are they vegetarians or carnivores?*

She needed to find out. The last thing she wanted on her hands this morning was a monkey with diarrhea. In the living room sat a low bookshelf next to Paul Stanley's reading chair, where resided his prized and much-used set of *Encyclopedia Brittanica*.

What kind of monkey is Eddie? There must be many kinds. She studied the pictures and decided this little mousy fellow, who looked sort of like a monk, his big frantic eyes peering from under what seemed like a monk's hood, was a capuchin. He had to be. They came from Central and South America, and that wasn't so far. *For Pete's sake, Gwendolyn! Eddie didn't migrate here.* She made a mental note to find out from Dixie where he actually came from.

She couldn't find any information about the capuchin diet. She mentally surveyed her latest grocery acquisitions for something that would make sense. *Bananas! Monkeys eat bananas, don't they?* It would have to do for now.

Returning to the kitchen, the first thing she saw was Franny's and Gilda's awe-filled expressions as they stood behind the kitchen table looking at something in front of them. Gwendolyn followed their gaze. It was Eddie. He had somehow escaped the basement and pinched a bottle of scotch from the nearby bar, opened it, and was now lapping up the amber liquid that had spilled all over the kitchen counter.

Gwendolyn surprised herself, and certainly her daughters, as she bolted toward Eddie, commanding, "Get back!"

Eddie lurched away from her and cowered in the corner under a cabinet as Gwendolyn cleaned up the spilled liquor. She fixed him with another don't-mess-with-me-buster look. "You're not going to be a booze hound in this house. No siree."

A split second later, the heretofore awestruck girls became activated. Gilda, blonde, blue eyed, and cool as a junior Grace Kelly, remained still as she dissected this strange addition to her otherwise familiar kitchen. Franny bolted forward in her best "Nurse Fran Fuzzy Wuzzy" manner—her father's affectionate nickname for his big-hearted daughter—intent upon enveloping this darling little creature in her pudgy arms.

Eddie would have nothing of it. With a screech, he fled the oncoming human missile and, to the shock of everyone, leapt onto Gwendolyn's chest. Clinging to its fine advantage, he made little threatening grabs at Franny, who stopped cold with a crestfallen look. She scooted behind Gilda, tears wetting her little face.

Gilda stood her ground. "Mother, who is that monkey and what is he doing here?"

Gwendolyn moved toward the basement door with Eddie in tow. "He's our new pet. A gift from your father."

After making sure Eddie had fresh water and two bananas, Gwendolyn, careful to ensure that the door was closed, returned to deal with her daughters and now Oliver, who had joined them. All three were staring at her as she entered the kitchen.

"Enough of all that. I need to get you fed," she said, bustling past them.

She got their poached eggs together, displayed on buttered toast with the crust cut off, and delivered them to her children where they sat at the kitchen table.

Gilda was first. "Why is that monkey in our house? You still haven't explained this adequately."

Gwendolyn sighed. "Your father has decided we need a monkey, so now you have one," she said. "His name is Eddie."

"He doesn't like us, that's clear," Gilda said.

"Why, honey, of course your father likes you. He loves you. That's why he's giving you a monkey."

"The *monkey*, Mother, *he* doesn't like us. Isn't that obvious to you?"

"Why would you say that?"

Gilda cast a meaningful glance at Franny, who was still whimpering.

Oliver spoke up. "Maybe he just doesn't like Franny."

Franny aroused from her despair. "Where did he come from? How did he get here?"

"We'll have to find out," Gwendolyn said, turning her attention to getting the children out the door and off to Lorimer Elementary School two blocks away. She made sure all buttons were properly engaged and hair pushed back out of their eyes. As they walked down the sidewalk, Gwendolyn watched them from the back porch, flushed with their adorableness.

She stood in her moment of mute apprehension in front of the basement door when Paul Stanley breezed into the kitchen.

"Hon, where's the coffee?"

She turned around and looked at him, not smiling. Quickly, her gaze softened. It amazed her how he could end his evening so coarse and witless and emerge in the light of the next day like that: crisp and smelling of soap, his head of thick auburn hair combed back like some windswept actor in *Photoplay*, smiling at her as if their life had been nothing but an endless walk on a beach.

She releveled her gaze. "Your coffee is in that thermos that you pick up every morning except Sunday, and by the way, you brought home a monkey last night."

He grabbed the thermos in one dashing swoop as he headed for the door. He stopped and turned to face her, his eyes bemused, his mouth turned into a crooked smile. "Really?" He looked down as if he were trying to recall something, then broadening his smile, he said, "Right. Cute little fella." He turned to exit. "Of course, you'll know what to do, Wendy. Good gal."

The screen door slammed shut behind Paul Stanley. She stared at it, arrested by a muddle of feelings. What was she going to do? She called Dixie and asked if she would come over and help her with the monkey. After all, it wasn't a situation that most women she knew had to deal with every day.

Dixie arrived around 4 p.m., dressed as if she were going to a party: a cocktail dress with a full-pleated skirt in cardinal red, a black cummerbund, and low-cut bodice—her signature look. Gwendolyn observed her friend, her best friend really, despite their obvious differences in temperament and looks. She was petite, enhanced by her pixie haircut but offset by her bountiful bosom, proudly hoisted, and by her comparison to Gwendolyn, who stood at a statuesque five-ten.

"What the hell are you waiting for," Dixie bellowed as she rushed past her. "Where're the rum 'n' Cokes and the little tea sandwiches?"

"Isn't that a mixed metaphor?" asked Gwendolyn.

"There is no metaphor intended. Okay, forget the tea cakes. Let's get down to business."

Gwendolyn knew this meant she had to produce something with alcohol in it, preferably genteel and Southern. It was, after all, not yet cocktail hour when brown liquor would be required. She made the drinks—lemonade and chilled vodka—and poured Dixie a large one and herself a polite one.

"Okay, Dixie. I would like to use a curse word here, but I won't. Who the heck is Eddie, and why is he in my basement?"

Dixie snorted. "Eddie? Now that's choice." She was already halfway through her poured drink. "As to your question, that is one you will have to ask your husband. Next question?"

Gwendolyn shifted in her chair. "Come on, Dixie, I need help. Please tell me what I'm supposed to do with this—"

"Monkey?"

"Yes, Eddie, the monkey, of course."

Dixie nodded toward the spiked pitcher of lemonade. Gwendolyn sighed as she reached for it to refill Dixie's glass. She had learned to squelch her judgments about the people in her life who "liked to drink."

"Well," Dixie said, settling into her chair now with her second libation firmly in hand, "Eddie doesn't like people. I don't know why, but he doesn't."

"That's comforting."

"Oh, don't worry. He does like the one who feeds him. That is, if you aren't afraid of him."

"He doesn't scare me," Gwendolyn said, knowing as the words left her mouth that she sounded tentative.

Dixie fixed her with a knowing look.

"What?" Gwendolyn asked.

"Maybe the little critter has something to teach you."

"Good lord, what could that possibly be?"

Dixie drained her glass and then looked at her friend over the rim. "Who the hell knows? But one thing that strikes me is your perfect looks and comportment are not going to be enough to tame that little fucker."

"You're talking silly."

"I know! He's come into your perfect life to fuck it up."

"What's to be learned from that?"

"Just speculating."

"Well, you can stop wasting your brain. A little monkey is not going to do that thing you said to my life."

"I like your confidence, sister." Dixie held out her glass for a refill. "Any further questions?"

Gwendolyn poured her some more from the pitcher. "How on earth did he become an alcoholic?"

Dixie looked at her with her classic amused smile.

"The monkey, I'm talking about," clarified Gwendolyn.

"How do any of them become lushes? They all like company when they drink, and I suppose Busby was no exception. Actually, I really think he thought it was funny. A drunk monkey can be a lot of fun."

"I wonder if they have an Alcoholics Anonymous for monkeys."

"Ha!" hooted Dixie. "Sometimes you pull off a good one."

Gwendolyn ignored this barbed compliment. "So, where did he come from? Franny wants to know."

"Hell if I know. He showed up at my house the same way he did yours—in the middle of the night, because of something Busby was up to."

"You have no idea?"

"I do, but I prefer not to spend too much time on it as I suspect it has something to do with a whore from 'cross the river." Dixie took a long sip from her drink. Gwendolyn couldn't tell if she was being snarky or simply recognizing her Bollinger husband. Gwendolyn had always secretly felt she had a lot to learn from Dixie, even though she was at least six years younger than her.

"Well, do you know how old he is at least?"

"Hell no. I didn't even know he was a boy monkey until I saw him masturbating."

"No!"

"Yes, Gwendolyn." She leaned in. "And he was staring right at me when he was doing it." Dixie paused then snorted out a laugh.

Gwendolyn tried to relax, hoping that this was just one of Dixie's crude jokes. She stood up and walked over to the basement door, looking at it as she said, "My children will be curious to know where he actually came from."

Dixie, who didn't seem wise at all on the surface, did often come up with some useful suggestions. She counseled her to have her kids write an essay on Eddie's origins. It was a good idea—a trip to the library would reveal more than Dixie could, with her louche ways of accepting odd things.

As she was leaving, Gwendolyn asked if she had any last words. Dixie took her hands in hers and said, "Bless your heart." As she watched Dixie's Thunderbird disappear around the corner, she wondered if Dixie, with her slippery tone, plump with innuendo, had just blessed her or cursed her.

That night, when she was putting the girls to bed in their shared room, she offered Dixie's suggestion. Franny feigned excitement about the project as she turned to her sister and said, "Gilda, you can help me!" As Gwendolyn left the room, she smiled, knowing that Gilda, with her cool eye on all matters, would be the one to do the research and present the results.

Two days later, Gilda presented her mother with the report, neatly bound between two blue pieces of plastic.

"Is this the report you and Franny did on Eddie?" Gwendolyn asked as she prepared dinner, a pea and tuna casserole, which was the Thursday night meal.

"Yes. I presented it at school today," Gilda said.

"Why don't you read it to me while I finish cooking?"

Gilda loved to read aloud, especially things that she had written. She began in her precise and clear style, "Two nights ago, my father brought home a monkey named Eddie. He got him as a gift from Uncle Busby and then gave him to Franny, Oliver, and myself so that we could learn to love and care for him. He is a capuchin monkey, and he looks sort of like we do, only with brown fur all over and a long tail that moves around a lot. Capuchin monkeys come from Central or South America, and they are the smartest of all the monkeys in the forest. They are not from Missouri, so they have to be brought here. I called Uncle Busby and asked him how Eddie got here. He said he didn't know. He got him from someone across the river who owed him money. I thought the debt was for some medical bill, but Aunt Dixie told me it was probably a gambling debt. There is still a mystery about his exact beginning in life. I went to the library and learned about this kind of monkey, and so I think I can guess about what happened and how Eddie came to live with us in Missouri."

She paused and looked around. Franny and Oliver had crept into the kitchen and were listening with rapt attention. Gwendolyn looked at Gilda with a smile and encouraging nod.

Gilda continued, "He was born in a forest in South America and his family was big, with at least twenty brothers and sisters. They all lived in the trees and had fun swinging from one treetop to another. Their father was what is called an alpha male, which means he can do what monkeys do to have babies with any of the lady monkeys in the family. The mother monkeys will also mate with any other men monkeys that they meet, which makes them different from other kinds of monkey girls. Eddie's family was very loyal to each other except for the lady monkeys, who would have sexual relations with other men monkeys."

Gwendolyn turned from the sink. "Where on earth did you learn that phrase?"

"What?"

"Sexual relations?"

"Oh, Aunt Dixie told me all about that. She used a different word, but I think it was a bad word that I didn't understand so when I asked her what that word meant, she said 'sexual relations.'"

"Oh, dear. Please continue, I think."

"Like I said, they were all loyal and would fight together to protect their part of the forest from other monkey families. They are like us because they will eat almost anything, like bugs, rodents, nuts, fruits, birds, even crabs. Actually, in our family we don't eat bugs or rodents, but still Eddie is what's called an omnivore just like we are, which means he could eat dinner with us if he wanted to."

"That's good to know," Gwendolyn said with a scintilla of sarcasm but was relieved at the possibility of feeding the monkey leftovers.

Gilda cut her mother off with an exasperated look then continued, "After Eddie was born, he became very in love with his mother. She would carry him around on her tummy and then, when he got a little older, he would ride around on her back as he learned more about how to be a monkey. When he was about three months old, which is probably older in monkey years than it is in human years, he started to learn how to walk. His mother held on to his tail while he tried to walk on his own. He was very happy with his mother and would have stayed with her for a long time, but a monkey hunter from Texas came to his jungle and grabbed him away from his mother and brought him to Missouri, where he needed to find a new mother."

Gwendolyn turned from her food preparations and stared at her daughter. Gilda looked up from her report. "Now what?" she asked.

"Where did you get that? The part about him being taken from his mother by some Texan?"

"Mrs. Sheets, the librarian, told me this happened to him because it happens to all these monkeys. She said this causes them lots of problems because they have damaged feelings about it."

Gwendolyn turned back to stirring the instant mashed potatoes. "Cheryl Sheets has some very liberal ideas."

"I have more, Mother."

"I can't wait," Gwendolyn said under her breath.

Gilda resumed her reporting. "Eddie was very cute as a baby, but he might not grow up to be so cute, especially since he was taken away from his mother he loved. He will find a new mother, who will probably be my mother, but he probably won't like anyone else. That's because he is still mad about being taken from his real mother. He can't talk like we do, but he will let us know about his feelings by being very messy, destroying things we have, throwing his doo-doo at us, and even giving us bad diseases like rabies and hepatitis. I saw Eddie open a bottle of my father's whiskey and that is because he is very smart, like all capuchin monkeys, and he likes to protect his territory by peeing on it. If we take good care of him, he will live to be fifty years old."

Gwendolyn realized she was holding her stirring spoon aloft as Gilda finished her report. She looked at her daughter, who was staring back at her with her familiar look of resolute confidence.

"That was really nice, dear," Gwendolyn said, "but don't you think you emphasized the negative just a bit?"

"I got an A plus from Mrs. Estes," Gilda answered, defiant.

Gwendolyn realized her mouth was tense as she pulled the pea and tuna casserole out of the oven and dished it along with the mashed potatoes on plates and set them on the kitchen table.

She consciously relaxed her mouth as she said, "Let's eat. Your father is still at the hospital."

"What a shock," Gilda said.

Gwendolyn gave Gilda her no-nonsense look. They all sat down without any further fuss.

They ate in silence until Oliver erupted with a protest. "Mother! This doesn't taste like your casserole!"

Both sisters endorsed this assessment by nodding in unison. Gwendolyn, who had been eating in a distracted state, realized they were right. Investigating with her spoon, she discovered that instead of peas there were briny canned olives in the dish. She went over to the trash can and fished out the can she thought had been peas but clearly wasn't. It had no label. She rushed down to the basement, followed by her children, and examined her well-stocked pantry, where she kept her canned goods arranged in alphabetical order. Not only were they in disarray, but most of their labels were ripped off. She was not amused, but her kids broke into giggles, soon joined by Eddie, who had emerged from elsewhere in the basement and added his distinctive chirping that sounded like it could be laughing,

"Come on, Mother," Oliver said, "it's not so bad. Now, every night will be like mystery dinner."

Gwendolyn joined them in laughter.

That night, as she went through her ritual of removing makeup and moisturizing her arms and legs, she realized that the report, which she assumed was accurate given Gilda's thoroughness, still disturbed her. She now knew that she had a monkey on her hands that most likely came from a South American jungle, had probably been traumatized from being removed too soon from his mother and therefore had emotional problems, and probably wasn't happy about being a long way from home. The worst thought of all: He would no doubt be a very difficult creature to deal with, and she would have to do so until she was a very old woman.

She looked up from these self-ministrations to the mirror and wondered, at another future point, would she look back at this day—the day when Paul Stanley appeared at their back door and handed her the leash of a drunken monkey—and realize that this was when it all began to change?

She returned to rubbing olive oil on her legs. She was not at all happy about the slinging doo-doo part either.

2

Animal Training

Gwendolyn hired her handyman to build a substantial cage on the back of the garage, complete with a miniature forest of branches for Eddie to swing upon. She equipped it with an opening into a small compartment inside the garage where he could sleep in comfort. All this effort was made, not because she had acquired any great affection for Eddie, but because of the obligation that came with knowing that he was a helpless animal and needed to be cared for. Despite her skepticism, Paul Stanley had sold Eddie to her by appealing to the great educational opportunities that caring for a wild animal could provide for their children. He failed to articulate his assumption that Gwendolyn would be doing that caretaking.

She wasn't so sure that these nature lessons needed to be provided by this unpredictable wild animal. Whenever the children tried to pick him up or even pet him on his head, Eddie would immediately shrink back, looking at first like a shy little boy. This briefly displayed cuteness would disarm his new human friends, who would then try to get friendlier with him. Inevitably, Eddie would bare his teeth, forming a rictus of terror, and lunge at his tormentors. It took only one time like this before Gilda decided that she would have nothing further to do with the monkey. Oliver, who at six was still innocent to the dangers of the world, had more success with Eddie, who let him wool him around like a favorite toy. This went on for a while, then one day Oliver showed fear, shrinking back with a shriek when Eddie pinched him hard. That was it for their playful relationship. Eddie treated Oliver now as an adversary, just like Gilda. That left Franny, still trying to snuggle the monkey like one of her stuffed animals. She couldn't believe Eddie meant anything untoward by his actions—he was just a scared little monkey boy who needed her love. She endured several scratches and a bruise because of this conviction.

One mild spring night, Gwendolyn was preparing the family's evening meal in her usual organized fashion when Paul Stanley arrived home from the barn wearing soiled jodhpurs and dusty riding boots. The familiar smell of horse sweat mixed with bourbon wafted behind him through the back door. He was usually immaculate and smelling of Old Spice, but Gwendolyn had to admit, this rank version of Paul Stanley had a certain appeal, one that made her blush under her foundation.

Franny looked up from where she was drawing at the kitchen table. "Daddy, you look like a lion tamer. I'm going to draw a picture of you."

"Be sure and let me see it when you're done, honey," he said as he walked by her to the bar to fix himself a drink.

Franny looked up at him with pleading eyes. "But I don't know how to draw a lion."

He turned around with a glass full of ice clinking in four fingers of bourbon. "Why don't you draw a picture of me and Eddie. You know what we both look like."

"Daddy, the monkey tamer!" She pursed her lips and concentrated her crayon on the paper before her.

Gwendolyn chimed in, "Eddie's a good boy. He's adjusting. Not sure he needs taming."

"Maybe with you, Wendy," Paul Stanley said. "He's an ass—"

Gwendolyn shot him a look.

"He's a mean little bugger to the rest of us and the only reason Eddie lets you touch him is because you feed him."

She retorted with a flirty smile, "Is that the only reason you let me touch you?"

He came over and put his arms around her, which she playfully rejected. "You smell like horse." He kept nuzzling her, which made her smile. "Seriously, Paul Stanley, you should get out of those clothes."

"You tolerate that monkey who stinks like hell." He downed his drink then turned to go upstairs

Gwendolyn went back to stirring the pot of her famous chicken and dumplings, enjoying a secret consideration of Paul Stanley Bollinger. He always reminded her of that old saying "Rode hard and put up wet," just like a character out of a novel by Faulkner or Hemingway. His love of hunting and horses made him somehow a romantic figure to her—so masculine. She smiled to herself recalling the story about when he was hunting from the back of his beloved stallion, a strawberry-roan American Saddlebred named Charlie. A misfiring of his shotgun took out Charlie's left eye. He galloped the horse back to the barn, the eye socket swinging in the wind like a bloody cartoon accident, and, grabbing his doctor's bag, surgically removed the mutilated eyeball and sewed up the eye socket. As gruesome as this story was, it somehow epitomized her husband, as did the one his Aunt Lilly always told at every family reunion about young Paul Stanley. As an already dashing boy of seventeen, she recounted him galloping up to the church in Patton Junction, located in the Bollinger family's crucible, the county that bore their name.

"He was late as usual, bless his heart," Aunt Lilly always said. "We knew he was pleasing his daddy by participating in the choir of Doc Ollie's childhood church. He would tie his horse onto the church door and barrel into the choir loft, smelling mightily of horse sweat. Some of the congregants recoiled, but most of us just shook our heads in recognition, so happy to have him there. When that boy picked up the hymnal and began adding his voice to the chorus, eventually soaring above the rest with his clear tenor, he had no detractors. He sang like he was on a first-name basis with the angels themselves!" At this point, Aunt Lilly would always blush like a schoolgirl, making Gwendolyn realize that this little homespun and oft repeated story pretty much captured Paul Stanley Bollinger. He was a complicated man. Everyone said so.

The smell of Old Spice interrupted her pleasant reverie. She looked up from stirring her chicken and dumplings and saw her husband looking relaxed in a short-sleeved shirt and chinos, but his expression was anything but.

"What that monkey needs is to learn who's boss," he declared, marching past her to the back door.

Gwendolyn gave him a glancing smile. "And you're just the man to do it, right?"

"Damn right. If you can break an American Saddlebred stallion and teach him to slow gait, you can teach a monkey to behave himself."

Gwendolyn began setting the dining table. "I've never understood that term—breaking an animal. It sounds cruel, like breaking his spirit or something."

"You wouldn't understand. Sometimes that's exactly what they need. And what that monkey needs is a bath."

"You're being crazy," Gwendolyn told him. "Eddie will not like getting wet."

"I don't care what he likes. He stinks, and I'm not having a stinking monkey in my house."

It was already obvious to everyone that Paul Stanley was not one of Eddie's favorites. This was in full evidence when he came back into the kitchen with Eddie in tow, dancing frantically on the end of a leash. Paul Stanley, red-faced angry, yanked the leash and growled, "Here now!"

All three children had gathered in the kitchen and stood frozen like frogs captured by a flashlight, eyes wide in amazement of the spectacle before them. Their father was dragging a protesting monkey across the linoleum floor and into the downstairs bathroom.

"Mommy," Franny cried out, "do something, please. Eddie doesn't want a bath!"

"I'm not getting in the middle of that," Gwendolyn said as she turned back to the kitchen sink and her dinner preparations. "You know your father. When he sets his mind to something, no one's going to stop him."

Gilda admonished, "Well, I wouldn't cook him dinner."

All conjecture on the matter halted as everyone stared at the closed door, where the most intense racket to ever visit the Bollinger household was in full eruption. Eddie screeching at the level of a tortured death knell, titanic water splashing, Paul Stanley cursing, "Hold still, you fucking little pissant!"

"Mommy, Daddy said a bad word!" Franny said, her distress rising.

Gilda chimed in, "That was two bad words."

"What's a pissant, anyway? What color is it?" Franny asked.

"Yellow for all I know," Gilda said. "What difference does it—"

They ceased their sisterly debate, once again mesmerized by the ruckus behind the bathroom door: "Cut it out, you bastard!"

Franny looked at everyone wild-eyed. "What's a bastard?"

"I'm pretty sure it's another bad word," offered Oliver.

The most awful cacophony then erupted, with repeated thumps punishing the closed door. And then: "I've had it with you, you little cocksucker!"

This last curse left Oliver silently aghast, Gilda smirking knowingly, and Franny downright confused.

Gwendolyn took charge. "All right, children, that's enough. Go upstairs while I finish dinner."

"What for?" retorted Gilda.

"Go play with your dolls."

"I'm too old to play with dolls," Gilda said, crossing her arms and planting her feet.

"I'm not," said Oliver.

"You're such a fruit," said Gilda.

Gwendolyn turned and shot them her serious look. "That is enough. That's not a nice word."

Franny spoke up. "What's wrong with that word? I thought it was a nice word, like broccoli."

"It's a word that describes a very sad kind of person, and we don't use words like that in this household."

Gilda didn't alter her stance. "Well, Oliver is a sad kind of brother, so I think it's accurate."

Gwendolyn held her spoon aloft, dripping brown liquid on the floor. "This family has a language problem. We don't use words like that in this house."

"That's not true," Gilda insisted.

Gwendolyn shot her most fierce look.

Oliver stepped in. "Gilda's right. Daddy just said cockfucker."

"That's not what he said," corrected Gilda, her chin lifted in full gloat.

"Go. Up. Stairs. Now!" commanded Gwendolyn.

Usually obedient, the three children were too paralyzed by the suspense—as well as the new vocabulary words—to obey.

Suddenly, the bathroom became silent, leaving the air heavy with apprehension. What seemed like an awful amount of time passed before the door opened. Paul Stanley stood there, hair plastered to his head, clothes drenched, a victorious smile. Beside him stood a soaking wet little monkey who looked dejected and exhausted.

Franny ran up to him and scooped the unusually docile monkey in her arms. "Oh, Eddie, you're so clean now." Then she looked at her mother, who came over to retrieve him. "But he still smells funny."

"I didn't get around to using any soap," Paul Stanley said as he stood at the bar pouring himself a bourbon. "But that little . . . the little critter did get wet."

"I guess we all know who's boss now, don't we?" Gwendolyn said as she left through the back door to take Eddie to his outside cage so he could dry out in the mild evening air. Her tone was flat, without the murmur of a breeze to lift her voice.

3

Separate but Equal

They stood in front of the monkey cage watching a frenzied Eddie leap forward, grab the wire front, bare his teeth, issue an angry warning bark, then leap back into the dark depths of the structure only to surge forward again with a repeat of his menacing aria.

"I don't know, Miz B. I just don't know about this."

Gwendolyn looked at Romaine, her housekeeper of ten years. She was a pretty, slender woman of similar age, with an upright posture in her starched white uniform that contrasted strikingly with her dark-brown skin. "What's the problem, Romaine?" Gwendolyn asked.

"That monkey animal just don't like me, that's what I'm seeing."

Gwendolyn looked back at Eddie, who was indeed acting strange. "Maybe he's not used to seeing a colored person."

As soon as she said it, she doubted herself. Romaine stiffened her posture even more and said nothing, but Gwendolyn could see that she'd hurt her. Or maybe this was her look that covered up anger. "I'm sorry, Romaine. I didn't mean to . . ."

Romaine looked at her.

"I mean he's not from Africa but somewhere in South America apparently, so I don't think he's used to . . . to people with your skin color."

Romaine turned back to look at Eddie, who was now calmer and studying her. "You're sayin' he's a racist monkey."

This confounded Gwendolyn. It was not the outcome she had expected when she brought Romaine out to see Eddie in his new housing and ask if she could please add cleaning his cage once a week to her duties. She decided to drop the request and do it herself.

"That's okay, Romaine, I'll find another way." She turned to walk back to the house.

"Why you put that little fella in a cage, anyway?"

Gwendolyn stopped and looked at her. Romaine was staring at Eddie, who was now staring back at her.

"Why? Why, he's a wild animal. He's not like a dog or a cat."

Romaine walked past Gwendolyn, toward the house. "That don't seem right then to keep a wild animal in a cage."

Gwendolyn stood there, silenced by an inarticulate disturbance. Was Romaine being ignorant? Or provocative? Or what? Hadn't she done a suitable job to provide Eddie with a safe and pleasant shelter? Not just a cage, for Pete's sake!

As she lay in bed that night with Paul Stanley, the afternoon's incident still troubled her. She asked him what he thought about it all.

He took his time to consider her question. "Well, you know Romaine's a proud woman. She's quiet about it, but you can tell by how she carries herself. I don't think she ever went to school, at least not high school, but she's smart. She observes; very little gets by her."

"Yes, I think you're right. I never thought about that. I feel so bad about it. I really think I insulted her. What can I do to make it up to her?"

"Maybe consider her more."

"What does that mean? Of course, I'm considerate with her."

"I know you are. You're always considerate of everyone. But I wonder if we ever take the time to think about what it's like to be her."

This stumped Gwendolyn. Had she ever allowed herself to think of what it was like to be a colored woman from Smelterville, the area on the south side of town that flooded when the waters of the Mississippi swelled with the spring rains? She lay awake that night, unable to shake off her unease. Romaine had called the monkey prejudiced, which seemed absurd to her—a monkey, prejudiced? But then she wondered if somehow she was the bigot. Could that be? She couldn't imagine it. She had even washed her son's mouth out with soap when he came home one day and described one of his colored classmates by that awful word that made her wince just like a curse word would.

She soon got her opportunity to rectify the racial incident, and it was Paul Stanley who presented that opportunity one morning in September. It was an Indian summer day, balmy and bright. But the nation was in turmoil, and it was being televised for all who had televisions to see. Little Rock, Arkansas, four hours away but seemingly a world apart, was turning out to be the epicenter of the school integration tensions fomented by the Supreme Court's *Brown v. Board of Education* decision three years prior. Nine Negro students would attempt to enter Little Rock Central High School for the first time to finally integrate the school system.

"I think Romaine might like to see this," Paul Stanley said as he was looking at the headline from that morning's *St. Louis Post-Dispatch*. He showed it to Gwendolyn, who glanced at it as she flipped pancakes in the stovetop skillet: "Negroes to be Escorted into Little Rock High School Today."

"Why don't you ask her if she wants to stay after work and watch the evening news with us? I don't think she has a TV."

Gwendolyn looked up from her pancake preparations. "Really?"

"Sure, why not?"

She slid the paper over and looked at it more closely. "Look, it also says here: 'Guns Force Integration as Tensions Reach Boiling Point.' Don't you think it could be upsetting to her?"

"Why don't you ask her?" He kissed her on the cheek before rushing out the back door.

When she did ask, it surprised her to hear Romaine accept the invitation without hesitation. All she asked was to call Percy, her husband, and let him know she would be later than usual.

※ ※ ※

Gwendolyn found Romaine in the utility room folding the laundry at a quarter to five and invited her to come have a seat in the living room. She sat alone while Gwendolyn busied herself in the kitchen, appearing a short time later with a tray of little canapés that she had retrieved from the oven.

"Let me help you, Miz B," Romaine said as she rose from her chair.

"No, sit, enjoy yourself. I mean, please, be comfortable."

Gwendolyn sat down opposite her. She crossed her legs at the ankles then recrossed them. Romaine looked at her with wide eyes.

"Please, Romaine, help yourself," Gwendolyn said, nodding at the canapés.

"Why thank you, ma'am, I will." She reached forward and picked up one. Gwendolyn offered her a napkin.

"Thank you, ma'am." Romaine looked at the canapé, hesitating, then plopped the entire thing into her mouth. She chewed it slowly, looking at Gwendolyn straight on as she did.

Gwendolyn recrossed her ankles. *Where is Paul Stanley? Why is he not here?* She glanced at the TV, it's hulking presence, it's sullen silence, vexing her.

She turned back to Romaine." Have I ever told you about the history of this house?"

"No, ma'am, not that I reckon."

"It's very interesting, as it turns out. During the Civil War over a hundred years ago, this was used by the Sisters of Mercy as their nunnery."

"Catholics?"

"Yes, Catholics. Missouri was a slave state, you see, and across the river, Illinois was a free state. Even though we were a slave state, there were a lot of sympathizers with the abolitionists, so a lot of slaves who escaped were aided by sympathizers to get to freedom across the river. The rumor is that this very house had a tunnel from its basement down to the Mississippi, right north of Cape Rock, a slave tunnel they called it back then, where the slaves could get to the river unseen and then to freedom in Illinois." She stopped, taking a breath, realizing she was getting sticky with her words.

With no discernible inflection in her voice or motility in her face, Romaine said, "I'll keep that in mind, ma'am."

The back screen door slammed shut, and Gwendolyn jumped up as Paul Stanley arrived, wearing a suit, his tie loosened. "Has it started yet?" he asked as he passed by and went to the alcove where the home bar resided. "Anyone want a drink?"

Gwendolyn seized up. This might not be the best time to start a party.

"What about you, Romaine? You're off duty," he said, peering around the corner.

"May I have a beer, sir?"

"Wendy, would you get two of those Buds in the back fridge?"

Gwendolyn relaxed. Hard liquor often signaled the beginning of a binge for Paul Stanley. Beer usually meant something more reasonable.

She brought the beers in and poured them into two glass mugs.

"Where're the kids?" Paul Stanley asked.

"They're in their rooms. Why?"

"Bring 'em down. I think they should see this."

Gwendolyn's hesitation was clear. "Don't you think this might be difficult for—"

"Come on, hon, history's being made today."

After the three children arrived, Paul Stanley turned on the television and everyone sat in a state of hushed awe as the light flickered on and the black-and-white image of Edward R. Murrow materialized before their eyes like a magical apparition. He leaned in, just like he was in their very own living room.

"Good evening, America. Today has been a most unusual and historic day. This September morning broke bright and clear in Little Rock, Arkansas, but storm clouds grew ominous as the start of what normally would be an ordinary school day at Central High School."

The picture cut from Murrow to the scene in front of the school. Armed National Guardsmen stood on two sides of a walkway. A sizable, all-White crowd stood behind them. It was eerily quiet, the air full of tense anticipation.

Back to a close shot of Murrow. "The crowd is awaiting the arrival of nine Negro students, the first to integrate the Little Rock school system. Today we see a much different assemblage than we did twenty days ago. Today, the spectators seem in awe of what is about to happen, or perhaps they are merely resigned. On September 4, these same nine students who are about to arrive made their first attempt to begin their schooling here but were dramatically thwarted."

Everyone, including the three Bollinger children, sat in a silent trance as the television switched to a much more raucous scene: Two young White boys sporting matching blond crew cuts held up a large Confederate flag, causing the eruption of cheers that unified the swirling, turbulent crowd. People were shouting, many shaking their fists, as eight young Negro students—five girls, dressed in light-colored blouses and full skirts, carrying tidily organized binders, and three boys, outfitted in collared shirts tucked properly into chinos—walked through a mob of agitated White people screaming obscenities, some yelling, "Lynch them!"

"Look at that." It was Gilda, who sat forward in response to a young woman appearing on the screen wearing sunglasses, a crisp white blouse, a starched full skirt with a gingham pattern appliquéd on the bottom, and a quiet, defiant look on her pretty brown face. She walked alone like an unintentional goddess toward the entrance of the school. Behind her stormed a throng of White girls, shrieking their protests. One surged forward, her mouth a snarl of hate, screaming, "Go back to Africa where you belong!"

Franny, who had been watching the television with rapt attention and had regressed to sucking her thumb, came over to where Romaine was sitting and crawled onto her lap. "Are you going to go back to Africa?" she asked.

"I was born and raised right here in Cape Girardeau just like you, and nobody gonna tell me to go nowhere. Don't you worry, Franny honey."

This seemed to comfort her, and they both turned their attention back to the unfolding drama on the television screen.

The distinctive voice of Edward Murrow resumed. "The mob on September fourth was estimated to be a thousand strong, but they weren't the only barrier to the nine children." A line of armed men in uniforms stood in an impenetrable line in front of the entrance. "Arkansas Governor Faubus called out the National Guard, ostensibly to keep the peace, but many charge it was to defy the 1954 Supreme Court order that ruled that the 'separate but equal' doctrine employed by all the former Confederate states to maintain segregation was now illegal."

The young girl in the sunglasses arrived at the steps going up to the front entrance. A solid wall of dead-eyed National Guard soldiers blocked her way.

Murrow: "That young woman you just saw was Elizabeth Eckford three weeks ago. Having missed the van that transported her future fellow students, she arrived separately on a public bus. She was forced to walk solo through an angry gauntlet toward the school that held her dreams of an education but was not yet willing to accept her. Today, she joins the other eight students who have strengthened their determination to integrate the Little Rock school system. Today, with the help of President Eisenhower, who ordered in twelve hundred troops from the 101st Airborne to enforce the order, they make their mutual walk into history."

There was a noticeable collective holding of breath as the Little Rock Nine, as they had come to be known, walked in a solemn line, accompanied by soldiers on each side of them, into Little Rock Central High School to begin their education in an officially integrated school.

Romaine sat ramrod straight in her chair. Silent tears ran down her face.

Paul Stanley walked up to her. He took his handkerchief out of his suit breast pocket and handed it to her. She pressed it against her cheeks as he turned off the television.

Gwendolyn asked Romaine if she would like to stay for dinner, making sure to clarify that the invite was for her to be a guest at the table, but she politely refused, saying that she needed to get back and feed Percy.

Later that night, after the kids were in bed, Gwendolyn and Paul Stanley lay together in the dark. Paul Stanley didn't fix himself another drink after Romaine left and willingly sat down to eat dinner with the rest of them, a definite signal that this was not to be another party night.

"Paul Stanley?" Gwendolyn asked, softly testing to see if he was still awake.

"Mm-hmm?" he answered.

"What did you mean when Gilda asked you about 'separate but equal' when we were all eating dinner?"

"What'd I say?"

"That it was one of those things people proclaim so they look like they are doing the right thing when they really aren't."

"I said that?"

"And you said there are people who just can't help doing what they do even if it's wrong."

"Mm," he murmured, his voice drifting away.

"Sometimes you surprise me, Paul Stanley."

She turned to see if he was awake. The deepening of his breathing told her he was at rest.

Paul Stanley at rest was a beautiful sight.

4

Apricot Pie

The next morning, Gwendolyn woke up feeling as warm and contented as a puppy in a puppy pile. She did not typically linger in bed like this. She and Paul Stanley had a wonderful and rare morning "snuggle," and he was now in the shower, singing something operatic in his fine tenor voice. She could smell the spicy scent of his vetiver soap. Smiling to herself, she decided she would do something special for him that day. Maybe she would treat him to his favorite pork tenderloin with her secret mustard sauce, maybe a special dessert. But now, she had three children who needed her help.

Alone in the house with the smells of bacon and fresh-squeezed orange juice, the flurry of morning departure activity settled, she turned her attention back to the desire to do something exceptional for her husband. This had been her daily intention in the first years of their marriage, but it had somehow dissipated with the children and their endless demands, the slight cuts and minor bruises of a lengthening marriage. As she enjoyed her post-children coffee, she wondered why this shelved impulse had returned. Was it the sweetness of their lovemaking that morning, rarefied because no alcohol was involved? Perhaps it was even the unusual experience with Romaine last night, watching the inspiring drama of the

Little Rock Nine. Or maybe it was about being reminded of how sensitive her husband, the great "monkey tamer," could be.

She shook off these speculations. No time for such analysis. The tenderloin was one of her specialties, so it would be perfect. But what kind of dessert could she make? It had to be particular as Paul Stanley had a nuanced sweet tooth. The thought occurred to her: This was probably because his mother baked pies for him, which was a rare offering of sweetness.

She glanced again out the kitchen window where the old apricot tree dominated the side yard. It was bursting with little peachy-orange orbs scattered high up in its branches. The light from the morning sun turned them on like Christmas tree lights. *Apricot pie!* She thought she remembered him telling her it was one of his favorites. Creating a nostalgic dessert could be a win for her. This old and fecund apricot tree, towering above the roofline of their two-story house, was a rarity in this historical part of town. Now, that would be exceptional—a pie made of fresh-off-the-tree apricots from your own backyard.

Romaine had already arrived and was ironing the sheets and pillowcases—it was Tuesday—when Gwendolyn breezed by her on the way to her car.

"You look right nice, Miz B," she said. Gwendolyn was wearing a springy print dress with a full gathered skirt and form-fitting top with an attached scarf creating a side bow. She wore pearl earrings, full makeup, her short brunette hair loosely curled and perfectly set, and low heels and stockings in the more modern seamless style.

"That's kind of you, Romaine. If the doctor calls, tell him I'm off doing my shopping and should be back in a couple of hours."

Romaine observed her. "I think you was going to church instead of the butchers."

"Let's just say I get a better deal from Mr. Blakely if I put on a little lipstick." And she rushed out to her DeSoto, leaving Romaine, with a wave, to her chore.

As she drove down the hill to head south toward the Good Hope section of town, Gwendolyn relished in her good mood. The Negro kids were safely integrated in their Little Rock high school, her three children were safe in their school, and she was going to treat her husband to his favorite pork tenderloin and a homemade apricot pie. Who knew? Maybe they would make love again tonight? She turned up the dial and sang along with Elvis' hit song "Don't Be Cruel (to a love that's true)."

Before she realized it, she was in front of Blakely's grocery. It was a dim, small store where she would never dream of buying vegetables or fruit, but Joe Blakely was the best butcher in town.

He stood in the back in a blood-stained apron, his wild ginger hair barely contained in a paper hat, hacking away at a slab of meat. This wasn't the kind of place Gwendolyn would normally feel comfortable frequenting, but she had to admit her almost weekly visits here were a bit of an undisclosed adventure, as if she were going across the tracks to a place where she wasn't expected to be.

"Looking scrumptious, as always, Gwendolyn Farnsley."

She didn't know exactly what he meant by scrumptious, but she quickly moved on from this. "How's your wife doing?"

"Ornery as ever. You know Sue."

Of course, she knew Sue; they all went to high school together. Joe Blakely never wasted an opportunity to talk about their upcoming twenty-year class reunion that you would think was a party for the Second Coming. "You'll have to make sure you flirt with me at the reunion, promise?" She knew he was referring to her being awarded "Most Flirtatious" in the 1937 yearbook. She offered him a polite smile. It was never easy with Joe, but she needed to change lanes. "I want to cook a special dinner for the doctor this evening. Do you have a good pork tenderloin for me?"

He broke out in a grin. "That strikes me as a mighty fine idea. Did I ever tell you your good doctor cured my mother of her lumbago? She thinks he walks on water. I think she's in love with him. Did I ever tell you that?"

"Yes, you did. He helps a lot of people. Now about that pork tenderloin?"

His grin expanded. "I just got some choice pieces from Perry County, a farm that makes the fattest, richest pigs you ever seen."

"That's convenient," she said.

He retrieved one from his case and showed it to her. It was beautiful. "Let me trim it up for you, a special Gwendolyn trim."

The lipstick was working.

Her next errand, Taveggia's Market.

Driving down Broadway toward the river, she came to a stop sign in front of the Idan-Ha Hotel. It was there, at the Rainbow Room, where Paul Stanley took her on their first official date for an ice cream soda. On an impulse, she made a right turn and drove down one block where a small brick chapel stood. It could have been a country church in the Cotswolds, but it was just the humble Christ Episcopal Church where she and Paul Stanley were married in 1941. She enjoyed a private smile as she drove by, remembering how dashing Paul Stanley looked in his Army dress uniform, just like a hero out of a storybook.

When she turned the corner, she arrived in front of the distinctive Common Pleas Court House—a two-story brick building with an impressive two-tiered cupola—that commanded the hill over the Cape Girardeau riverfront. Looking at the old-fashioned bandstand brought forth another memory. Her family had just moved to Cape Girardeau from Los Angeles, where she was born and had only known up to that point. She was twelve, and her parents brought her and her brother, Thomas, to the courthouse park for a summer bandstand concert. She couldn't recall the music, but she did remember the fresh smells of the summer night, especially the exotic perfume of new-mown grass, the twinkling lights from the bandstand, the wonderful strangeness of it all.

As she drove past, she also realized how her heady experience of this new land was different from her parents'. Her father, who had grown up here in the wealthy Farnsley family, set out to make his own fortune building houses in the far-off land of opportunity, California. When the Depression hit and he refused to foreclose on the many mortgages he held, he went bust and endured the humiliation of returning to Cape, forced to take a subordinate job with his family business—no doubt a punitive measure meted out by his cousins for his folly of leaving the grand Farnsley family in the first place. She had been so filled with the fun of her burgeoning social popularity that she didn't even notice that her mother, who never lost her gracious smile, was burdened by the terrifying and all-consuming diagnosis of her brother, who had polio. Or how mortifying it was for her father to return to his hometown, a failed California real estate mogul, now having to assume the role of the poor relation.

All of these thoughts cascaded through her mind, and by the time she arrived at Broadway and turned down the hill to the riverfront, they had lost their complication, creating a scrim of nostalgia where her life past and present harmonized.

She soon reached Mr. Taveggia's Italian restaurant and market, a modest store on Water Street which, as its name would suggest, bordered the historic levee on the Mississippi. As she disembarked from her parked car, she could smell the river before she saw its lugubrious brown flow. The local joke was, "St. Louis, flush your toilets—Cape Girardeau needs water." This crass quip didn't diminish her awe of the river, the "mighty Mississippi" that eternally surged with increasing force to the southern portal of the country. She took an indulgent moment to step out on the levee and breathe in the distinctive smell. It reminded her of old socks, yet nothing could diminish her reverence. She looked up the river and saw the limestone cliffs of Cape Rock, where she and Paul Stanley would park when they were courting, and then down the river to where Cape Bridge crossed over to Illinois. She could almost feel the power of the river from the cobblestone levee where she stood. On one of those first dates, Paul Stanley told her that he had swum across the river to the other side, a feat that he claimed made him locally famous. That story and this landscape, so green and arcadian, were gorgeous to her. She was a long way from the arid landscape of her native California. In an instant, she realized that even though she was so distracted by her girlish follies, she was surely impacted by the undertow of her parents' displacement from their dream, their humiliation of returning to Cape Girardeau empty handed. A flush of warmth bloomed over her, her eyes smarted with salty wetness: Paul Stanley had secured this for her—this place, this home.

And he darned well deserved a great apricot pie!

Mr. Taveggia, a big, burly man with wavy, dark hair and magnanimous eyebrows, greeted her heartily. She considered him the purveyor of her secret culinary weapons—garlic, handmade pasta, and real Italian olive oil. These were novel ingredients in local cuisine, and it always impressed Paul Stanley when she made her garlicky pasta con piselli.

The first thing she needed to attend to after arriving home was the apricot pie. She made herself a cup of tea and took it out to the backyard, where the huge apricot tree commanded the space. Looking up, she could see that most of the fruit was in the top branches. How was she ever going to get them? From the garage, she brought out the biggest ladder and propped it up against the tree trunk. Climbing up, she realized that her arm's reach was just shy of the lowest hanging fruit. Eddie's chirping coming from his shelter in the nearby garage commandeered her perplexity.

On a whim, she went there and snapped the leash on his collar. He danced at the end of his tether as she made her way back to the apricot tree. She was only going on some vague assumption that monkeys like to climb in trees. How was this going to work? With coaxing, she got him to follow her up the ladder. At the highest rung, they were near the lowest limb. Gwendolyn, with little forethought, unsnapped Eddie from the leash and watched as he scrambled up to the higher branches, where he began swinging from limb to limb. So far, so good.

Gwendolyn hurried down the ladder and went to get a wicker basket that was stored in the shed.

Standing at the base of the tree, she sang out, "Come on, Eddie, throw me an apricot!" As soon as the words came out of her mouth, she realized the absurdity of her request. He wasn't paying attention to her, more intent on the apparent thrills of his acrobatic pursuits high among the branches. Hauling her basket, she climbed back up the ladder, calling to Eddie. Once at the top, she did seem to get his attention. He had already discovered the apricots and had tried to eat one, but apparently it was not to his liking as he threw it to the ground. When he plucked another one, Gwendolyn called his name, holding her basket out for him to see. This seemed to engage his curiosity. She called his name again. He looked at the little golden orange orb in his hand and then to Gwendolyn and her basket. He surprised her when he tossed it at the basket. It almost made it but bounced off to the ground.

"Good shot, Eddie," she encouraged.

This seemed to do the trick. He plucked another apricot and threw it at Gwendolyn. This time, she moved her basket to intercept the tossed fruit. Her elation at the score was infectious. Eddie became more animated, hurling apricots toward Gwendolyn, which she attempted to capture in her basket. His chirping became more excitable. Except, it wasn't his game-on chirping. It was more like distressed screeching. It was the last sound she heard when the world suddenly turned upside down, as if she were tumbling into a dark dream.

❖ ❖ ❖

From a place of blackness, her eyes fluttered open. The first thing she focused on was Eddie running around in frantic circles, surging toward her then darting away only to return. Her first thought was, *Why is he so distressed?* Then she realized, *I'm on the ground, and I can't breathe.*

She tried to get up, and then pain shot through her upper body like a thunderbolt, knocking her back to the ground.

The next flash of consciousness came when she opened her eyes in her own bed. Paul Stanley was next to her, taking her pulse. Romaine stood on the other side of the bed holding a cold compress, which she had just removed from her forehead.

"What's going on?" Gwendolyn mumbled. Fragments of memory began gathering in her mind: Paul Stanley and Romaine picking her up from the ground, Eddie expressing torment somewhere around her, the pain piercing her like a spear lodged somewhere in her upper body, Paul Stanley's voice coming at her in shredded pieces through the veil of her consciousness: *You fell off the ladder... what on earth were you doing up there, Wendy? Eddie alerted Romaine. She called me at the office. I came right over...*

Another bolt of pain caused her to convulse. "What's wrong with me?"

Paul Stanley leaned forward, holding her hand. "Wendy, you have to be brave. I've got to do something to you, and it's going to hurt."

"But why? Why would you do that?"

"I have no choice. Please forgive me."

Hearing this, the adrenaline must have brought her to full awareness so that she could absorb the reality that her fall off the ladder had not only blown the breath out of her but also dislocated her left shoulder. "I've got to relocate your shoulder," he said. "There's no time to waste, and this is going to hurt like hell."

Without waiting for her consent, Paul Stanley went into ER mode. "I'm going to give you some morphine. Not much though because I need you to give me feedback."

The shot had an immediate impact, putting her into a pleasant swirl. It was short-lived. Paul Stanley told Romaine to hold her down on the right side as he gently took her left arm and folded it across her chest. This slight movement caused a visible stab of pain.

"That's a good girl, Wendy. You're tough. Hang in there." He bent down and smiled, his wondrous, healing smile that could put everything right.

The morphine was kicking in; she returned him a hazy smile. "You'll make it better, won't you?"

Without answering, he pulled her arm toward him. Then in one swift move, he rotated it. A popping sound erupted, alarming Romaine. "Doctor, give her one of them shots. Look, she's in terror!"

Silent tears ran down her cheeks as she clenched her teeth.

"She's all right." Her breath came in shallow gasps. "Wendy, I just popped your shoulder back in its socket." He was rubbing her exposed shoulder that was florid with inflammation. "Is the pain better?"

Her eyes winced shut then fluttered open after a moment. "You saved my life."

"Hardly, but I saved your shoulder from a messy surgery, so you can thank me for that."

Gwendolyn felt floaty, like she was in a dream. "I was going to make you an apricot pie."

"You relax, Wendy darlin'." He started putting his doctor bag back together. "Don't worry about that. My mom used to make apricot pie, and I got bored with it long ago."

1959

5
Show-and-Tell

It was Oliver who convinced her that she needed to bring Eddie to show-and-tell day at Lorimer Elementary. Gilda had feigned indifference but was secretly curious about the social currency it might offer her—that is, if all went well. Franny, who was distracted by the marvels of addition and subtraction that she was learning in her second-grade class, didn't offer an opinion.

"But, Mother," Oliver implored, "no one has a monkey. Most of them haven't ever even seen a monkey! And school is only two blocks away."

It was this last comment—so naive, as if walking two blocks with a monkey on a leash would make a difference—that softened Gwendolyn's inclination to refuse this entreaty.

The day arrived, a Friday, which the principal felt would be best. He knew that this would be a very exciting event and the parents would be better at quelling the inevitable arousal than his overworked staff. As Gwendolyn walked up the front steps to the two-story brick building with its distinctive two gables, a strange mixture of pride, nostalgia, and doubt overcame her. This was the elementary school she had attended when her family first moved to Cape Girardeau in 1932 from Los Angeles. It was also the same school Paul Stanley had attended. She first laid eyes on him there, although she barely remembered that event. Now, all three of her children were attending the same school.

As she approached the glass front doors, she paused and checked herself out in their reflection. She wondered if she was overdressed. She dismissed the thought, knowing that the teachers expected the mothers to dress nicely when they came to school functions, and, after all, she was known for her simple but elegant taste in clothes. As she admired her image in the glow of this last thought, she realized she was wearing a smartly tailored beige silk suit accessorized by a leashed monkey on her shoulder, and thus all bets were off.

She arranged her itinerary at the school in consultation with the three teachers whose classrooms she would be visiting. Best to start with Gilda's sixth grade class, which might have more decorum. She could feel Eddie dithering more than usual on her shoulder.

As she walked down the second-story hallway to Mrs. Estes's classroom, she noticed a miniature head poking out of the door. As soon as the boy it belonged to saw Mrs. Bollinger with a monkey, he quickly sucked himself back into his classroom.

At her destination, Gwendolyn looked through the glass pane in the door and saw Mrs. Estes speaking to her class with a stern expression. The veteran teacher exuded an air of authority; a stout woman with glasses hanging on a chain and a gray-haired, no-nonsense bun. She looked up and smiled at Gilda's mother, holding up a finger as a signal to wait a moment. The entire class looked wide-eyed and expectant. Gwendolyn could see that Gilda's desk was on the front row. She sat there, looking down at her folded hands.

Mrs. Estes came over to the door and opened it with a welcoming smile. "Hello, Mrs. Bollinger. How nice of you to come for this very special show-and-tell day. Gilda has been quite excited to show everyone her most unusual pet. Isn't that right, Gilda?"

Both women looked at Gilda. "Not really," she muttered under her breath.

Mrs. Estes led Gwendolyn and Eddie over to the front of the room, where she addressed the class that remained composed despite a notable increase in the atmospheric tension in the room. Gwendolyn focused on a little Black girl sitting in the second row, pretty in a starched, white dress, her eyes wide and her hands folded neatly in front of her on the desk. This pleased her. *Little Rock has nothing on Cape Girardeau!*

"Girls and boys, please welcome Mrs. Paul Stanley Bollinger and her pet monkey, Eddie."

In unison, as if rehearsed, the entire class said, "Welcome Mrs. Bollinger and Eddie the Monkey."

"Hello, class," Gwendolyn said with her most bountiful smile. As soon as the words left her mouth, Eddie did a little hop and let out a whoop.

Gwendolyn startled but recovered quickly. "That's Eddie saying hello to you all."

The class burst out laughing, but Mrs. Estes was quick on the draw. "Now, class, remember what we discussed. Monkeys are cute and we may look alike, but we must remember that they are unfamiliar with us and so we have to remain calm to make them feel safe." The titter silenced as the class came to heel. Gwendolyn relaxed. Mrs. Estes clearly had control of her domain.

"Gilda, dear, would you like to tell your classmates about your special friend," instructed Mrs. Estes.

With a sigh, Gilda lifted herself up from her desk and walked by her mother and Eddie without looking at them. She assumed her place in front of the class.

"First of all, let me get something straight. Eddie is not my special friend. He doesn't like me, and I don't like him." This got a rise out of several in the class. "This was not my idea for my mother to bring him to show-and-tell. It was my little brother Oliver's idea. He's only ten and doesn't know any better. My sister Franny, a second grader, used to like to play with him when she was younger, but then I don't think she even realized Eddie was from a different species."

Mrs. Estes put her hand gently on Gilda's shoulder. "Didn't you tell me you went to the library when you first got Eddie and made a report on him to help your family understand more about him—what kind of monkey he is, where he came from? I bet your classmates would love to hear about that."

"Yes, ma'am," Gilda said and then launched into the report about Eddie's origins.

Gwendolyn watched her with the same amazement she often felt about her eldest daughter's poise and determined spirit. Even Eddie had stopped his fidgeting and seemed enraptured by the story of his history. But this was just "anthropomorphizing," as Paul Stanley always accused Gwendolyn of doing. All was going well. How silly it was of her to have been at all concerned by this nice educational experience for the Lorimer Elementary students.

It was a false respite.

As soon as Gilda got to the part about a monkey showing anger by slinging his doo-doo, a few snickers erupted. This began a swell of excitement, causing laughter to spread throughout the classroom. The noisy exhilaration made Eddie dance around on Gwendolyn's shoulder.

"Children, please!" scolded Mrs. Estes. "Remember what we talked about."

Barney Macalister, a reliably hyperactive boy, jumped out of his seat and in an excited voice asked, "When do we get to pet him?"

"Children, calm down. Get back in your seat, Barney. It is important to remain calm. Remember, Eddie is a wild animal."

The class erupted in a tsunami of excitement, with some boys jumping around like they imagined a monkey would, scratching their sides and making *woo-woo* sounds.

Eddie responded with a fierce shriek as he leapt from Gwendolyn's shoulder to the top of her perfectly coiffed hair. From that perch he commanded the room, punching his scrawny little arms at the erupting classroom, howling his protest in the most piercing way. Gwendolyn stood ramrod stiff, not knowing what to do as Eddie gripped tighter with his feet into her increasingly disrupted hairdo. Before her was a swirl of unfocused enthusiasm.

Oh no. He didn't!

That was Gwendolyn's immediate thought when she felt it. She may have even said it out loud as Mrs. Estes looked at her in horror.

The only thing she could think to do was turn around and stroll out of the classroom. She did exactly that—and with the grace of a nervous, but intent, contestant in the Miss America Pageant who might have had a shrieking monkey perched on top of her head. It was then that the classroom let out a collective gasp as they saw the monkey diarrhea streaming down the back of Mrs. Paul Stanley Bollinger's fine beige silk suit.

At the door, Gwendolyn turned and, with a tense smile, gave a slight wave to the classroom that was now mute with astonishment. She paused, not knowing what else to do, so she turned back to the door, opened it, and left. You could hear a pencil drop.

6

Haviland China

"You have got to be fucking kidding me!"

"I am not what-you-say kidding you," said Gwendolyn.

They were in Dixie's kitchen, working on that evening's dinner. Busby and Paul Stanley were by the bar, drinking whiskey sours and smoking cigars.

"But shit in your hair? Monkey shit in your hair, I might add."

"It wasn't that bad. My hairspray kind of kept it on the surface."

"But what did Mabel say?" Dixie was referring to their mutual hairdresser, who did Gwendolyn's weekly washout and set.

"I took care of it myself. I wouldn't subject Mabel to monkey . . . you know."

Dixie guffawed. "Very Christian of you, dear. It's about time you started going more natural anyway instead of shellacking your hair like you are some kind of classy mummy. I cannot wait to tell the bridge club about this!"

"You will be telling no one about this. I don't want people thinking of me in this way. Do you understand?"

At that moment, Busby breezed in. "Dixie darlin', you got any bitters hereabouts?"

Many assumed that Busby, with his often-flamboyant clothes—some of them made from textiles he wove himself—and florid

Southern manners, was a homosexual. However, his reputation with his many female conquests over the years usually quieted those rumors, and Dixie was always willing to confirm what a heterosexual stud Dr. Busby Bollinger was in the sack. None of this speculation ever concerned Busby, who loved to drive around Cape Girardeau in his bright-red Thunderbird convertible, his black cape with a red silk lining blowing in the wind, two large Airedales riding in the backseat. He even sported an unusual goatee that, along with the red-silk-lined cape, gave him a devilish look.

"What are you men jabbering about in there?" Dixie asked as she handed him a bottle of bitters.

"Whether or not Leontyne Price is the greatest mezzo-soprano in the world. Cousin Paul Stanley claims she has a magnificent Negro voice, which I say is not only demeaning to her powerful talent but patently bigoted."

As soon as he left, Gwendolyn and Dixie looked at each other and shared a giggle. They were surely the only two women in Cape Girardeau with husbands who argued opera.

"At least they're not talking about duck hunting or frog gigging," said Dixie.

"Or politics," Gwendolyn said as she took a bubbling Pyrex tray out of the oven. "Are you ready to put this casserole on the table?"

"Let it cool a bit. Let's go in and see what they're really talking about."

When they arrived in the den, the two men had their backs to them and seemed to be looking at something Busby had in his hand.

"What're you two rascals up to?" Gwendolyn asked.

Busby showed her the large, framed photograph he was holding.

Gwendolyn walked over to take the photo and scrutinize it. "Oh, you're kidding me! Where did you get this?" It was a colorized photograph of her, standing in a statuesque pose between two pillars, her chin held slightly up, and her scarlet-red and strapless gown draped to the floor in a figure-flattering style.

Dixie came up and took the photograph from Gwendolyn. "Maybe you'd better ask *what* he does *with* it."

Busby plucked the photo from Dixie's hands. "This is precious to me as it is to every man there that night in 1940." He turned to Paul Stanley. "You missed it, cousin. The night of the Savitar Ball, and this vision appears at the top of the staircase, a goddess in an unforgettable red dress. This photo took up practically the whole front page of the paper next day. A legend was born."

"I missed that all right," said Paul Stanley. "Heard about it all the way up at Mizzou and ever since, mostly due to your obsession. That's why when I came home for a weekend soon after, driving down Broadway in my Ford Roadster when Gwendolyn Farnsley practically leapt in front of my car, waving me down, I knew it was none other than the girl in the red dress, and I had no choice but to stop and take her to Finney's Drug Store for a soda."

"Oh, for Pete's sake, Paul Stanley, in your dreams," Gwendolyn said with a sportive smile. "You boys exaggerate. Come on, let's eat before the food gets cold."

As soon as they sat down at the dining room table, Paul Stanley, who seemed intent upon drinking his dinner, said, "Did you all hear about the shitstorm Wendy got herself caught in?"

"Paul Stanley!" Gwendolyn said.

Dixie roared with delight. "Literally, from what I hear. I laughed so hard I blew milk out my nipples."

Gwendolyn shifted her look to Dixie. Evidently, she was also drinking her dinner.

Busby reached over and put his hand reassuringly on Gwendolyn's that rested limply beside her untouched spoon. "Hon, you better get used to it. This story's not going anywhere."

"Forget it, cuz," said Paul Stanley, "Wendy is an unrepentant prude."

"I am not a prude," Gwendolyn said, her head lowered, her voice quiet and serious.

"Busby's right, darlin', this will not go away," said Dixie. "They're already talking about it at the country club and down at the Last Chance Saloon, you just know it." Her face was an eerie mixture of glee and concern.

"I've got a dandy idea," proclaimed Busby. "Let's help Gwendolyn make up a great story about it. You know, take charge of the situation before it takes charge of you."

Dixie picked up her fork and pointed at Gwendolyn; she obviously wasn't going to use it tonight for its intended purpose. "I've got it! Eddie got into your laxative bottle. Little did you know when you got him, he's a laxative addict."

"I do not take laxatives," Gwendolyn murmured.

Busby added, "How about denying it, just claiming it was a fresh look for you, a hairpiece. What do you call them, a fall?"

"Yes," Dixie almost screamed, "and you use a new hair product from France—a distinct smell but all the rage on the continent."

"How about"—Busby was practically choking on his glee—"how about deny it altogether? You just say old Mrs. Estes is senile and kids make up shit."

"Or maybe you could just be bold and tell the truth: that the monkey was scared shitless by a rowdy gaggle of sixth graders," became Paul Stanley's contribution.

Everyone howled at this one, alcohol emerging victorious. Even Gwendolyn laughed. She was starting to relax, realizing she needed to defang this humiliating incident. "I think I'll use that one," she said, which sent everyone else into almost full hysterics. This surprised Gwendolyn as she realized it was almost impossible for anyone imagining her ever saying a thing like that.

"Can't you just see Wendy's reaction when she realized what was going down," Paul Stanley said. "And I bet she never even broke stride!"

This erupted even more hilarity. "That should be on Gwendolyn's tombstone, don't you think?" said Dixie. "'And she never broke stride.'"

The night progressed on the wings of the usual chatter and imbibing—talk of hospital gossip, horse racing (they were all going to Louisville next week for the Bollinger annual trek to the Kentucky Derby), and all the usual fluff of small-town America. But the talk always came back, like some recurring exclamation point, to the subject of Eddie and his mishap on Gwendolyn's head.

At one point, Gwendolyn answered one of Busby's ripostes. "You know, this is really all your fault. I should beat the poop out of you for letting Paul Stanley take that monkey home with him."

"Then, dear Gwendolyn," Dixie said a little too loudly, "you will need to haul your fine ass across the river and beat the 'poop' out of the East Cape whore who gave it to him."

"Be nice now, Dixie, hon," Busby admonished.

Gwendolyn was wondering if she herself may have had a bit too much to drink, but she was relaxed now and laughing, not even paying attention to the rising tide of tension between Dixie and Busby that usually predicted a coming storm. She finished Dixie's beautifully prepared meal certain that she was the only one who did.

Driving home, she was quiet in the passenger seat. She had long ago given up insisting that she drive when Paul Stanley had had too much to drink.

Finally, she punctured the silence. "Paul Stanley, I am not a prude."

"I know that, sweets. I was just joking." He reached over and caressed her hand. "I tell you what, you can prove it to me tonight."

She looked at him with his winning smile. Maybe he wasn't so drunk after all. Maybe their Saturday night "date" would turn out enjoyable for them both.

And it was. At least until the phone rang.

Paul Stanley looked at the clock. It was 1 a.m.

"You'd better answer. It could be the hospital," said Gwendolyn.

He picked up the phone. "Dr. Bollinger here."

"I know who the fuck you are." It was Dixie's unmistakable guttural drawl. "Get over here. I think I've killed your cousin."

Gwendolyn insisted on going with him.

When they arrived at the Bollinger's two-story brick colonial, the back door was open and Dixie was sitting on a stool by the bar, legs crossed, a large drink in her hand, the other holding a cigarette aloft. Spotting Paul Stanley with Gwendolyn standing behind him, she said, "Brought reinforcements, I see."

She took a fierce drag on the cigarette and then pointed toward the corner of the den.

"Check him out. He may still be breathing for all I know."

Their eyes followed her gesture. They saw Busby on the floor, looking unconscious, a trickle of blood oozing from his head and a large pineapple nearby.

"Good god, Dixie, what did you do now?" Paul Stanley asked as he hurried over with his doctor bag to the fallen cousin.

"What does it look like, Dr. Bollinger? I threw a goddamned pineapple at the son of a bitch."

Gwendolyn looked at Dixie openmouthed. Dixie was the only woman she knew who used curse words so freely; even at all, for that matter.

She put a hand on her shoulder. "Are you okay? Let me get you a cup of coffee."

"Only if you put brandy in it." Dixie lit another cigarette off her last one.

"What happened? Why did you throw a pineapple at him?"

"Good shot, huh?"

While Gwendolyn put some coffee on the stove, Dixie told the backstory. Evidently this had to do with that "White trash whore" that had given the monkey to Busby. Only she wasn't from East Cape, as originally purported, but the wife of Busby's male office nurse.

"I know, ironic, isn't it?" declared Dixie. "A twist on the whole nurse-fucking-doctor stereotype, but in this case the nurse is a guy who's evidently a little light in the loafers and didn't care if his whore snatch of a wife was screwing his boss. Hell, as far as

I know, that perverted son of a bitch over there was probably screwing them both."

"Tell us what happened." Gwendolyn handed her a cup of coffee without the brandy, trying to get Dixie to focus.

"I didn't tell you this, did I? We went to a party two nights ago at that couple's dumpy house. I didn't want to go—fraternizing with the help is not my thing—but Busby was suspiciously adamant. At one point, I noticed he and the slag had disappeared. Much to my surprise, I found them in the kitchen. And what did I find that asshole doing? Helping the slut wife of the homosexual male nurse wash the dishes! Now ask me, has he ever, *ever* lifted a hand to help me with the dishes around here? Hell fucking no!"

Gwendolyn looked over and saw Paul Stanley propping Busby up and dressing his head wound. He had already checked his vital signs. "How is he?"

"Lucky for Dixie, he's going to live. I don't know about lucky for him."

"Does this mean I'll have to change his diapers from now on?" Dixie said with a coarse burst of laughter.

Gwendolyn nudged her with the cup of coffee. "Come on, Dixie, please drink this. You need it."

Dixie took a sip and then continued, "So, fast-forward to tonight. You leave, and of course there're dishes to be done. But tonight, I was going to make sure it was different. I was gonna make sure I made a point." She thrust her index finger forward, almost tipping off the stool, then righted herself with an exaggerated propriety. "In my most prison matron-like voice, I commanded him to come over and help me with the dishes. Busby did, no doubt knowing he would be in big ass trouble if he didn't, and I do know the great Southern feminine art of intimidating your man." She took another sip of the coffee, grimaced and put it aside.

"So, what happened?" Gwendolyn prompted.

"I told him to wash, and I would dry. These are our good dishes, the precious Haviland china that belonged to his priggish old fart of a mother. She gave them to us for our wedding. I've always hated them. But you know how Busby is, just like a woman, appreciating the finer things, and he was especially proud of those dishes. When he handed me a plate, I just let it slip through my hands, shattering on the floor. Oops! He hands me another one. Same thing. Oops! We're staring at each other like two prizefighters, neither one about to give in. I don't know what was going on in his pea brain, but you know those Bollinger men, they're stubborn as jackasses. Soon enough, he threw down his dishrag and walked off. I told him that in no uncertain terms, we were not done with the dishes. And you know what that fuckwad said to me? 'Reverence, Dixie Renee Bollinger!' *Reverence*? Well, that did it. I picked up the first thing I could find, which happened to be that pineapple right there, and I hurled it at him as he was trying to escape, the chicken shit bastard."

Gwendolyn and Paul Stanley were both trying to keep a straight face. "That's quite a story you have there, Dixie," Paul Stanley said as he gave Busby a sip of brandy.

Sliding off her barstool, Dixie wavered and then righted herself by staring hard at Busby. "Just because her husband won't fuck her doesn't give her the right to take my husband. And then, if that weren't enough for her, that hungry, voracious twat has the gall to seduce that bastard over there to wash her dishes."

She staggered over to where Busby was now sitting up with his head bandaged. He grinned at his wife, who was peering down at him. "Hi, darlin'," he said.

She pulled herself up into a majestic stance and moved her hands up and down her tightly sheathed, voluptuous body. "You see this? You see it?"

Busby nodded stupidly at her. She turned and as she was walking out of the room, said over her shoulder, "You're not getting any of that tonight, so don't try. Paul Stanley, put him in the downstairs bedroom."

On the drive home, Gwendolyn said, "Dixie sure curses a lot, don't you think?"

"She's a wonderful gal, that Dixie. She may get into her cups on occasion, but she knows how to handle Busby. Gotta give her credit for that."

Gwendolyn immersed herself in the passing landscape. The moon was bright and almost full, and she could feel its sensual embrace, pulling them toward their home, their bed. She might be stained forever with the enduring anecdote about her ill-fated show-and-tell at Lorimer Elementary, but at least she wasn't Dixie, charged with the compulsion to talk so crudely about her life.

7

Running for the Roses

The annual trip to the Kentucky Derby always began with a brunch at the Colonial Tavern, the traditional place to go in Cape Girardeau for breakfast. Dixie and Busby had the station wagon, so they drove. Gwendolyn and Paul Stanley provided the bar. After doing it for twenty years, the cousins, and now their wives, had the system down pat.

Brunch at the Tavern comprised the usual: three eggs over easy, ham hocks, buttermilk biscuits and gravy, Bloody Marys. It was an important meal as it would probably be the only way to fortify themselves nutritionally for what was to come.

The drive over started with crossing the Mississippi on the rickety Cape Girardeau Bridge. Each year, the bridge crossing spawned a festival of nostalgia. First came the toast to Gwendolyn—crowned Miss Cape Girardeau Bridge Queen at its dedication in 1938—inevitably followed by the retelling of the time the four of them had been partying at the Purple Crackle Night Club in East Cape on the Illinois side of the bridge when Gwendolyn, who had her own car, followed Paul Stanley back home. On that black night, a dense fog rose off the river. Suddenly, Gwendolyn emerged from a fog flow to find Paul Stanley's Chrysler stopped in the middle of the bridge. She slammed on her brakes and before she realized it she was heading back across the bridge toward the Illinois side. She turned around in the Purple Crackle parking lot and began heading back to the Missouri side when she spotted Paul Stanley emerge suddenly from the fog, calling her name plaintively over the railing. The recalling of this story always brought a gendered difference of opinion about stopping in the middle of a bridge to take a leak—both men agreed that made sense, especially when you had to "piss like a racehorse"—and an amazement that never diminished about how it was even remotely possible for a large Buick Roadmaster to do a total 180 on such a narrow bridge.

"I had three little children who needed me still," Gwendolyn said, as she did every year.

"And don't forget about that fucking monkey," rejoined Dixie.

"He's not easy to forget!" said Gwendolyn as they all laughed easily at the rituals of conversation that bonded them together.

The trek continued through the lowlands of Southern Illinois, past the slowly dying town of Cairo, and emerging finally into the rolling verdant beauty of western Kentucky. It was always at Paducah where the men made a "piss stop" at the eastern edge of the city. The women, who were somehow blessed with larger bladders—or at least more decorum—remained in the car. "I think they just like to hold their dicks at least once an hour," observed Dixie.

Gwendolyn, already feeling in high spirits, added uncharacteristically, "Maybe they just like to compare them."

Dixie hooted. "Well, I can assure you Busby would win that contest."

"How on earth would you possibly—"

Gratefully, this conversation that could have been dangerously dodgy even for a Derby exchange was derailed by the men's sudden reappearance.

"Tallyho!" proclaimed Busby as Paul Stanley swerved the car out onto the road leading to Louisville.

Gwendolyn knew what this meant, even though she thought it was a little early to start pouring the mint juleps that she had prepared in a Tupperware carafe. Knowing they would outvote her, she made the preparations, pouring three modest portions. As for herself, she hated to "drink and ride."

They arrived in downtown Louisville on schedule, around 4 p.m., just in time for cocktail hour 'Looville' style. The front desk at the Galt House passed them through the throng, given that they were regulars, and soon they ensconced in their adjoining rooms.

The décor was adamantly early riverboat, which made Gwendolyn wince every time she first encountered it after a year away, even though it never changed. The ubiquitous olive-green and muddy-brown wallpaper, with its dizzying riverboat-themed pattern, was enough to exacerbate even the mildest hangover. Paul Stanley loved it. He liked its homely familiarity, admitting that it reminded him of his parents, with whom he had begun the annual trek to the Derby in his teens and who always stayed at the Galt House, perhaps because it was the only decent accommodation offered in their era.

It was Friday night, and the town was in full party swing. Fridays were traditionally Louisville Locals Day and the main event at Churchill Downs was the Kentucky Oaks, the "ladies" race, as it featured fillies. The treacly smell of bourbon pervaded the lobby, teeming with gents in stained seersucker suits and ladies in elaborate hats now haphazardly worn. The decibel level was booming; high-pitched women's voices shrieking in drunken merriment, deep drawling male voices adding a bass line to the cacophony.

Up in their rooms, Gwendolyn and Dixie freshened up while the cousins went in search for their dressing drinks. They returned with supplies, and everyone gathered on their balcony that overlooked the Ohio River as well as the festive entrance to the Galt House.

"Do we dare?" Gwendolyn asked, nodding toward the whirling crowd below.

"Tallyho!" exclaimed Busby.

The ladies snagged seats at the lobby bar, something Gwendolyn preferred as it offered the advantage of a prime view of her long, shapely legs. Dixie just liked being close to the source of libation.

The evening surfed along in a lovely, liquor-infused twilight. At some point, Gwendolyn noticed that Paul Stanley and Busby were nowhere to be seen and hadn't been for some time. She brought this up to Dixie, who was staring past her with vacant eyes. She nudged her. "Dixie?"

Rousing as if from a dream, she answered, "Oh, them. You know how they are when they get Kentucky Oaks fever."

"What's that?"

"Don't be so naive—not one of your most endearing qualities, my dear."

"I still don't know what you're referring to."

"The Kentucky Oaks is about the fillies, the females. You know that, right?"

"Yes, but what does that have to do with—"

"For chrissake! How many times have you been on this little Bollinger bacchanal?"

Gwendolyn was feeling cautious. She was well aware of the dangers stalking her when Dixie got this way.

Dixie jabbed a finger at Gwendolyn's shoulder, almost sliding off her barstool. "You do notice, don't you, how the boys disappear almost every damned Oaks night?"

Gwendolyn didn't say anything, now on alert. "They're in high spirits, this being their annual and all."

"Yeah, high spirits. If that's what you want to call it, if that makes you feel all better. Let's just hope the boys have the sense to wear rubbers."

"Oh, come on, Dixie. You always go there."

"I'm not the one who goes there. Our husbands do. Turn down Main the wrong direction, and you'll find those horny fuckers in high spirits all right, high as kites at the Wildcat Club, or as they like to call it, the 'Wild Pussy.'"

Gwendolyn turned to her VO Press and took what she hoped

looked like a thoughtful but uncommitted sip. "You know, I've always thought Paul Stanley was born in the wrong age."

"What the hell does that mean?"

She was slurring her words, so Gwendolyn wasn't sure why she should proceed. "He would have been better in the Wild West, where there weren't any rules where men could, you know?"

"Fuck whores and shoot anyone they wanted? How you romanticize your husband. He's just a spoiled, entitled boy who wants what he wants and doesn't want Mommy to be mad at him for it."

Gwendolyn realized she must have been frowning as Dixie slapped her hand on the bar. "Drink up, dammit, and get that serious look off your face before you wrinkle up!"

◆ ◆ ◆

Later that night, Gwendolyn lay silently in her bed. Noise from the street had subsided finally. She had been like this many times before, alone, waiting for Paul Stanley to stumble in. That wasn't what was keeping her up, though; it was her conversation with Dixie. Normally, she would tell herself that Dixie was just crazy as a bullfrog. Yet once again she wondered if Dixie possessed a wisdom that she should listen to.

The Wild Pussy! Why would Paul Stanley need to go there? Don't I make myself available to him whenever he wants? Oh, of course Dixie would say she was a prude. But that was just not true. She wasn't exactly innocent. When Paul Stanley was consumed with his residency at Barnes Hospital in St. Louis and she was working as a receptionist at a local radio station, she would often join the boys at the nearby Chase Hotel Bar for drinks and enjoy flirting. She was good at it and knew it would not lead to anything further. But still, she wasn't exactly innocent. She was a "technical virgin" when they married, for Pete's sake!

As the dawn was encroaching on their room, she roused slightly, enough to see Paul Stanley next to her, snoring rhythmically. She smiled despite herself. He was home, safe.

◆ ◆ ◆

May 2, 1959, the First Saturday in May, the 85th Run for the Roses

The day broke sunny and bright, which was not always the case in this often atmospherically turbulent part of the world in spring. Everyone gathered, per custom, in the large Galt House Restaurant where a sumptuous buffet was offered. It was a waste of money for the most part, as the Bollinger cousins always chose instead to drink their breakfast with the passable Bloody Marys that were on offer. Gwendolyn avoided this liquid breakfast, wanting to save her calories for the Churchill Downs signature mint juleps, which she looked forward to every year. She already had a prized collection of fifteen commemorative mint julep Derby glasses and was always eager to add one more. Occasionally, she even indulged in the ardent fantasy that one day her Derby glass collection would swell to more than fifty, proudly displayed on her custom built-in sidebar in her custom-built house on a hill overlooking the Mississippi River.

She found them spread out at a table with a panoramic view of the Ohio River. The cousins were poring over the *Daily Racing Form* while Dixie, looking hungover, smoked.

"Have we picked any winners, yet?" Gwendolyn asked as she sat down with her small plate of scrambled eggs.

Dixie practically snarled at the eggs. "How should I know? They haven't said a word."

"How 'bout it, Paul Stanley, got a hot tip for me?" Gwendolyn asked, leaning in and looking over his shoulder. His form was marked up with all kinds of esoteric-looking numbers.

This roused Busby from his scratchings. "I've got a hot tip for you anytime you want it, Gwennie, but you're going to have to get past that one over there," he said, casting a nod at Dixie, whose only response was a *harrumph* and a swig of her Bloody Mary.

"Settle down, cuz," said Paul Stanley as he turned toward Gwendolyn. "You know you always bet the long shots."

"Yes, but this year I really want to win. I've got my eye on that new divan at Patrick's Furniture, and I plan on getting it with my winnings."

Paul Stanley tossed her his vanquishing smile. "And I want you to have it, so I'm going to give you the surefire winner of the Derby—Sword Dancer."

Busby hooted. "Don't listen to him. When has he ever been right? If you want the winner, bet on Tomy Lee."

Dixie chimed in, "That sounds like a rockabilly singer. I'm going with the filly."

"There's a female horse in the Derby?" Gwendolyn asked.

"Damn straight. Silver Spoon." Dixie jabbed at her racing form. "That's her name, and it says right here she's owned by Cornelius Vanderbilt Whitney. That sounds like a winner to me."

"Gold digger," muttered Busby without looking up from his form.

"If I'm a gold digger then I'm a piss poor one by the looks of it. Besides, I'm a Democrat, so I'm voting for the filly."

Paul Stanley looked up at her. "What does that even mean?"

The good times kept rolling as they headed out to the Downs. True to custom, they skipped the first few races, giving all the amateurs and Derby virgins time to crowd in through the gates. The verbal battles continued about who would win the big race. Only Gwendolyn hadn't firmly encamped with her choice. Busby was usually a good handicapper, so that made Tomy Lee look promising. Paul Stanley always derided this assessment, claiming his cousin had the luck of a fool. And then there was a certain appeal to Dixie's pick, the filly, Silver Spoon. But the gender-based choice seemed to be a weak logic, so she swerved back to her husband's pick, Sword Dancer. She liked the name. It had both a masculine and a feminine sensibility, so that took care of any gender issues. Besides, hadn't she always benefited from throwing in her lot with Paul Stanley? Look at where she was now—Louisville, Kentucky, on the first Saturday in May!

"Let's get some music on the radio," said Busby from his driver's seat. Paul Stanley was riding shotgun, and the two women sat in the backseat, per usual. Paul Stanley turned on the radio and sifted through the static until a woman's perky voice came through, singing a catchy tune.

"Connie Francis! Turn that up," Dixie demanded. 'Lipstick on Your Collar'—I love that song." She began singling along,

Paul Stanley suddenly turned the dial, muttering, "She sounds like a damned cartoon." He finally came to rest on Bobby Darin singing "Mack the Knife."

"That's better," he said.

Gwendolyn stared out the window at the shaded street and once-grand brick townhouses. She could sense Dixie sneaking her one of her teasing looks, but she didn't acknowledge it.

All was back in gear as they arrived at the backside of Churchill Downs, where they parked their car in the front yard of the Graboski family, who greeted them once again while gathered on their front porch, barbecuing short ribs and drinking Pabst Blue Ribbon beers.

Third floor Club House, finish line. That was the privilege the Bollinger cousins enjoyed year after year thanks to their fathers, who obtained the box as a result of a rare Depression-era good fortune: One of their patients couldn't afford to pay for his appendectomy and instead bartered with his box seat tickets that renewed automatically year after year.

When they arrived at the box, Busby summoned Johnny Smith, their man with the mint juleps in an always-full tray. "Keep 'em coming, Johnny boy!" Busby declared, slipping him a twenty.

"Yessir," Johnny said, distributing four ice-sweaty juleps with tufts of mint sprouting from their 1959 memorial glasses. Gwendolyn took special note of the striking black and gold depiction of a jockey on a high-headed horse—a stunning modern design. She thought it would make a brilliant addition to her collection.

While the Bollinger cousins continued their intense handicapping and betting, and Dixie continued her intense drinking, Gwendolyn focused with great delight on the colorful fashion scene swirling around her. It was always an opportunity for men to peacock, usually with bow ties, pocket scarves, and seersucker suits. Paul Stanley, uninterested in fashion, always wore the same beige suit and maroon Countess Mara tie depicting miniature blue horses in flight. Busby, however, was a treat to behold on Derby Day. She had never known a man who took such an interest in dressing with flair. This day was especially flavorful. He wore a purple felt fedora with a paisley headband of clashing hues that matched an ascot. His signature cape had an equally purple lining. His pants were jodhpurs; his brown-top, knee-high riding boots sported a pair of spurs. Gwendolyn thought he looked like a cross between a pimp and a jockey. This was in committed contrast to the conservatively tailored suits with narrow lapels that almost every other man was wearing.

Everyone looked at Busby, which never seemed to bother him. But to Gwendolyn, the women were always the most visually interesting. The hats! They swooped low like Garbo's and sprouted high like birds in flight. Halter-style, brightly patterned dresses with cinched waists, dropped just below the knees, were all the fashion that year. As she perused the women parading by their box, she began to feel uneasy as she realized her dress, although in a bright, springlike color, was one of the only dresses that covered the shoulders. One consolation? She didn't need to wear a girdle like a lot of these women to fit into her cinched dress.

There was always a trend to the day in terms of winning and losing. Either Busby was winning or Paul Stanley was, and whoever it was claimed ascendancy on the "peter meter," as Dixie termed it. But there were some Derbies when the long shots were coming in, and that was when Gwendolyn and Dixie could claim the bragging rights. When this was the case, as it was last year, Busby was always a good sport. Paul Stanley claimed to be, congratulating the women for their good sense, but Gwendolyn knew by the way he said it—in a slightly higher voice than normal—that he wasn't too happy about this outcome.

They worked their way through the undercard, fueled by Johnny's attention to their needs. No one was getting all that drunk, except for Dixie. It was hot—someone said ninety-four degrees, the hottest Derby on record—which must have accounted for the unexpected sobriety as they sweated off the effects of the mint juleps.

Then the moment came.

A man in a red coat, riding cap, and boots stepped out in front of the winner's circle, raised his bugle, and played the familiar "Call to Post." The horses emerged onto the track for the post parade and the announcer, in full throttle, proclaimed, "And now, please rise as the University of Louisville Marching Band plays 'My Old Kentucky Home'!"

The Bollingers were already on their feet as the horses passed by. Paul Stanley took Gwendolyn's hand, making the annual gesture seem like a moment of reverence as they sang along to the familiar lyrics . . .

The sun shines bright on my old Kentucky home, 'tis summer, the children are gay,

The corn top's ripe and the meadow's in the bloom, while the birds make music all the day.

Gwendolyn could sense the emotion gathering in her husband. She glanced at him sideways, his handsome, regular-featured profile, his tenor voice swelling. She could feel his hand on hers, tightening . . .

Weep no more my lady, weep no more today.
We will sing one song for my old Kentucky home,
For my old Kentucky home far away.

He hugged her and then flashed a smile that made her forget everything except the joy of being there, at this moment, with him.

As the horses loaded into the starting gate, the crowd's energy amplified to an overwhelming level, as if a current of adrenaline connected the thousands of people throughout the grandstand. Paul Stanley and Busby stood at the front of the box, side by side with their racing forms rolled in their clenched fists. Busby had stuck with Tomy Lee, and Paul Stanley, true to form, had gone with the favorite, Sword Dancer. Dixie, shorter than all of them, scrambled to mount one of the folding chairs, which she somehow accomplished while shouting "Go, girl" in support of Silver Spoon.

Paul Stanley turned to Gwendolyn and asked, "Did you get your long shot tickets?"

She showed him her one ticket. It was for Sword Dancer. "I'm going with yours."

"Good choice, hon. Goin' with a winner this year."

Gwendolyn never really cared if she won or lost; it was all about being part of this electrifying world that, before Paul Stanley, she had never imagined.

"And they're off!" whooped the announcer as the crowd let out a collective cheer. The horses thundered by them toward the first turn, the noise of sixty-eight horse hooves hitting the ground sounding like thousands. At sixteen hands and with his dark bay coat glistening almost black in the heat, Tomy Lee was easy to spot, stalking the lead horse as they rounded the first turn. On the backstretch, he commandeered the lead, which earned a whoop from Busby, but it was short-lived as Sword Dancer overtook him at the milepost. Paul Stanley pounded his rolled-up program on Busby's shoulder, shouting for Sword Dancer, who now appeared to own the race.

A bawl of sound from the crowd announced the thunderous herd as they came around the home turn and down the stretch, with Tomy Lee not giving up the race. The entire human population of Churchill Downs was on its feet, roaring with excitement as the horses battled for the lead. Tomy Lee crossed the finish line in front of the Bollingers' box by a nose.

Dixie threw her arms up and head back in one long yowl of glee as she seemed to leap off her chair into the middle of the box, where Busby caught her and planted a big kiss on her already lipstick-smeared lips. "My winner," she exclaimed.

Paul Stanley looked at Gwendolyn with what she knew was meant to be his "oh well" philosophical good-sport look. "Sorry," he said. "I thought he had it in him."

She held up her ticket and shrugged. "You know me. I only bet two dollars."

"That's my Wendy, sensible to the last," he said then turned away to glare at the track, where Tomy Lee was parading by on his way to the Winner's Circle. Gwendolyn knew that her husband's "two-dollar ticket" surely had at least three added zeros.

That night, back at the Galt House, they were having a hazy dinner of prime rib and twice-baked potatoes when Paul Stanley stood up suddenly and announced, "I'm ready to call it a night."

"Sore loser, cousin," said Busby.

"Actually, tonight, I feel like a winner, and I'm going to prove it." He leaned down and took Gwendolyn's hand. "Come on, hon, I've got some making up to do with you."

She gave them a raised eyebrow and coquettish shrug as she turned to follow him out of the room to hoots of encouragement from Dixie and Busby.

Paul Stanley was already in bed when she turned around from getting some supplies from her suitcase. He was often amorous after the excitement of the Derby had subsided but usually only when he won. This year was unusual, but she wasn't complaining. Clutching a sheer negligee to her chest, she paused at the doorway to the bathroom. "Why don't you put some music on while I get ready—something from that station that plays the top ten?"

While in the bathroom, she heard some random noise coming

from the radio then settling on a song by The Platters that she recognized, "Smoke Gets In Your Eyes."

She opened the door and paused, hoping the back light created an enticing tableau with her sheer negligee. "I'm ready," she said.

Paul Stanley pulled the covers off him. He was ready all right. The Platters continued to sing. She walked through the darkened room toward him, feeling like a star in her own movie with an enchanting soundtrack.

8

Hero

Everyone was in a slackened state on the drive home, all grudges of winners and losers mellowed in the mist over the Ohio River. Busby drove with determination and played with the radio to find as much opera as possible—a distinct challenge in western Kentucky—while Dixie turned quiet and remote. In the backseat, Gwendolyn curled up under Paul Stanley's arm as she dozed in and out of awareness.

With a jolt, she came out of her slumber. The radio was turned way up. Dixie and Busby were dancing in their seats, Dixie with bombastic jazz hands. Both were singing at the top of their voices.

"Turn that damn song off!"

It was Paul Stanley, causing Gwendolyn to shoot him an irritated, quizzical look. "Why? 'Boogie Woogie Bugle Boy'—I like that song."

Busby turned the radio down. "Yeah, why, cuz? Too close to home?"

"Why would you say that?" Gwendolyn asked with a laugh.

Dixie chimed in. "Did Paul Stanley play the bugle in the Army? I didn't know."

Gwendolyn turned to her husband with an expectant smile and a tease on the tip of her tongue. She swallowed it when she saw darkness descend on his face.

Gwendolyn was confused. "What is it, honey?"

Busby turned around. "Yeah, what is it, cousin?" he asked in his teasing voice.

"Dammit, keep your eyes on the road," demanded Paul Stanley.

"What's going on here?" asked Dixie.

Busby answered, "Come on, cuz, you don't have anything to be ashamed of. You did your part—splendidly, it would seem. You got the Soldier's Medal."

Dixie chirped, "Is that the same as your Silver Star?"

"Not exactly, no. That was for combat," said Busby with a lilt to his voice. "Soldier's Medal was for heroism not involving conflict with an enemy. Cousin was stunning as the medical procurement officer at the New Jersey Quartermasters. Important job, for sure."

"But I thought . . ." Gwendolyn trailed off as she glanced at Paul Stanley, who was darkening even more. She had always thought of her husband as some kind of war hero, and this swirled her once-secure picture of Paul Stanley. He had never spoken about his war experiences, which she had accepted as his way of dealing with the trauma. She shrank into silence.

Dixie broke it. "Am I to understand that the fearless Paul Stanley Bollinger doesn't have anything like that sexy slash of a scar over your chest just under your right nipple?"

Paul Stanley said nothing as he looked out the backseat window at the endlessly rolling green of western Kentucky. Gwendolyn did the same on her side, and they rode forward in the sludge of an uncomfortable silence.

◆ ◆ ◆

Busby and Dixie dropped them off with awkward felicitations, and Paul Stanley dragged their valises into the back patio of the house.

That's when they saw it. Eddie's cage was open, and he was nowhere to be seen.

"My lord, what's happened?" Gwendolyn whispered, even though her heart was screaming.

"Look," Paul Stanley said, pointing up to the second-story bank of windows belonging to the girls' room that overlooked the patio. Six widened eyes were focused on something to the west. They followed their children's gaze but could only see the high, slatted fence that separated them from their neighbors. A distressed screech coming from that direction grabbed their attention.

"Where's Aunt Sally?" Gwendolyn hissed, more loudly than she intended. She was referring to Paul Stanley's aunt, who they hired to stay with the children when they were out of town. She was not known for her mental stability, having been an occasional resident of Farmington, the mental hospital in the next county.

From the back door came the answer. It opened slightly, enough for them to see Aunt Sally peering out, her watery blue eyes full of terror. "I couldn't stop them," she said, her voice wavering.

Paul Stanley stepped forward. "Aunt Sally, don't be afraid. Tell us what happened."

"There. That monkey." Her gesturing hand looked useless as it flopped toward the fence.

A scream pierced the air. It sounded human, female. And then another, almost in harmony with the last one. Eddie's staccato screeching accelerated the cacophony.

Aunt Sally stuttered, "The sisters!"

That pinned it. The next-door neighbors were two crotchety spinster sisters. "I'll see what's going on," Paul Stanley said as he jumped to grab the top of the fence and hurled himself over, disappearing into their yard.

Gwendolyn rushed inside to find her children, all clearly upset. "What happened?" she asked. Gilda had the most coherent answer. "Those nasty Simpson boys, from the next house over, started throwing rocks over the sisters' fence and one hit Franny and then Oliver let Eddie out so he could help us, and he did by jumping across the fence and then—"

"He saved us, but the sister ladies started screaming," Franny injected, her upper lip quivering.

Gwendolyn looked at Oliver, who was silent but seemed content with his participation in this drama.

"Oliver," Gwendolyn commanded, "what's happening?"

"We needed Eddie's help, so I set him free, like Gilda said. He yelled at those boys and then chased them away."

"Eddie protected us," Franny added.

More screams. More monkey screeches. And now, Paul Stanley's roaring curses.

From the upstairs windows, they could see into the next-door house where Eddie was jumping from one ceiling fixture to another and then lunging in full shriek at a woman—the more submissive sister—who was trembling while balanced on a dining room chair. Then they could see the other sister leap into view, wildly thrashing a broom at Eddie, which further agitated him into a fury. Paul Stanley had somehow gotten into their house and was yelling at Eddie while grabbing at him. The sisters retreated to cower in the corner while Paul Stanley continued his efforts to grab the leaping monkey, who was obviously not inclined to be grabbed. Then came a crash, followed by Eddie flying across the fence and straight into his open cage.

Gwendolyn raced down the stairs and outside, where she found Eddie shrinking into a dark corner. His big, brown eyes studied her. It always seemed that he was pleading with her.

"Oh, Eddie," she said in a soothing tone, "you're being such a rascal."

His tail started waving around him, settling into an embrace of his trembling little body. When Paul Stanley appeared on the back patio, he found Gwendolyn feeding Eddie.

Scratched and bruised, he said, "That little bastard doesn't deserve any food."

She continued with her ministrations to the monkey, filling his water dish and fluffing his sleeping pad. "How're the ladies doing?"

"They're pissed. What do you expect?"

The vitriol in his voice got Gwendolyn's attention and even more so Eddie's. He leaped forward, baring his teeth and lunging toward Paul Stanley. He somersaulted back to the middle of his cage, where he grabbed on to a branch that had been installed across the top. Performing a rapid succession of pull-ups, he locked eyes with Paul Stanley.

"What the hell?" Paul Stanley said.

"I think he's trying to show you who's boss." Gwendolyn said this with mirth, but when she got no response, she turned to look at her husband. "Oh dear," she said when she saw him glaring.

"You care more for that monkey more than you do me."

Confused by this outburst, Gwendolyn made a split-second decision to ignore it and reach out to put her hand gently on Paul Stanley's cheek, saying, "You saved the day, didn't you, sweetheart?"

He jerked away and started back to the house, muttering, "Fuck Busby, and fuck that damned monkey."

Gwendolyn stood there in the darkening gloom of the evening, watching as Paul Stanley retreated. An unfamiliar feeling of rejection enveloped her. She turned toward Eddie to make sure he was secure in his cage. He inched closer, grasping his skinny, hairy fingers on the wire barrier.

"Don't mind him, Eddie. He's sore he lost the Derby, but you really have to be a better boy."

She turned to her house, all aglow with the early evening lights and her children chirping hungrily like little birds in their nest. The new knowledge about Paul Stanley's war service gave her pause. Then it dawned on her that it explained more about why he came back from the war with an increased need for alcohol.

Besides, he was still her hero—he had leapt across the fence and saved the terrified ladies from that scamp Eddie.

1965

9

Sex and the Married Lady

It was the 1965 edition of the Charity Bridge and Golf Tournament at the Cape Girardeau Country Club, and Dr. and Mrs. Paul Stanley Bollinger were one of the sponsoring couples. Gwendolyn organized the bridge tournament while Paul Stanley oversaw arranging the foursomes for the men's golf tournament.

Gwendolyn asked Dixie to help her set up.

"Why do we have to have this event here?" Dixie grumbled as she set out the petite vases of flowers Gwendolyn had arranged from her garden.

"What're you talking about? This is the best place in Cape to have a bridge party." She gestured toward the view, which was indeed spectacular for Cape Girardeau; a vista stretching across manicured greens to the Mississippi River flowing in the distance beyond Cape Rock, the original promontory of their historic town. "Where else are you going to get a bridge party with that view?"

"Maybe some place that allows Jews."

Gwendolyn paused her task of putting out place cards and looked at Dixie with exasperation. "You know I don't agree with that discriminatory policy, but still—"

"But still what? This whole thing is so bizarre. Our husbands are all out there getting ready to drink and golf, we're getting ready to drink and play bridge, all to benefit poor Negroes who can't even step foot on this property!"

She was referring to the beneficiary of this annual event, the Smelterville Baptist Church of the Holy Redeemer, which provided the only social services available to the disadvantaged Negroes who lived in the south of town.

"I asked Romaine to come . . ." Gwendolyn trailed off, unsure of what she was saying.

"Romaine? Your maid?"

"Well, yes, I thought—"

"What? That she could enjoy serving the fancy White ladies while they play a game of cards that she never heard of?"

"Romaine always wants extra work. She has lots of family responsibilities." She said this knowing full well she would get nowhere with Dixie when she was on this trail.

"Did you ever think of asking her to join us, not serve us?"

Gwendolyn almost gasped with what seemed like the absurdity of this. "Why do you always go there? You know that's impossible."

Dixie went back to her task of placing the flowers on the tables, seemingly satisfied now with her point. "You know I'm a Democrat."

"I never know what you mean by that. Besides, aren't you Southern Democrats the ones who are always trying to maintain segregation?"

"The good Lord did not put me in your life, Miss Gwendolyn, to dignify your misguided assumptions."

Like so many of Dixie's oblique comments, Gwendolyn didn't know what she meant by this, and today, she had no time to spend on it.

Romaine popped her head in from the adjoining kitchen. "Miz B, your ladies are startin' to come."

She glanced approvingly at her, looking so pretty and well-groomed in her starched white uniform. "You look so nice today, Romaine."

"Thank you, ma'am. Would you like me to start serving anything?"

"Just make sure the ice teas are filled and when we take our break that the buffet is set up. Oh, and Romaine?"

"Yes'm?"

Glancing sideways at Dixie, she answered, "Better make sure there is a pitcher of vodka lemonade available."

Gwendolyn turned back to her chores and came up short with Dixie in the middle of a miniscowl. "I sure hope you treat that Negress well," Dixie said.

"Of course I do! She's a jewel. And you keep your hands off her," she said as she headed for the door to greet the first of the women to arrive. "She's mine."

The Ladies' Bridge Tourney went splendidly. The chicken à la king was excellent—Campbell's mushroom soup was the secret ingredient—and the best part for Gwendolyn was that she won. She had never seen herself as particularly talented at anything, except perhaps housekeeping and mothering; but she had to admit, she was pretty darn good at playing bridge.

After the ladies had departed, Dixie suggested that they get a couple of VO Presses ordered and sit out on the balcony overlooking the golf course. The golfers were returning from their nine holes to their kegger setup below.

"We can find out what they're really up to," Dixie suggested as they took their seats with drinks in hand. They were hidden from view unless they peeked over the half wall.

"Are you sure they can't see us eavesdropping?" Gwendolyn asked.

"They can't, as if they would even be interested."

They could hear the basso murmurings of the men gathering in the twilight. The women listened, enthralled by this secret bugging of their uncensored conversation. Now and then, they heard something that caused Dixie to whoop and then slap her mouth shut with her right hand.

Gwendolyn had to admit, despite her ethical reservations, she was enjoying this illicit view. It was like they had snuck into a private meeting of the Masons and were learning all their secrets. She could hear Paul Stanley's voice rise above the rest quite often, possibly because of her deep familiarity with its timbre.

That last putt was PGA perfect . . . Let's get something harder out here than this Busch Bavarian . . . No kidding, that's an epic ass. This last comment referred to Bonnie, the well-known cocktail waitress at the Ninth Hole Bar. Everyone knew her as Bonnie Buns, and most of the wives took no real umbrage at their husbands' teasing about her, having decided that she was harmless. Besides, she made the husbands happy—and perhaps even more amorous—and they respected her for her industriousness at getting better tips.

After some party progression, the latest auditory balloon arriving from Paul Stanley caught Gwendolyn's attention. Responding to something indistinguishable that was said to him, she heard him say, "You got that right, bud. She's a beauty, my Wendy, but it takes more than a pretty face to make it great in the sack." There were whoops and muddy expressions of disbelief. "Settle down, fellas. I can vouch that she is adequately available."

"Adequately? Available?" Dixie looked over at Gwendolyn, who was staring straight ahead, revealing nothing. "Honey," she said, taking her hand, "we need to talk."

※ ※ ※

Of course, the confab would involve drinks, so they agreed to have a ladies' luncheon at the Petite N'Orleans, what passed for a fancy restaurant in Cape Girardeau. Located in the historic opera house, it overlooked the Mississippi River beyond and possessed a brick-walled, white-cloth, red-velvet-curtained, elegantly quiet atmosphere. Bands of dusted light streamed in through the narrowly parted curtains.

Dixie was already seated at a discreet booth by a large window overlooking Broadway when Gwendolyn appeared at the entrance and paused to adjust to the dusky light. She was wearing a bright-yellow A-line dress that came right above her knees. She carried a patent leather handbag, also bright yellow.

As she arrived at their booth, Dixie greeted with a whistle that embarrassed her as it echoed in the mostly empty room. "Cape's very own Jackie Kennedy!" Dixie said. "Let me see that divine purse. Where did you get that? Surely not local."

"It's Pierre Cardin." She smiled as she took the cloth napkin from the table and placed it over her knees. "And yes, as a matter of fact I got it at Hecht's, right there on Main Street."

"What I wouldn't do to have legs like yours," Dixie said, shifting focus suddenly as she often did.

"Why do you say such a thing? You have very pretty legs."

"You're a thoroughbred. I'm a pony. But never mind, I have other assets," she said, cupping her rather large breasts with both hands. *"Las magníficas!"* she exclaimed with self-referential mirth.

The waiter appeared, and since martinis were their specialty, Gwendolyn decided it was only appropriate to join her friend in partaking. The implied purpose of this luncheon might have also had something to do with her forsaking her standard of not day drinking. She made a quick survey of the room and was relieved to see only two men in the opposite corner, leaning into each other, engaged in what looked like a business lunch. Another two men, recognizable to her as an editor and a reporter from the *Southeast Missourian* housed across the street, were leaving. That left old Mrs. Themis, Cape Girardeau's uberdowager, who always ate her beef stroganoff lunch at the Petite, every day except Sundays. Thankfully, she was deaf, shortsighted, and in possession of a vanity that left her without any compensations.

They settled in with their Waldorf salads and martinis, Dixie's with two olives and Gwendolyn's with a lemon twist.

Dixie began the conversation in earnest. "You are of course upset with what you overheard your husband say about your sexual talent."

Gwendolyn took a long unthinking sip from her drink and then almost spit it out. "Good lord, that burned my tonsils!"

"I'm waiting," Dixie said with an unwavering eye on her friend.

"Okay, you might be correct about that. It was hard to hear, and I really don't understand how—"

Dixie put a hand up. "Let me save you some grief. Of course, no one wants to hear their sex skills critiqued. We're not whores, we're wives. But is there really a difference when it comes to this kind of assessment?"

"Are you serious?"

"When am I not? Look. I know what you're going to say: You are a good wife and do everything you can to please Paul Stanley. You would do anything he wants. Anal even."

"Good lord, Dixie."

She let out one of her signature hoots. "That's even a stretch for me. I'm just havin' my fun with you." She leaned forward with a conspiratorial smirk. "But let's face it, we all have vices."

Gwendolyn decided to play. "Even her?" she asked, with a nod over her shoulder at Mrs. Themis.

"Beef stroganoff, perhaps?" They both stole a glance at their subject, who was staring vacantly at her plate.

"That could count," Gwendolyn said, and they both snickered.

Dixie downed her drink in one gulp, then in one deft move raised it up only to have it quickly whisked away by the waiter and replaced with a frosty new glass. After a reverential sip, she put the glass down and cradled it with her hands. "Well, that was fun. But now what about you?"

"What about me? Are we still trying to uncover my supposed vices?"

Dixie maintained her purposeful look.

"I don't know..." Gwendolyn trailed off.

"Blah fucking blah, Gwennie. Let me spell it out for you. You are a simple woman, a deliciously simple woman."

"You make me sound like a snack or something."

"You're hardly a snack, Miss Gwendolyn. Now listen up, this is important. You are what you are. What you see is what you get. Unlike *moi*, you have no layers. But that is precisely your charm. That's why men are crazy for you. They don't particularly like intricacies." She took a slow sip of her martini.

"That doesn't sound like some kind of sexy vice, now does it?" said Gwendolyn. Her answer was a raised eyebrow from Dixie. "But they get bored, I'm guessing you'll say."

"I could say that."

"What're we talking about here?" Gwendolyn asked, lowering her voice as she took a more discreet sip of her drink. She was feeling a strange sense of danger coupled with an excited interest.

Dixie leaned forward but didn't lower her voice. "We're talking the third hole here."

"What?"

"Oral. Pecker in mouth."

Gwendolyn looked at her. She wasn't exactly speechless, but she couldn't think of anything to say.

"Jesus, Gwendolyn, this is 1965. Don't act like you've—"

"Yes, I know."

"Here's the deal. It's not so difficult to do, and men love it."

At that point, the waiter showed up to refill their ice waters. Gwendolyn took the break to glance over at Mrs. Themis, who was staring blankly out the window, barely touching her beef stroganoff.

When the waiter withdrew, she leaned forward and whispered, "Do you, you know, you and Busby—?"

"Good god yes!" Dixie said, not in a whisper. "He demands it almost every time. As you can imagine, Busby Bollinger is very phallic-centric."

Gwendolyn winced. "I prefer not to imagine."

"Really, Gwendolyn, you have to get with it. You heard what Paul Stanley said. Of course, that was hard to hear, but consider it a gift, or at least a challenge to up your game. I'm here to help." She turned to retrieve her purse, which was sitting on the floor next to her. From there, she produced a crisp new magazine and placed it in front of Gwendolyn.

"What's this?"

"*Cosmopolitan*. It's a new magazine for today's woman. See? It says so right there on the cover. It's yours to keep."

Gwendolyn glanced down at it. She had the inclination to scowl at what she was seeing but made sure she didn't. The cover featured a young woman with long, lustrous hair, her head thrown back with a magnificent smile that dominated her face. It was almost lurid. And there it was, right on the cover in large pink lettering: "How to Please Your Man Orally!"

Gwendolyn looked up at Dixie and caught her cockeyed, grinning.

"Don't worry, Gwennie. You don't have to swallow."

❖ ❖ ❖

When Gwendolyn got home, she immediately placed the magazine at the bottom of her sweater drawer and followed up with a self-check on why she was being so furtive. *I am NOT a prude!*

It was the third Wednesday of the month. That meant Paul Stanley would be bowling with the Lions Club and then closing down the Town Pump (jokes always ensued) on Broadway. It also meant that she wouldn't see him until the next morning. She sometimes wondered about this but had gotten used to her husband's penchant for all-night drinking sprees. She used to question him about it but gave up when he would answer her by singing, "Gentleman songsters off on a spree, doomed from here to eternity, Lord have mercy on such as we." His charm offensive was usually successful in quelling any concerns her questions revealed, but more recently, they resulted in vague confusion.

She made sure her children were asleep in their beds and then turned her focus to the magazine at the bottom of her sweater drawer. She settled into bed with the magazine on her lap. Feeling flushed, she opened it and began reading the article on what promised to make her a more pleasing lover to her man. She had a moment that was like looking at herself through a keyhole. How could it be that Gwendolyn Bollinger of Cape Girardeau, Missouri, sitting in her comfortable bed, her three children snoring and sputtering nearby, was reading about giving a man *head*?

It was fascinating.

She learned that men relished having the head of their penis attended to by the lips of their sexual partners. She learned that it was a good thing to put her hand on the shaft and do a rotating motion. She found out that taking their testicles into her mouth—gently!—would send them over the moon. This last instruction was just a bit too much for her; she didn't trust herself to accomplish that particular action safely.

She closed the magazine and put it back in its hiding place underneath her prized collection of cashmere sweaters. Back in bed, in the dark, she considered her options.

The banging of the back door or the clomping up the stairs that woke her wasn't a surprise, but the time on the bedside clock was: 12:45 a.m. Paul Stanley was never this early on bowling nights. Stumbling into the room, she could hear him stripping off his clothes in the dark.

The flicker of inspiration sparked for Gwendolyn. She lay still, trying to calm her breathing as Paul Stanley lay down beside her. She heard him starting a soft snore. When he flopped over in her direction, she reached down and found his penis through the slit in his boxer shorts. It was squishy. She kept her hand there. It started to thicken. Emboldened, she rotated her hand on the shaft and began enjoying the power she felt bringing his penis to life. He roused with a pleasured moan. She increased her ministrations, just like the article had suggested, and the shift from tumescence to hard felt like a reward. She had always enjoyed the normal sex they had, but this was different; experiencing the pulsing sensation of the fiery penile veins brought forward a strange gratification. Without a thought, she slid down under the covers and found his hard penis doing a strange up and down dance.

She did it, just like *Cosmo* instructed.

It lasted maybe twenty seconds before Paul Stanley intervened.

"What the hell are you doing?" he barked.

She bolted up off him, her head spinning.

"Where did you learn that?" he demanded, his breathing heated.

She said nothing, looking down, unable to speak, her cheeks flushed.

He wouldn't look at her. "How did you know about that? Who taught you?"

"I . . . I thought you might like it. I heard—"

"You heard what?"

"That men like that, that you might like that."

"Who've you been with?" It was a threatening accusation.

"What're you talking about? I never—"

"There's no way, no way you could know about this. Is it Sam?"

"Sam?"

"Sam Jones, don't pretend you don't know who I'm talking about."

"The plumber?" She was horrified at the thought.

"He's always sniffing around you. It's him, isn't it?"

"You are so wrong, Paul Stanley. So wrong." She hoped he couldn't see her tears in the dark. The feeling of vulnerability was overwhelming. They lay side by side in a scorching silence, both staring at the ceiling. Gwendolyn did her best to quiet her breathing and quiet her mind, which was busy spinning a sticky web of humiliation: *Did I do it wrong? Maybe I am a dud, a prude! Does he know the feel of other women who do . . . that?*

Almost as if he were reading her mind, Paul Stanley reached out through the darkened space between them and put his hand on hers. Startled at first, she began to feel reassured. Her breathing returned to an easier cadence.

"Paul Stanley?" she said, her voice sounding to her like it was in a tunnel.

"Yes?"

"I'm sorry. I didn't know..."

After a moment, his voice wafted over from the dark. "It's just that... that it's so not like you."

That's the point!

But she didn't say it. Instead, she said, "I know."

She turned over and pulled the covers up over her head, clenching her eyes shut in some vain attempt to blot what had just happened from her reality. She knew then that this was futile, that she would never forget this night and what had happened.

10

Through the Woods

Anyone traveling north on County Route 651 toward Trail of Tears State Park will eventually come to the entrance of the Bollinger family farm. A small sign announcing Flora Creek Farm signaled the turn onto a bucolic lane bordered by two dozen walnut trees, promising the entrant a fine prospect of Missouri arcadia. On the left side of the lane was a three-acre field where a small herd of mares and their foals, corralled by whitewashed fences, grazed. On the right lay a larger field with acres of newly planted corn, flowing in the spring breeze. The bright smell of new-mown grass perfumed the air. This was the farm that Paul Stanley's parents had acquired many years ago and where they had raised their two children along with Dr. Ollie's prized Tennessee Walking Horses, his herd of Angus cattle and Miss Belle's award-winning daylilies.

The lane arrived at where a large two-story brick farmhouse commanded the hill. It was a congenial example of traditional German farmhouse architecture, so common to this countryside—a white, wooden wraparound porch, deep and wide, old red brick, a many-gabled roofline. Beyond, more than three hundred acres of rolling hills stretching back to the West, embraced by stands of old growth oak, silver maple, and American elm. To the east flowed the majesty of the Mississippi River. Now, the farmhouse was the temporary housing for Gwendolyn and her family while they built their dream home on the highest hill of the farm.

The move to Flora Creek Farm earlier than planned had a lot to do with Eddie, or at least that was what Gwendolyn would tell everyone who enquired. His escapades in the neighborhood made him locally infamous and therefore rendered the story credible. The kill shot came when he showed up at the Catholic church three blocks away and aborted a Mass by gobbling the Eucharist wafers and draining the chalice of wine. Gwendolyn found out when she was at Mabel's sitting under the hair dryer. A frantic call came from the church secretary, so she had to forgo her standards of public presentation and rush to the church in curlers. When she entered the dimmed nave, she expected to see Eddie leaping from one beam to another. Instead, an anguished scream greeted her. The first thing she saw was a small gaggle of midday Mass worshippers standing near the communion rail. She followed their horrified stares to a nearby nun in a traditional habit, the author of the scream who was then reduced to pathetic whimpering.

It was soon revealed that Eddie had crawled under the habit of Sister St. Charles—a place where no man, let alone a monkey, had ever been—and cinched tight on to her left calf. Once Gwendolyn realized this, she had a frozen moment, unsure of how on earth she was going to dislodge Eddie from underneath a nun's habit. She hadn't been raised Catholic but nevertheless, nuns intimidated her. She got a hold of herself and mustered an authoritative voice. "Eddie! Enough of that." In a flash, he bolted out from under Sister St. Charles's habit, leaving her shuddering in the wake, and flew over to Gwendolyn, where he found purchase on her right shoulder. An apologetic Gwendolyn and her unapologetic monkey quickly left the church.

Still, Gwendolyn had her reservations. The farm was remote although a pastoral delight. She wouldn't admit this to anyone, but it bothered her that it was on the road to Trail of Tears State Park. *Trail of Tears! Could that be a bad omen?* It was named after the tragic forced march of the Cherokees from the Southeastern states to

Oklahoma. She knew the story from her Central High School history class: How Andrew Jackson signed the law that forced the removal of "Five Civilized Tribes," which resulted in the displacement of sixty thousand people. Sixteen thousand Cherokees crossed the Mississippi a half mile from what would be her new house—she could actually see it from that hill. She could never get over that four thousand of these tragic humans perished in the harsh conditions of the trek.

She needed to shake off these thoughts as "bad thinking" (as her Grandmother Farnsley would put it), getting her nowhere. If she were going to be honest about it, the move to the farm had more to do with the increasing encroachment of Paul Stanley's drinking. Gwendolyn figured that the farm would be a healthier environment for him. There would be the proximity of his beloved horses and the role of gentleman farmer to keep him occupied and out of trouble. Then there was the further goal of getting him away from the rummaging eyes and ears of the neighbors. Temporarily living in the drafty old farmhouse with smelly and unreliable plumbing was an easy price to pay for such anticipated benefits.

They were already accruing. Soon after their move, Paul Stanley began organizing Sunday horseback rides. He worked with Gwendolyn and his children on improving their equestrian skills, assigning a horse from his stable to each.

This Sunday was to be a special ride. It was Gilda's birthday, and she insisted that she wanted to take a family ride through the woods, literally, to Grandma's house. Paul Stanley's parents had built a more modern house on the other side of the forest, and that is where Gilda insisted upon going. Willing to indulge his feisty eldest daughter, Paul Stanley pulled himself out of his hangover bed, sloshed water on his face followed by a bracing sting of Old Spice, pulled on his jodhpurs, his riding boots, and in his best Master of the Hounds impersonation, gathered his pack to head down to the barn.

Dusty streaks of sunlight streaming through the windows greeted their arrival. So did the earthy smell of the hay stacked at the end of the breezeway and the pungent smell of horse dung piled up like an ancient Indian burial mound outside the barn. Paul Stanley got all five horses out and tied them up to crossties, instructing everyone to curry their horse then bridle and saddle them.

While the others busied themselves with these tasks, Oliver stared at his horse, hesitating.

Paul Stanley walked up to him. "What's the matter, son?"

The others stopped what they were doing and looked at Oliver. Things didn't always go smoothly between father and son. Oliver stammered, "What happened to Redhead?"

"Time for you to move on from a pony to a quarter horse."

They looked at each other in a frozen moment, Oliver wary and Paul Stanley tensing his jaw.

"Come on, you're a fine rider. Stop being such a—"

Gwendolyn broke in, "Honey, why don't you help him get used to his new horse?"

Oliver looked from his mother to the horse, who stood with his head dropped, ears in neutral.

"His name is Willie. He's a good boy," Paul Stanley said. "Come on. I'll help you tack up."

After working silently side by side to do so, Paul Stanley coupled his hands and bent down next to Oliver to give him a leg up. "Up you go, son."

Soon everyone was mounted—Gwendolyn on her ugly but reliable mare, Candy; Franny, on her Shetland pony, Fats; Gilda, on her sleek Morgan horse, Go Boy; Oliver, still tentative, on his new Willy; and Paul Stanley, on his American Saddlebred gelding, Samuel Clemens. They filed out of the barn and down the road. Still in single file, they came to Miss Belle's famous daylily garden on the west side of the old farmhouse, walking carefully on the garden path that bisected it, heading for the levee that guarded the pond, crossing over it at a trot, and picking up the pace with Paul Stanley in the lead. Though it was a month away, it felt like Easter to Gwendolyn, the air fresh with the verdant smells coming in on a breeze, the radiant colors shimmering in the morning light, the renewal of possibilities.

Clearing the levee, they entered an alfalfa field that abutted the hardwood forest known as Belle's Woods. Samuel Clemens broke into a canter as they headed up the hill rise to the woods, sorting out the lineup as Go Boy overtook Candy, Gilda displacing her mother at the left flank of her father's horse. Willy and Fats brought up the rear, with Oliver struggling on his unfamiliar steed but hanging on.

Gwendolyn breathed in the heady greenness of it all as she took a secret, delicious scan of her pack: her healthy, beautiful children; her husband who was looking almost heroic as the lead in the charge across the field. It was one of those wondrous moments when the brain feels drenched in a bright-golden honey.

At the perimeter of the woods, Paul Stanley guided them to a trail leading through the dark-green curtain of the trees. To Gwendolyn, the perimeter looked forbidding, unknowable, but she trusted her husband as he grew up on this farm and knew its secret pathways. The horses walked through the silent forest in a single file, the crunch of fallen leaves the only sound. No one spoke. The sunlight fractured into radiances on the forest floor, creating a starry path. Gwendolyn breathed easier then more deeply the pungent ozone of the woods.

After a while, they emerged onto a dirt road that brought them to a modern house surrounded by towering trees. As they approached, Gwendolyn renewed her bafflement about her mother-in-law. She possessed an awe-inspiring intelligence even though she had grown up in the hinterlands of Bollinger County. She had never finished high school and was completely self-taught. She was a classic beauty, yet she seemed dedicated to a modest plainness. Quiet in her demeanor, she still observed her world with a keen eye that cast the unsettling shadow of disquieting judgmentalism. Gwendolyn found her genteel and polite, but she always left a chill in the air.

They tied their horses to the fence behind the house and trooped in to find Miss Belle standing in the kitchen. Her three grandchildren lined up like dutiful supplicants as she acquiesced to their proffered cheek kisses. Gwendolyn observed Paul Stanley as he stepped forward to put his arms around his mother and kiss her on the cheek. Miss Belle stiffened at the show of affection, causing Paul Stanley to wrench back.

"What's the matter?" Miss Belle said with what looked to Gwendolyn to be a sarcastic smile. "Too big and important now to kiss your old mother?"

Paul Stanley looked like a wounded child, confused. Gwendolyn never understood why her husband, usually so assured in his choices, could persist in going to a dry well. Why would he keep wanting his mother's affection, her confusing rejection, and the need to replay this sad song over and over? It just didn't seem fair.

"I've got to take a piss," Paul Stanley said, turning away and heading to the hallway by the kitchen.

"Language, son," Miss Belle said to his retreating back.

Dr. Ollie sat in the living room in a worn-leather Lazy Boy recliner, a stark contrast to the sleek built-in furniture. Upon spotting his grandchildren, he threw out his arms, commanding hugs. His face was jolly, but his voice was loud and gruff.

Franny rushed up to him first. "Hi, Granddaddy! I rode my pony all the way here and didn't fall off."

He met this with a hearty chuckle and a pinch on her robust cheek. She squealed, either in delight or pain, then scrambled to move away.

Gilda was standing next in line. She kept a safe distance. "It's my birthday today. I'm eighteen."

"You don't say. All grown up, are you?" Dr. Ollie said. "Then you get a special birthday hug from me."

She quickly received a bear hug from her grandfather then moved away.

Oliver stood back.

"Ah," Dr. Ollie said once he saw his grandson. "My namesake. How did you make the ride?"

Oliver hesitated then spoke. "I didn't fall off, either."

"Why would you do that? You're a Bollinger, born to ride."

Oliver remained still, his right hand covering his left hand below his waist. Gwendolyn thought he looked vulnerable.

"What's the name of your horse, son?"

Oliver stuttered his response. "Her name is Willy."

"Willy? *Her?* What kind of sissy talk is that?"

Gwendolyn sensed that Oliver was about to sink into the floor. She loved her father-in-law but knew he could be frighteningly gruff, especially when dealt cards that didn't make sense to him. She looked around for Paul Stanley, hoping he would step forward and break the tension. He wasn't there.

And then he was, coming out of the bathroom. "What's going on?"

Gwendolyn could smell it, the fermented odor wafting around him like some familiar cheap cologne. She knew he would only side with his father, whom he idolized, and especially in his newly altered state he would not intervene on behalf of his son. He often tried to be tolerant or even supportive of Oliver, who didn't always make sense to him. When alcohol hijacked his brain, however, all bets were off.

"Nothing," Gwendolyn answered the question. "Nothing at all."

They all endured some of Miss Belle's dry baked goods and stilted chatter before Gwendolyn, a bit too early, said that she thought they should get back on the horses. "We have some cake and presents at the house."

When they remounted, Paul Stanley took charge again. "Let's head over to that new road and take a gallop."

"Don't you think we should get back?" Gwendolyn asked. "You know, for cake and presents?"

Paul Stanley pulled out a flask from his back pocket and took a long pull from it.

"What're you doing?" Gwendolyn tried to be casual, but there was tension in her voice.

"What do you think I'm doing? Enjoying a Sunday ride with my family."

"I think we should go back," she said with even more tautness.

Just then, a motorcycle appeared on the gravel road in front of the house and roared past like sudden thunder in a summer sky. Oliver's horse, closest to the road, reared up in a panic, causing Oliver to squeal in terror and lose his balance. He was hanging at the side of the horse by only the reins, further agitating Willy. Paul Stanley was there in an instant, grabbing his son just as he was about to fall to the ground, righting him in the saddle as he took control of the reins. He transferred them back to Oliver, who was now squarely seated on Willy. Tears appeared and cascaded down his face.

"What's the matter with you, son?" Paul Stanley's expression had suddenly transformed from urgent concern to cold anger. "Didn't I tell you no fear! You squealed like a little girl."

Franny giggled, and Gwendolyn gave her a shushing look as she rode over beside Oliver.

"Okay," Gwendolyn said. "I've heard all of that I want to hear today." She turned to face Paul Stanley. "I'm taking the children back to the barn." And then to her children, "Follow me."

Before they could mobilize together, Paul Stanley, who had already grabbed another draft from his flask, wheeled his horse around and galloped off in the opposite direction, shouting over his shoulder, "Anyone who wants to ride with me better get in gear!"

They watched him disappear around a bend in the road.

Franny was clearly distressed. "Mommy! Daddy just wants someone to ride with him."

"Okay, kids, time to go. We've got cake waiting for us back at the house."

❖ ❖ ❖

Later that night, after her children were in their rooms asleep, Gwendolyn allowed herself a nightcap, a light rum and Coke. Paul Stanley was nowhere to be seen. She knew she should be worried sick, but he always seemed to survive whatever risky exploit he stirred up, and she assumed he would this time as well. As she sat on the back porch listening to insects create a familiar symphony, the awareness that she had challenged her husband and taken charge overcame her. She had led her children back through the woods, finding her way, getting the horses properly put away, her daughter's birthday celebration accomplished. Today seemed like a novel victory for her.

Around 5 a.m., she woke up with a start. Shaking off her sleep confusion, she realized that not only was she still in her clothes but that Paul Stanley was not snoring beside her. She checked on all three children in their respective bedrooms and, satisfied that they were safe and asleep, got into her car and drove down to the barn.

The day was dawning when she arrived, and slanted rays of dusky light barely lit the breezeway of the stables. When Gwendolyn entered, she heard the snorting of horses, some of them pawing the ground, expecting their morning feeding.

Then she saw him, sitting slumped on his snoozing horse, back lit by the rising sun beaming in the open eastern doorway of the barn. Gwendolyn paused and tried to focus on what she was seeing.

There he was, her great provider, the man who had earlier bathed her mind in honey. There he was. Snoring. Passed out.

Pathetic.

The thought startled her. It was a strange judgment for her to have about her husband, so bold it made her catch her breath. But she had no time to dwell on this. He needed her help.

11

Man Stuff

Gwendolyn heard the whole story from Oliver as she sat on the edge of his bed one night. It tumbled out of him in excitement. She tried to piece it together as best she could.

He had been alone in his bedroom, he said, immersing himself in the rhythm and earthy delight of Tina Turner's voice. He knew all of Ike and Tina's songs by heart and was happily lost in his perfect lip-synch of his current favorite, *A Fool in Love.* His legs were pumping in an earnest effort to replicate Tina's famous pony trot when he suddenly became aware that his father was observing him from the doorway.

"So now you're going to be a Las Vegas dancer?" Paul Stanley had asked, only it didn't sound like a question. "I guess this means you're not going to be my first-string quarterback, are you?"

Oliver stared at his father, not at all sure of himself.

"Lights out, son. We've got a big day tomorrow, early start."

He had no idea what his father was talking about, but it left him with a slight shiver of dread.

Oliver could smell the sourness of a night of drinking on his father when he rousted him out of his bed the next morning. It was dark and cold, adding to his apprehension. Some calm returned to him when his mother appeared in the kitchen, still in her nightgown. She set about preparing a breakfast of eggs and bacon. To Oliver, she seemed different. It wasn't just her appearance in the kitchen wearing her nightgown—he had never seen that—but the set of her mouth, the seriousness with which she fed him. "Here you go. You'll need this for the day ahead," she said, her voice tight as she placed the plate in front of him.

"Where're we going?" he asked.

"It's a surprise, you'll see," his father said as he poured a wallop of brandy into the mug of coffee he held.

The sun was lightening the sky as they drove northwest on unfamiliar, twisting roads. Paul Stanley was singing in his cracked tenor, a song that Oliver recognized from the scratched records his father played late at night. After he crescendoed, he turned to him. "You know what that's from?"

Oliver shrugged.

"It's *Pagliacci*. You know it, right?"

"No." Oliver wasn't sure where this was going.

"It's about an actor named Canio. He plays a sad clown in a traveling play and his wife is also in the acting group. Her name is Nedda. In the play Canio discovers Nedda's being unfaithful to him with another actor, and this mirrors the play they're both acting in. In the play, the clown kills his wife at the end with a dagger. But what happens is Canio actually kills his wife on the stage after singing the most heart-stopping aria."

Oliver really didn't know what his father was talking about.

"*La commedia è finita!*" Paul Stanley said, almost as if he were singing the phrase. He glanced over at Oliver, who looked lost. "It means the comedy has ended."

"Oh," Oliver mumbled.

"I've got a lot to teach you, son. That's what this little outing is all about."

"Where're we going?"

"I told you. A surprise."

Oliver watched as he took a swig from a flask and then turned his attention to the road as it climbed higher through deepening woods. The unrelenting dark-green landscape and the endless curves in the road made him increasingly anxious. It was a familiar experience, this anxious feeling as his father took him into some strange and scary place, usually involving the hunting and killing of animals. Oliver would even feel terror at times, though his mother had told him that his father was only trying to teach him about the "art of being a man."

At some point, Oliver must have dozed off, as he woke up with a jolt when the car pulled to an abrupt stop. They were in front of the Marble Hill Diner.

Oliver hesitated. Paul Stanley laughed. "Nothing to worry about. You'll see. Fat people eat here, so it's gotta be good."

After they entered and took a seat at the counter, Oliver sneaked a look around. The people looked familiar: large women with flattened faces and merry, rosy cheeks; and men, also large, wearing buff-colored coats with dirty fake fur collars, dark-brown pants with lots of pockets, and big, menacing boots covered in dust and mud. It was a place that Oliver had been before, probably on one of those hunting trips his father imposed on him. While Paul Stanley drank his coffee, endlessly filled by a chunky waitress who always called him "hon," and he enjoyed his Coke, a rare treat only possible because they were out from under the vigilant eye of his mother, he let memory flow through him… early-morning duck hunts, freezing for hours in a duck blind while the men drank brandy and waited; coon hunts, even worse, happening in the middle of the night, with the yowling dogs chasing raccoons up a tree, and shotgun blasts causing dead animals to rain down like a nightmare. The quail hunting wasn't so bad because of the dogs, who searched out coveys hiding in the tall grasses, posing still as statues when on point. The birds would flush up into the sky like a rapturous fan before the lethal spray of shotguns brought them down. The dogs, still in control of their instincts, rushed off to retrieve the dead birds and bring them back, held in their slobbering mouths. It was all like a rustic ballet to Oliver, and he grew to like hunting quail, except for the kickback of the twenty-gauge shotgun against his shoulder when he pulled the trigger.

They left the diner and drove on farther into the countryside. They rode in silence for some time, and then Paul Stanley began talking. "Do you know why your Grandfather Ollie became a doctor?"

Oliver was pretty sure he had heard why but said nothing, knowing he was going to hear about it anyway.

"Dad was working in the field one day—you know our people were farmers, having come here from Switzerland. He was harvesting watermelons when he saw a man drive by in a splendid buggy drawn by a high-stepping horse, and he asked his dad who that was. 'It's the horse-and-buggy doctor, come to see your sister for her rheumatism.' That's when your granddaddy decided he was going to be a doctor. It sure beat picking watermelons. So, eventually he and his brother Layton—that's Busby's father—took their best two horses and rode all the way to St. Louis. It must've taken them several days, and when they got there, they found themselves in the middle of the 1904 St. Louis World's Fair—"

"'Meet me in St. Louis, Louis, meet me at the fair,'" Oliver sang, off key.

"What?"

"You know, the song from the Judy Garland movie. 'We will dance the Hoochee Koochee, I will be your tootsie wootsie, if you will meet me in St. Louis, Louis.' You know?"

Paul Stanley telegraphed he didn't know with a scowl. "Anyway, the brothers eventually pulled themselves away from the excitement of the fair and signed up for medical school at nearby Washington University. Back then it only took two years, and soon enough they were back on their horses, riding back to Bollinger County, bona fide medical doctors."

"Oh," Oliver said, not knowing really what to say.

"You come from simple stock, son," Paul Stanley said, "but

noble in their simplicity. They cared about each other and this land. There's nothing more important than that."

Usually, his dad talked about where they had come from with a catch in his throat and sometimes tears in his eyes, which he would wipe away with the bandanna that he always carried when he came up to Bollinger County. These were the rare times when Oliver felt for his dad—felt close to him instead of afraid.

"Are we going duck hunting?"

"Not the season. I've got something even better in store for you."

Not too long after that, Oliver noticed a terrible smell. He commented on it, and Paul Stanley told him not to worry, he would take care of it soon enough.

An hour or so later, after traveling through roads gradually more remote and a terrain so dense with hills and trees that it seemed ominous and unfamiliar to Oliver, they turned off the paved road onto a rough dirt one that caused the car to toss about. Oliver noticed an intermittent, high-pitched sound, like a squeal, coming from the back of the car. By the time they pulled into a clearing, where there were other cars and trucks, the sounds were anguished.

The mystery was soon solved. Paul Stanley opened the trunk. There was Eddie, cowering in the corner, baring his teeth. He had defecated everywhere. "Nasty little beast," Paul Stanley said as he snapped a leash onto his collar. The leash kept Eddie from bolting, which he was clearly intent upon doing.

After giving Eddie some water, they walked toward a weathered barn. The raucous noise coming from within frightened Oliver and agitated Eddie. Paul Stanley moved forward with resolve.

He flung open the double barn door. Men in overalls and John Deere caps crowded around in a circle. The air was thick with smells, and the sounds were fierce. Oliver hung back until Paul Stanley pulled him forward. Eddie was leaping around on the end of his leash. When it became apparent that they were present, there was a lull in the noise as the men turned toward them with curiosity.

When they saw Eddie, who was now holding on to Paul Stanley's leg, a collective murmur of interest arose. "Hey, doc," one man with ruddy jowls said, "we didn't know if you'd get here."

A fat man with a bright-red beard stood in the middle of the circle. He had a hulking dog with a huge slobbering mouth. The dog strained against a chain attached to a spiked metal collar.

It all came at Oliver like a tornado: Two big dogs, both with teeth bared, huge haunches with muscles rippling as they stood against the restraint of their owners' chains, lunging at each other, the yowling of the dogs as blood splattered, teeth gnashing on necks, the throaty cries of excitement from the men.

But it was what came next that made his eyes widen and his voice hollow out with the remembrance. "The big man with the red face asked Dad if he was ready. Then Dad yanked on Eddie's collar and then he asked him, 'Are you ready, little buddy, to show your stuff?' With so much happening, I'd forgotten all about Eddie. Dad pulled him to the center of the ring. Eddie got more and more crazy acting, leaping and baring his teeth at the men who were yelling at him. The red-faced man was collecting money from everyone, including Dad. They were placing bets on Eddie or the new dog brought out to the ring. This dog looked less scary, a thinner kind of dog, but as soon as he saw Eddie, he bared his teeth and growled like crazy. This got Eddie mad. He jumped at the dog."

Oliver paused. Gwendolyn could see his eyes losing focus, his mouth moving as if he were chewing on something tough.

She put her hand on his knee. "Go ahead, honey, tell me what happened."

"Eddie," Oliver said then looked up at her, "was awesome!"

Gwendolyn tightened up. "What on earth do you mean by that?"

"This big ugly dog didn't scare him at all. Dad held Eddie back on his leash, but he was snarling and jumping at the dog that had this awful sound coming from him. You could see both of their teeth as they flared at each other. It was awesome."

"You said that, Oliver. Tell me what happened."

"Everyone was yelling. It was loud. Eddie leaped onto the dog and rode his back. His claws dug into the dog's neck. He was making the most awful screechy sound. The dog suddenly seemed confused. He was whirling around like a crazy dog. Eddie looked like he was in one of those rodeos, like he was a cowboy riding a bull. Then the dog just gave up. A lot of the men were mad, but Dad was happy. When Eddie came back to where we were, he and Dad looked like friends."

Gwendolyn leaned forward and put her hand on his head. "Please, Oliver, put all of this out of your mind."

"Why? They were having fun. It was like when men were men and women wore Kotex."

Gwendolyn gasped. "Where did you get that, for Pete's sake?"

Oliver's wide-eyed look transfigured into an oddly self-contained grin. "I heard it from the red-bearded man. I thought it was funny. What does it mean?"

"Eddie was scared, and I'm sure that dog was too. The only ones having fun were those men betting on their animals like they were gladiators in ancient Rome . . ." she trailed off, realizing that Oliver wasn't tracking what she was saying. "Never mind. Just try to put all of this out of your head and get some sleep."

Later that night, Gwendolyn lay in bed, her eyes closed, but she couldn't fall asleep. The violent images that Oliver had bequeathed to her were too agitating.

Paul Stanley arrived at the side of the bed, taking off his watch to put on the nightstand.

"I thought you were going hunting," she said.

"Oh, you're awake." He got in bed. "It's not hunting season. Why would you think that?"

"I don't understand why you did it."

"Did what?"

"Take him to that place, that barn, where they do those things."

"Oliver's going soft. He needs to be exposed to more man stuff."

"That's what you call 'man stuff'—a poor monkey fighting a dog?"

"You should have seen that little bastard. He was a wily beast. The way he leaped out and over the head of that snarling dog before it even knew what hit him. His fingers dug into the dog's neck, riding him like a broncobuster. It was no time before that dog was simpering out of the ring. You shoulda seen it."

"No, I shouldn't have, and neither should have Oliver."

"That's what's wrong with him, and that monkey too—you coddle them, make them into mama's boys. Pansy asses."

"I don't understand you sometimes, Paul Stanley. You can be the most tenderhearted man. And you can be so cruel. Oliver is just artistic; he has an artistic temperament."

"What're you talking about? He doesn't even draw."

"You don't understand."

"What I don't understand is having a son who would rather be a Las Vegas showgirl—"

"Than what? A Golden Gloves boxer?"

"I don't know where you're going with this."

"What you don't understand is having a son who isn't you."

"I've had enough," he said as he reached over to switch off the bedside lamp. "I've got early surgery tomorrow."

12

Driving Lessons

Gwendolyn was proud of her driving skills. Her father taught her in the family Packard when she turned sixteen, and it was one of her fondest memories. When she shared this with Gilda, who rode in the front seat with her as they crossed the Mississippi River Bridge at Memphis, Gilda shrugged, not impressed.

Eyes firmly on the road like she was taught, Gwendolyn enjoyed the mental smile brought forth from the memory of her father spending hours teaching her all the nuances of driving an automobile. It was 1936, and as difficult as it was for Gilda to imagine, girls weren't usually taught to drive back then. She knew she received this benefit because her brother, Thomas, who had been stricken with polio, couldn't drive. She only knew this in retrospect. Then, her father's attention and faith in her made her feel special and capable.

The memories slid easily through her mind as she took the turn on the highway leading toward Tupelo, Mississippi, en route to Tampa, Florida. She hadn't seen her parents in several years. They moved there when her father retired from his unhappy job at Farnsley Lumber, and she missed them terribly.

She glanced in the rearview mirror and spied Oliver absorbed in one of his Archie comic books. Franny was asleep, cuddled with Romaine, who stared out the window. Romaine had a look of wonder on her face, which Gwendolyn understood. When they left for their trip, she had told Gwendolyn that she'd never been anywhere outside of Cape Girardeau, let alone all the way to Florida.

Gwendolyn had called ahead to the Howard Johnson Motel in Tupelo for two rooms. They arrived at 5:30 p.m., as planned. Leaving at dawn, despite the loud protests of her children, had paid off. Pulling into the parking lot in front of the motel, she turned off the DeSoto, put on the parking brake, and told her children to hold their horses; she would be back shortly.

As she approached the pretty, young, pink-cheeked woman at the front desk, she felt a sense of pride that she was managing this trip well on her own. Paul Stanley had surgeries he needed to complete and was scheduled to fly down and meet them in a couple of days.

The desk clerk greeted her with a big smile. "Hello, ma'am, how may I help you?" she said, startling Gwendolyn with her thick Southern accent, so different from the milder mid-South accent she had become used to in Southeast Missouri. Her name tag proclaimed, *Hi! My name is Suzy!*

"Hello, I'm Mrs. Paul Stanley Bollinger. I called ahead to reserve two rooms."

"Yes, ma'am," Suzy said as she drew her index finger down the page of her register. "Oh, here we go: Mrs. Bollinger, Cape Girardeau, Missouri." She looked up at her curiously. "Are you traveling with your husband?"

Gwendolyn smiled. "No, I'm traveling with my three children and my maid. My husband . . ." she trailed off as she realized that she had lost the young woman's attention. Suzy was looking out the glass door to where Romaine sat quietly in the backseat of the car.

"Your maid?"

"Yes, she's helping me with my children."

Suzy shut her registration book. "I'm sorry, ma'am, but we don't serve the colored at this establishment." Her features, formerly soft and pink, reddened as they scrunched up into defiance.

"But this is 1965!"

"So what?"

"So, what about the Civil Rights Act, you know? They passed it last year. You aren't allowed to discriminate any more."

"I don't know what you're talking about, ma'am."

"It's the law of the land. You should know that."

"I don't know what land you're talking about. Now, if you'll excuse me." She turned her back to Gwendolyn and picked up the phone.

When Gwendolyn got back in the car, she slammed it into gear and overpedaled the gas, making the tires squeal as she pulled out onto the highway.

Franny demanded from the backseat, "Why are we leaving? I'm tired."

"Aren't we going to eat?" added Oliver.

Gwendolyn said through clenched lips, "They don't have any more rooms. We have to keep driving."

Gilda turned to face the disappearing motel. "But, Mother, it says 'Vacancy' on that big sign."

Gwendolyn noticed the knuckles of her hands gripping the wheel had drained of color. Realizing that she was overgripping, she relaxed her hands. *I guess that's where they get that thing about white knuckles.* It occurred to her that possibly Mississippi was exempt from the Civil Rights Act—she didn't really know—and if that was the case, then they were probably never going to find a place that would accept them.

Romaine leaned forward. "Miz B?"

"Yes, what is it Romaine?" *God, I hope she isn't going to bring up the motel!*

"Why don't I get out some of those sandwiches I made, and we can have a picnic in the car while we drive on?"

She breathed easier. "That's a great idea. Thank you."

They drove on into the night across Mississippi. Gwendolyn's stamina surprised her, and she realized that her fury at Suzy and all she represented fueled—almost chemically—her endurance.

Dawn was breaking as she pulled into a gas station in Tuscaloosa, Alabama. They were making good time. Oliver offered to pump the gas, as there was no attendant on duty, while Gwendolyn headed for the snack shop. Both girls were behind her in obvious need. They paused, unsure.

"What's the matter?" Gwendolyn asked. She knew when she followed their gaze: There were two women's bathrooms, one marked *White* and the other *Colored*.

She looked back to her daughters, who were hopping from leg to leg in dire need. She made a rash decision, probably because of her exhaustion. "Go ahead, girls. Each take one."

"But?" Gilda said, unsure.

"It's all right," Gwendolyn said as she entered the store in search of coffee and donuts for her famished children.

Gwendolyn returned with a Styrofoam cup of coffee with sugar, which she handed to Romaine and told her, with an apology, that there was a bathroom that was okay for her to use. She scrambled out of the car. "Why be sorry?" said Romaine. "I'm in a fearsome need." Gwendolyn watched her stride to the bathroom marked *Colored*, her head held high, her white uniform a little rumpled but well modeled, and felt confused as ever about her.

They drove forward through the day, windows down, blowing in hot air. Gwendolyn worked to stay focused on the road while suggesting car games. She engaged everyone with the one about who could spot the most license plates from different states. Gilda won.

She drove for another six hours, enduring her children's complaints until she couldn't anymore. By the time they reached Dothan, Alabama, it was too much. She had to stop; they needed to eat, and she needed to get out from behind the wheel. When she saw the Dothan Chicken Shack in the near distance, she thought it might be a safe bet.

She pulled into the parking lot and parked between two trucks, which gave her pause. *Is this a truck stop? Is it safe for a woman traveling alone? With a colored maid?*

She gathered herself. She would not give into this kind of fearful hesitation. No more. She told everyone to sit still while she checked on something.

Greater calm didn't greet her at the door. Inside, she saw mostly men, big men, rough-looking men, and several of them turned to look at her as she stood in the doorway. This was familiar to her, and she knew what to do: She smiled her pretty smile back at them.

A waitress, all hair and lipstick, approached and asked what she was looking for. "My children and I are traveling to Florida, and we're famished. Can you seat us?"

"Of course we can, honey. How many?"

Gwendolyn clutched but tried to breathe through it. "I have three children. They're all well behaved, and I'm traveling with my colored maid."

"Is the colored woman wearing a uniform?"

"Why yes, yes she is."

"Okay, but she'll have to eat in the kitchen."

Gwendolyn forced confidence as she told Romaine about the necessary dining arrangements. "Okay, Miz B," she affirmed as she walked back into the kitchen area as if she had expected to do so.

They washed up and sat at a table in the middle of the room. The children fussed, probably because they were hungry, except Gilda, who she assumed was just being difficult and would eventually eat the extra helping of fried chicken that Gwendolyn ordered.

The grousing didn't abate. "What are you all so upset about?" she asked the table.

"It smells in here," said Franny.

Oliver spoke next. "Why can't we eat with Romaine?"

Gilda came out of her pout and leaned forward. "Don't you get it? These are all racists, and because of the color of Romaine's skin, she can't eat with us White people."

Gwendolyn shot her a look. Gilda was a freshman at the University of Missouri, and she and Paul Stanley had shared a concern that she might be unduly influenced by the famously liberal college professors. Yet, Gwendolyn easily realized that she had a point.

"Let's try and enjoy our meal so we can get back on the road," Gwendolyn said, trying hard to be soft.

Gilda stood up. "I'm going to go eat with Romaine. This is insane."

She turned and walked with determination toward the kitchen. Oliver followed her. "Me too," he said with less determination as he glanced at his mother.

"Don't worry, Mother," Franny said. "I'll keep you company."

Gwendolyn barely noticed her dinner of fried chicken parts, mashed potatoes piled high with a puddle of gravy in the center, and grayed green beans. Franny gobbled her meal, unthwarted. In fact, she even said so—"This is the best ever!"—which brought a smile to Gwendolyn as this sounded just like Paul Stanley, who often described anything he was involved in with that exact phrase.

After she paid the bill, she and Franny went to gather the others from the kitchen. They were all sitting around a big wooden table, laughing as the two Black cooks provided them an endless supply of cornbread and fried chicken. Romaine was laughing and flirting with the male cook. Oliver and Gilda, for the first time, appeared relaxed.

According to Gwendolyn's calculations, it was a seven-hour drive to Tampa. She was beyond exhausted, but she wanted to avoid further problems related to Romaine's skin color. Fortified with a pitcher of iced sweet tea, and pleased to see her children well fed, happy with their restaurant adventure, and too drowsy to complain, she decided to forge forward.

She pulled her weary brood into the driveway on Parkland Boulevard at 10:30 p.m. Everyone was asleep as she set the parking brake and leaned over the steering wheel in a moment of surrender. *How did I ever do this?*

It didn't matter. She was here, in front of her parents' Spanish-style house, the newest but smallest one on this pretty street in Tampa. She looked up at this house that her father had built as their retirement home. They'd moved here to escape the oppressions of his wealthy family, who had never forgiven him for leaving the family business to make his failed fortune in Los Angeles. Her eyes moistened with tears that refused to flow. She missed them terribly.

Her parents emerged into the splaying light of their porch: Maurice, her father, was handsome, perpetually tanned, intense; her mother, Mildred, was tall and elegant, with a radiant smile that Gwendolyn had inherited. Tears started to seep. She quickly swatted them away; there was no time for that. She needed to get her children washed up and to bed.

The week flowed by. Every morning, Maurice picked a gardenia from his prized bushes and brought it in for Gwendolyn to place behind her ear. The children seemed happy to play endless games of badminton at the court their grandfather had set up for them and gorge on the homemade popsicles their grandmother provided. Romaine settled into the utility closet that had been set up for her with a cot and fresh flowers to soften the utilitarian space. Mildred, apologetic, explained that they had dedicated their guest quarters to her daughter's family, but Romaine seemed happy to have her own space. Mildred also commented on how clean and well turned out she looked in her white uniform. "Yes'm," she said. "I wash it out every night in the sink and hang it up to dry, and then I get up an hour early, before I have to help with the childrens, and iron my dress. I always like to look proper."

"What a gem!" Mildred told her daughter later that day.

Once Paul Stanley arrived, the plan was to go to the La Playa, a small hotel on Redington Beach that they had been to many times. There was the large pool in the center of one courtyard, a shuffleboard court in another, as well as the gentle waters of the Gulf to safely frolic. For the adults, there was the small cocktail lounge with Herbie, the genial bartender who quickly learned their preferred drinks, and the seawall bordering the beach that provided the best gathering spot for sunset happy hours with Gwendolyn's good-time cousin, Helen, and her grandly mustachioed husband, Sammy. Gwendolyn always joked that they were the Florida versions of Dixie and Busby.

Relaxation finally embraced Gwendolyn, happy in the sunshine of this familiar summer place. Paul Stanley was enjoying himself somewhat soberly, tossing the kids in the surf, playing shuffleboard with them, racing them in the pool. Cocktail hour started early, around four in the lounge, and then continued out on the seawall at sunset. Paul Stanley kept pace with the others but didn't blast off into his own dominion. Despite the reprieve, Gwendolyn couldn't ignore the intrusive thoughts about the other shoe dropping.

As expected, Paul Stanley and Sammy would take off on their favorite outing, deep-sea fishing for tarpon, renewing their contest for landing the biggest one. Sammy was the current winner, and Paul Stanley was champing at the bit to take the title away.

Gwendolyn felt relief with his departure. This had been a perfect vacation so far, and she was loathe for it to veer in a different direction. Her mother renewed the tradition of her sunset serenade by strumming her ukulele and singing jolly ditties from her ingenue years, but this didn't mitigate the worry Gwendolyn held about her father. Maurice, usually intent on hosting everyone for the splendid memory he and Mildred wanted to create, had been taking long, solitary walks on the beach, often returning with a dour expression.

On one such return, Gwendolyn wondered if he had been crying. There was always a whiff of melancholy about her father that his smile, with white teeth beaming from olive skin, obscured for most people. He gave a weak wave as he passed by her and Helen when they were sunbathing on the beach.

Helen could see the distress on her cousin's face. "You look surprised," she said after he had walked past.

She paused, contemplating this. "I just worry."

Helen, always empathetic in contrast to her cigarette-coarsened voice, turned to her. "I've never known Uncle Maurice to be anything but sad. Oh, he tries to hide it well. He tries to seem engaged when he and Mildred are square dancing or he's fussing with his gardenias, but the whiff of dejection is always there, underneath."

"Mother told me once that Dad changed with the Depression, when they had to leave California and come back and work for his Farnsley cousins. They treated him like a bastard relation. That must've humiliated him terribly, his dreams of making it on his own blown up." She looked out at the horizon over the Gulf. "I was so full of myself back then that I didn't really notice." She paused, lowering her head. "I feel ashamed of my selfishness. I was so focused on being popular."

Helen turned on her side to face Gwendolyn, resting her head on her plump arm. "Why're you being so hard on yourself? You were born to be the belle of the ball."

Gwendolyn knew what Helen was trying to do—shift her out of her morose mood—but she was drifting in her shame. "What I remember thinking was my dad was nice and decent but sort of uninteresting."

"Well, you certainly didn't marry your father, now did you?"

This one worked. "God no. Hardly!" Gwendolyn laughed. It felt good to laugh.

The week flew by, and Gwendolyn experienced her own increasing melancholy as she anticipated the return of Paul Stanley from his fishing trip and the subsequent departure from her parents. The return trip through the Deep South also worried her. Paul Stanley was going back with them by car, but this agitated her more in a surprising way.

She decided that Romaine would take the bus back to Missouri, something Romaine agreed to do.

"You know you may have to sit at the back of the bus," Gwendolyn said, but it was more of a question.

"It's okay. I figure that. Probably less noisy, and I can spy on the White people." She said this with a merry laugh, which helped Gwendolyn with her uncertainty about this request.

Everyone piled into Maurice's car to take Romaine to the Greyhound station in downtown Tampa. She had shed her uniform for a modest blue dress and low white heels. Mildred had prepared a picnic basket for her—fried chicken, fruit, a thermos of iced tea, and some home-baked cookies. Gwendolyn thought Romaine looked relieved as she smiled and waved to them from her window seat in the back of the bus.

It was the next day that they planned to start the two-day drive back to Southeast Missouri. Gwendolyn made sure everyone was packed up and ready to go at dawn. The problem was that Paul Stanley hadn't returned from his fishing trip as scheduled. Trepidation entrapped Gwendolyn like a sticky spiderweb.

When he finally arrived around ten on the morning of departure, it was obvious that he was still on a bender. The family sat in the Florida room eating tuna fish sandwiches when he burst into the house like a squall off the Gulf.

"You're looking at the tarpon fishing champion of Hillsborough County!"

This resulted in tepid praise. "That's wonderful, honey," said Gwendolyn. "Maybe—"

"What till you see it," Paul Stanley said, stumbling toward her then veering over to where Gilda was seated. "Taxidermist got it now. It's going to look swell over the mantel. You're gonna love it."

"I doubt that," Gilda said as she turned away from him.

"Dear, we're late getting on the road," Gwendolyn intervened. "We have a reservation at Montgomery, and I don't think we're going to make it, even if we leave right away."

"Let's get on the road then. What's everyone waiting for?"

Figuring that Paul Stanley would stay true to form and insist on driving, she asked that he take a shower and drink some coffee. He took the shower but refused the coffee.

Gwendolyn couldn't look at her parents when they were all in the car preparing to leave. She knew they worried, not only about Paul Stanley driving drunk, but about her unusual nervous state, which had become more and more evident to them over the week.

Paul Stanley got them sufficiently on the road to Tallahassee, and all seemed to be going well. Gwendolyn sat in the back, trying to not chew on her knuckle and to be a comforting presence for the two restless daughters, seated on each side of her. Paul Stanley had insisted, for reasons that were unclear, that Oliver sit in the front seat with him.

As they approached Tallahassee, Paul Stanley declared, "Florida is a great state. There's no speed limit." He punched the gas pedal hard. "I'm going to drive this tank a hundred miles an hour. Hang on!"

Protests erupted from the backseat as the car groaned in the effort. Gwendolyn went into a strange trance. She shut her eyes and tried to remember the Lord's Prayer.

Somehow, they made it to the Alabama border without incident. Paul Stanley continued to drive and nip at his brandy flask. An hour into Alabama, the DeSoto swerved and almost ran off the road. At the last minute, Paul Stanley righted the car. The tension in the air was palpable. Only Oliver, his eyes intent upon the road from his perch in the front seat, didn't seem bothered.

Paul Stanley pulled over at a gas station outside of Dothan. When they were ready to resume the trip, he surprised everyone by declaring that Oliver would drive.

"But he's only fifteen!" Gilda protested. Then she mumbled, "At least I'm eighteen."

"It's about time the boy learned something useful," Paul Stanley said as he slid into the shotgun seat.

"Mother!" Gilda called out as Oliver assumed his position behind the wheel. "He can't drive!"

"I know how to drive," Oliver retorted. "I've been driving around the farm all year."

Paul Stanley tossed him the keys. "Everyone, calm down. I'm gonna teach him what to do."

Oliver lurched the car forward when he stepped on the gas, but he quickly recovered and pulled safely onto the highway. He drove with determination, eyes riveted to the road. "You can go faster, son," Paul Stanley said.

Gwendolyn held tight to her daughters' hands. She felt paralyzed, as if she were in a nightmare and needed to scream or flee the danger but couldn't.

She softened as the trip proceeded without incident. She saw Oliver with both hands clenching the wheel, leaning forward, and sensed he was feeling proud of steering them safely toward home.

Paul Stanley, still nipping at his flask with regularity, had begun to drop his head then jerk it back. When Oliver reduced his speed behind a livestock truck, his father jolted upright. "Come on, stop being so chicken. You got plenty of room to pass that hillbilly."

Oliver pulled out into the oncoming lane. "Come on! Step on it!" Paul Stanley said in a loud enough voice to rouse Gwendolyn from her snooze.

What she saw, she would never forget: A large green sedan appearing out of nowhere from behind a blind hill rise, charging right at them. Her voice returned. "Oliver!" A horn blared as he wrenched the steering wheel to the left and the DeSoto skidded onto the hard shoulder. The green sedan whooshed by, so close to the tempest that it rocked their car. Oliver brought the DeSoto to an abrupt halt. A stunned silence followed, then Gwendolyn found her voice. "You saved our lives, Oliver, but I'll take over from here."

Gwendolyn could not remember much of the rest of the trip back to Cape Girardeau. Images of her family—her entire world—being annihilated on an Alabama highway had confiscated her mind. Why had she felt so throttled, so incapable of protesting her husband's recklessness? The image of Paul Stanley as her roguish hero was slowly unraveling. And it left her feeling lost.

13

Independence Day

It had been a rough year for the country. As Dixie had become fond of saying, "The time for sex, drugs, and rock and roll is at hand." But not everyone shared her enthusiasm. Or, in this culturally cloistered part of Missouri, understood what she was even talking about.

All the more reason, Paul Stanley decided, for them to have a good old-fashioned Independence Day celebration. Fireworks, homemade ice cream, fireflies caught in a bottle, cousins, pony cart rides, American flags swinging in the breeze on the porch, the scent from an ancient and still fecund lilac tree dominating the front of the old farmhouse perfuming the air. It was the perfect setting.

Both of Paul Stanley's parents arrived early. Dr. Ollie assumed his customary spot in his favorite rocking chair on the porch, chomping ferociously on ice cubes, lunging forward to pinch a grandkid racing past, waging war against all flies with his giant fly swatter. Miss Belle maintained her usual stern expression that warned the rowdy grandchildren not to invade her personal space with any unnecessary notions of frivolity. Paul Stanley's sister, Anna, had come down from St. Louis with her four children and her husband, Hector, who Paul Stanley maintained was "light in the loafers." This was a designation Gwendolyn found ludicrous. Bad blood simmered between her husband and his sister, another outcome that she held their mother responsible for with her parsimonious doling of love.

Gwendolyn was, as usual, in charge of all preparations, but her labors kept getting interrupted by her nephews and nieces tugging at her to see Eddie. She wiped her hands on her apron and went down to the basement to retrieve him from his cage. Snapping the leash on his collar, he jumped onto her shoulder. He seemed quiet and content until they rounded the corner to where the throng of kids awaited. Having learned from her disastrous show-and-tell day experience at Lorimer Elementary, she prepared them with instructions to be quiet and, for goodness' sake, no fireworks. Eddie was uncharacteristically calm, letting a couple of the older cousins lead him as he walked along the fence railing in front of the old farmhouse, his prehensile fingers balancing on the plank like an Olympic gymnast. Maybe Eddie was more mature, maybe less wild? Surprisingly, all was going well. Until it wasn't.

Screams rended the buzzy quiet, bringing Gwendolyn's attention to heel on what was happening in front of the house. As she rushed out, she could tell these were screams of delight, so her heartbeat went back into normal sync. That only lasted seconds when she emerged on the porch to see Eddie mounted securely on the back of Anna and Hector's golden retriever. He had a death grip on the dog, who was darting erratically around the front yard. Despite the cousins' excited cheers, Gwendolyn could see Eddie's terror in his wide-eyed grimace, which evidently only she could read. She swooped in and grabbed his leash, which was dragging on the ground, and once in hand, Eddie leapt into her arms. As she brought Eddie down to the basement she was sure he must have thought he was in a rematch of that horrid dog fight. When she returned him to his basement cage, he seemed unusually grateful.

Back at her perch at the sink, as she prepared the barbecue fixings, she gazed out the window to the back of the farm. She became immersed in the memories of the Sundays when her family would ride across that field. She could see them in her mind's eye silhouetted against the light, cantering rhythmically together toward the leafy wall of the woods. She smiled; there was such beauty in that memory and no remembrance of any aftermath to spoil that poetical image to spoil it. Things looked good to Gwendolyn, who was always looking for such a view.

Busby and Paul Stanley tended the barbecue: cuts of sirloin butchered from the farm's Black Angus cattle, fresh corn on the cob from the fields, big juicy beefsteak tomatoes from the vegetable garden. Hector picked flowers from the garden and made loose arrangements for the tables set up on the big wraparound porch. Anna helped Gwendolyn prepare the "fixin's" while Dixie sat in the corner and commented with the aid of her gin and tonic. It was going to be a feast and, Gwendolyn hoped, a celebration for a new beginning.

Around 5 p.m., Gwendolyn, roused by some commotion, looked out the open door. A huge American flag posted on the porch waving in the breeze obscured what was going on. She squinted. Gilda came into focus, running with more-than-usual determination toward her. She banged through the kitchen screen door.

"What is it? What's the matter?" She couldn't tell if Gilda was terrified or gleeful, so strange was her bifurcated expression, her eyes lit up (with fear? excitement?), her upper lip trembling yet with what could be construed as a smile. It was almost eerie.

Gilda manifested a dramatic intake of breath, her eyes widening. Gwendolyn put her hands firmly on her daughter's shoulders. "Honey, tell me what happened."

Gilda sputtered, "It's Franny."

"What about Franny? Is she alright?"

"Scotty kicked her."

Oliver appeared behind her. "It's real, Mom." He paused and looked at Gilda, as if he were seeking permission to speak further.

"And then what?" Gwendolyn demanded.

"Dad . . ." Oliver couldn't get it out.

"What did Dad do now?" There was more edge to her voice than she wanted to allow.

"Daddy killed Scotty," blurted Gilda.

It was true. Scotty, a Shetland pony that Paul Stanley had hitched up to a cart to give the kids pony cart rides, wasn't used to pulling a cart and evidently didn't like it. As Gwendolyn got the story from a tearful Franny, she could see that she was floridly bruised on her left arm but otherwise not physically injured. It all started with Scotty kicking at the rigging of the cart in protest. This infuriated Paul Stanley, who tried to bring the pony into line by using his buggy whip. This made Scotty even angrier.

"Daddy kept cussing Scotty and that made him mad, you know, like when he got mad at Eddie and said bad words at him," Franny said as her mother cuddled her on the living room couch. Pops from firecrackers and sizzles from sparklers sounded from outside along with shrieks of delight from the cousins.

"What happened then?"

Franny's big brown eyes widened. "He kicked me! It hurt awful. I know Scotty didn't mean it. He was confused 'cause he didn't like the cart. But Daddy didn't care. He got out of the cart and picked up a board that was on the ground and hit Scotty with it, right between the eyes, and then Scotty stumbled, and white stuff started coming out of his mouth and then he fell and then he was—" She stopped and it seemed like she was seeing it all anew. "And then he was, he was dead!"

That son of a bitch, Gwendolyn thought. A tense moment passed where she thought she might have said it out loud, but when she looked at Franny, she appeared more mollified than she did before.

"Mother, don't be mad at Daddy. He was just trying to save me from Scotty."

This really struck Gwendolyn. Franny, thirteen, seemed like a little girl untainted by the furies of puberty. She still had her big, uncorrupted heart, her desire to not only save every winged bird she came across but to forgive her father for killing an animal.

Gwendolyn wondered if she could do the same.

She looked out the window and saw the dusk glowing. The luscious aroma of grilled meat infused the night. "Come on, Franny," she said. "It's the hour for fireflies. Let's go make some lanterns. We have mason jars."

Though Gwendolyn could barely look at her husband, the zest of sparklers illuminating the night soon swallowed up the Scotty affair. Everyone gathered on the porch to watch fireworks going off haphazardly in the front field. Fireflies flickered brilliantly before dying in their glass prisons. When everyone laughed at the men doing their ritual dousing of the fireworks by turning their backs to the house and peeing together on the smoldering remnants of their pyrotechnic display, Gwendolyn cheered and clapped with the rest. She looked as fresh as she did when she began the day of labor, her dress unsoiled and remarkably unwrinkled, her makeup intact, as was her easily luminous smile. No one could sense the black cloud of despair gathering around her.

Anna kept pace with the imbibers, eventually breaking from the pack, accelerating to a whole different level, even from Dixie, who had become mellower as the evening wore on. Gwendolyn stood at the sink with her tipsy sister-in-law, cleaning up. Anna handed her the dish she was supposed to have washed, which resulted in Gwendolyn needing to rewash it before she could dry it.

"I was talking to your mother the other day," Gwendolyn said, "and I was struck, as I often am, with how intelligent she is."

"She *can* be," Anna said through compressed lips.

Gwendolyn wanted to keep things light, but she quickly realized that talking about Miss Belle wasn't the right move to meet that goal. However, the ensuing silence was too much to bear. She persisted. "She didn't even finish high school, did she?"

"She was a poor girl from Bollinger County. Probably not."

"I wonder what she would've become had she had more . . . more modern opportunities."

"Probably a prison matron."

Thinking this was a joke, she glanced over at Anna. It was no joke.

"You don't much like your mother, do you?" Gwendolyn asked before considering the trajectory of the conversation.

"You might recall she pulled a gun on me."

"The way I heard it, you began a fist fight with her."

"That surprises you, doesn't it? Remember, I'm her one and only daughter. Apples. Trees. You get the memo, right?"

Gwendolyn had forgotten how spiteful her sister-in-law could become when she got her snoot full.

"I hope you're enjoying the farm," Anna said, practically spitting out the words as they both turned from the sink, now abandoning the dishes even though the water was still running.

Gwendolyn looked at her sideways, wary. "Yes, the farm is lovely. We're looking forward to building the new house on the hill."

"Heard you got Frank Lloyd Wright. Fancy-shmancy."

"Well, I think it's someone in his office. Busby arranged it. You know Busby." Her voice lilted as she tried to ease the building tension.

"Of course, I *know* Busby. He's my cousin."

"I didn't—" Gwendolyn drew up, not sure how to proceed. "This is about the farm, isn't it?" As soon as she said that, she knew she shouldn't have. The farm was a source of enduring animus for Anna. Doc Ollie and Miss Belle had deeded the three-hundred-acre farm to Paul Stanley and compensated her with some worthless stock in the local cement factory.

Anna threw down her sponge and wheeled on her. "Are you taking hormones?"

Gwendolyn turned off the water and faced her. "What on earth are you saying?"

"You're practically menopausal, and look at you. It's not natural."

"I have no idea what you're talking about, and no, I am not menopausal. You might recall I'm only forty-five."

"Only forty-five, huh?"

Gwendolyn stared at her. She felt like she was in the presence of a poisonous snake. She had been there before with her sister-in-law.

A mocking laugh erupted from Anna's distorted face. Her lipstick was smudged, and her eyeliner had expanded to make her look like an evil raccoon. "I wouldn't get so cocky if I were you."

Gwendolyn felt a clutch in her gut. "What're you talking about, Anna?"

"You don't know, do you?"

"No, and I still don't know what you're talking about."

"My brother, more importantly, your husband, is double-dipping again."

"Again?" It was all she could manage to say.

"This isn't speculative gossip, by the way. Joan—you know my best friend from high school, the one who's in charge of food and beverage at the hospital—she told me, and she knows everything that goes on there."

"I don't know what you or your friend Joan are talking about." She already felt defeated.

"She's a nurse, of course, easy pickings for a doctor. And French, by the way. You know how they are."

She didn't know "how they are," and she certainly didn't want to imagine this further. She stared at Anna, hoping that her expression didn't reveal what she was thinking: *Who is this family that I married into?*

"But not to worry, dear Gwendolyn," Anna said. "Your ever accommodating father-in-law, my less than accommodating father, ran her out of town. Problem solved."

"Good night," Gwendolyn said, her voice flat, as she turned from the sink and left the kitchen.

Upstairs in her dressing room, she removed her makeup, brushed her teeth, brushed her hair, moisturized her body—her unwavering ablutions for another day lived, even a day like this one. She got into bed but didn't close her eyes or invite sleep even though she was bone tired. It was a lovely night, simple in its beauty, with moonlight from the three-quarter moon streaming in the window, the sound of frogs flirting with each other in the pond nearby. But she was alone in the double bed, tense with an unwelcome alertness. She had heard Paul Stanley leave after everyone else, his car retreating down the lane. He often did this, more so lately it seemed, disappearing into the night without explanation. She used to assume he had a hospital emergency. How could she be so naive! It all sort of fell into place. Paul Stanley seemed distracted lately and had started drinking more.

At around 2 a.m., she heard the distant sound of gravel crunching, getting louder until it stopped, and a car door slammed. She listened as the front door opened and shut. Realizing that she was holding her breath, she let it out in a slow exhale.

When Paul Stanley opened the bedroom door, trying not to be noticed, she sat up in bed and turned on the light.

"Hi, hon," he said with a startle then recovered with his once-disarming smile. "Still up?"

"Yes. I'm waiting for you."

Paul Stanley looked at her, cocking his head in an unspoken question but didn't wait for an answer as he turned and disappeared into the bathroom. When he emerged, he found Gwendolyn sitting up, expectant. He got into bed and turned out the light. She reached across him and turned it back on.

"What're you doing?"

"I want to talk," she said, surprised by her calm, low voice.

"What about? Can't it wait? I've got surgery tomorrow early."

"No, I can't wait any longer."

He settled back on his pillow, not facing her. They stared at the wall in front of them, side by side.

"What is it?" His voice took on the tone of a contrite little boy, one who knows he is about to be brought to task. It was a tone that could soften Gwendolyn's resolve in the past. Tonight, she felt resolute.

"I know all about it."

"What are you talking about?"

"You know what I'm talking about. Don't waste your time trying to deny it."

Paul Stanley was quiet, but his face collapsed into a puddle of uncertainty.

"How did you find out?" he asked in a subdued voice.

"That doesn't matter." She made a sudden turn to face him. "Why? Why did you do it?"

"I don't know what to say," Paul Stanley finally said after a long, tortured silence. "It just happened."

"That's hardly an explanation."

"Well, what do you want me to say?"

That you're sorry that you hurt me? That you will never, ever, EVER do that again? That you know I never signed up for this life of hurt you've delivered to me?

Instead, she said nothing.

After another long silence, Gwendolyn finally said, her voice soft with inquiry, "I don't understand. I don't understand why you would do this to me. Haven't I always loved you faithfully? Haven't I been a good wife? Don't I always make myself available to you? Do I ever deny you?" She sounded plaintive, and she immediately regretted how this made her seem weak, as if she were begging for her own forgiveness. Her words hung in the emotionally thickened air, abandoned by Paul Stanley's silence.

14

The Sticky Days of August

Gwendolyn had never kept a secret from Paul Stanley, but now the house seemed moldy with them.

It was an oppressively clammy day in August when she stayed in bed while Paul Stanley left for surgery. That should have told him something and maybe it did, as it was the first time in the twenty-three years of their marriage that she hadn't fixed his coffee and to-go thermos. She had explained it by saying she was not feeling well.

This wasn't a lie.

She managed to get to the bathroom before vomiting. After, she cleaned up and applied her makeup. She put on a tailored gray suit. It was the most somber outfit in her closet. When she arrived at her father-in-law's office, she entered through the back door as instructed. Dr. Ollie personally greeted her. He was a big moose of a man, with a square jaw that was almost cartoonishly imperial, a bristly fan of silver hair. Despite his gruff ways, she was enormously fond of him.

She had contacted him two days before, telling him what she should have been initially sharing with her husband. She was pregnant.

His response shocked her. "Do you want to keep it?"

"Why would you say that, Dr. Ollie? You know how much Paul Stanley wants another son."

"Yes, I know. He hasn't spawned his quarterback yet, but that doesn't address the question."

"I still don't know why you would . . ." she trailed off. She knew he knew.

"I'm guessing you've heard," he said gently, not with his usual bluster.

"Yes," she said, looking down.

"Well, you don't have to worry about her anymore. I wouldn't exactly say we ran her out of town on a rail. But I could say I convinced her that Southeast Missouri Hospital, and therefore Cape Girardeau, was not the best place for her anymore. Let's just say I have some influence."

"I've heard," she said without any whiff of triumph.

"You know this wasn't the first time my son's weakness got the better of him."

"I didn't know," she said after a moment of absorption.

She looked up at her father-in-law, who observed her with soft eyes. She knew he revered his son, who became a doctor and returned to Cape Girardeau to carry on the Bollinger legacy. But he wasn't blind to his son's "weaknesses," as he referred to them.

She never thought the day would come when she would stand in front of Dr. Ollie as she was on this muggy summer day. But she had woken up that morning with a rare sense of certainty. She didn't want to have another child with Paul Stanley. It would feel like a trap. After the night of the Fourth, things had noticeably cooled between them. She remained dutiful, getting up earlier than him, making his toast and filling his thermos, even receiving his peck on the cheek as he hurled himself out the door, late as always for surgery. But she was cold and removed, even rejecting his offers of sex, and this agitated Paul Stanley, who was used to having unfettered access to his wife.

At least a week had passed without him getting his way with her, and she knew she was taunting the devil. And one night he arrived, breathing the fire of too much whiskey. She knew it would happen, and so she didn't fight him. As she lay there after he was finished—it was rough and didn't take long—she listened to his fierce snores and thought: *Is this what it feels like to be raped? This disembodied feeling? This empty fury?* She also knew, in an instant, that this was Paul Stanley's unconscious way of trapping her. He didn't use a condom, and it was the dangerous time of month for pregnancy, something they both kept track of. He felt her slipping away, and this was his way of preventing it.

But it wasn't going to work. Here she was in her father-in-law's office, considering a choice she had never even imagined having to make.

※ ※ ※

A week later, Gwendolyn awoke and found blood on her nightgown. She was alone in bed as she had been more and more these days. She knew it wasn't her period; she had been feeling listless and feverish since the procedure.

She got up to wash off the blood and change her nightgown when, in a flash, she felt a sharp pain that literally knocked her backward onto the bed. Difficult thoughts rushed her mind. Did she bring this on because of what she had done? Did she deserve this?

The pain wave passed, and she managed to get up and take care of herself. Exhausted, she lay back down, worrying about all the tasks that she had outlined for herself for that day. The pain returned, as did spotting on her new nightgown. As it increased, she thought about driving herself to Dr. Ollie's office but quickly remembered that he, being semiretired, was only in his office two days of the week and this wasn't one of them.

The pain persisted and worsened. Gwendolyn questioned herself again. Was this her conscience attacking her? She didn't know how that could be possible, but she couldn't keep the thought at bay. By noon, she was still in bed, her nightgown drenched in sweat. She felt her forehead—it was hotter than before. She didn't want to, but knew she was being foolish. She called Paul Stanley at his office and told him her symptoms.

"I'll send someone over right away to pick you up and take you to the hospital. We need to check this out."

She dressed and waited for her ride on the front porch. The atmosphere changed perceptively when a green Dodge Dart pulled up to the side of the old farmhouse. It turned out to be Paul Stanley's new surgical nurse, who introduced herself as Maureen. The woman was pleasant enough, but the ride to the hospital was awkward. She was nice looking, even pretty, in a countrified kind of way—dark, shiny hair, long lashes, a fulsome figure. Gwendolyn wondered if she was from Bollinger County. Paul Stanley had a sweet spot for anyone from there. She was in too much pain to bother asking her.

Once there, Maureen helped get her admitted and situated in a private room before she retreated.

❖ ❖ ❖

Gwendolyn was dozing in her hospital bed.

"Hi, Wendy."

It was Paul's voice, rousing her with an unanticipated smile.

"What's going on? What's all this?" she asked, referring to the tubes connected to her.

"You're losing blood and dehydrated. We're trying to figure out what's going on. It's not like you. You're healthy as a mare in the field. That's why I chose you to be the broodmare for my colts and fillies."

This line had always melted her. Not so much now, but maybe a little.

She hadn't intended to, but she blurted it out. "Paul Stanley, I was pregnant."

"What?"

"I was pregnant but . . . now I'm not."

He looked stricken. "You had a miscarriage? Why didn't you tell me?"

She knew she had to say it. The burden of the secret was too much. "No, not a miscarriage. I had a procedure."

He held on a minute to absorb this. Then, "You had an abortion."

The word spoken out loud made her blanch. Paul Stanley turned around and walked out without saying another word.

Later that day, he returned with the curt declaration, "I want Busby to investigate."

"Investigate? For what?"

"We have to go in there and see what's happening."

"Surgery? Busby?"

"Your bleeding hasn't stopped." Paul Stanley said in a strangely cold, clinical way. "It could be serious."

Gwendolyn took this in, trying to process what he was saying, trying her best to stay away from the muddle of guilty thoughts so she could think clearly. "But, Busby? He's a urologist, not a gynecologist."

"It's not a problem. He's the only one I trust and I'll be there, assisting."

It all sounded so strange to Gwendolyn, but he was the doctor and it never even occurred to her that she could say otherwise.

When she came out of the ether, nestled in the whiteness of her hospital bed, it took her awhile to figure out where she was. It was the sudden awareness of pain in her stomach area that brought her out. She let out a whimper when she saw Dixie sitting next to her. Anyone who knew Gwendolyn would know a whimper from her would be a full-throttle scream from anyone else.

"I'll be right back, honey," Dixie said as she rushed out of the room, returning soon with a nurse who immediately gave Gwendolyn a shot. This put her back into a welcomed stupor.

Consciousness returned before the pain. There was Dixie again, sitting in a chair next to her bed.

"Where's Paul Stanley?" Gwendolyn asked.

"You haven't seen him? Or Busby?"

"No. Why? Is everything all right? Where are they?"

Dixie muttered something to herself that Gwendolyn couldn't make out. "What? Is everything okay? What is it, Dixie?"

"You might as well hear it from me."

Gwendolyn lifted up. "What? Tell me!" The pain knocked her back onto her pillow.

Dixie took her hand. "Honey, you don't have your parts anymore."

"My what? My parts? What does that mean?"

"Your woman parts, you know . . ."

"What're you talking about?"

"Your baby oven, you know. Your uterus, I think it's called."

"It's called a hysterectomy." It was Paul Stanley's voice, his clinical one. He was standing in the doorway.

Gwendolyn looked at him in disbelief. Behind him stood Busby, still in his surgical scrubs. She looked at both of them in turn. "But why?" she asked, barely audible.

Paul Stanley was now at her bedside, yet he seemed far away to her. "We had to do it. There was an infection. It didn't look good. It had to be done."

Gwendolyn looked at him, speechless.

"Shouldn't matter, should it?" Paul Stanley said with his askew smile that was always meant to set things right with her, but this one twisted differently. "You're obviously not wanting any more babies."

Then he turned and walked out of the room.

1972

15

This Unexpected Life

She had been sure she would leave Paul Stanley once she recovered from her unexpected hysterectomy. It had been yet another lesson in the folly of certainty.

That was seven years ago! What was she waiting for?

Their hilltop home had been completed, and although it was a spectacular house (old brick, slate roof, leaded-glass windows) in an even more spectacular setting (overlooking the Mississippi River) it didn't bring her the expected joy. Yes, she had "arrived," as one of her bridge club friends proclaimed at their inaugural gathering at the newly completed house. And although she appreciated the privilege of it all, she was strangely unmoved.

And the children were no longer the excuse she had clung to. Oliver was in his inaugural year at Yale grad school and creating an alternate life that he was sharing less and less with her. Franny was in her junior year at the University of Missouri and headed to medical school a year early. And Gilda was enjoying her job as an interior decorator for a prestigious Chicago firm. As much as Gwendolyn privately wished otherwise, she knew that they didn't need her much anymore.

Paul Stanley was more complicated. It wasn't all philandering and endless nights of marathon drinking. There was his keen mind, full of curiosity about the wider world, that he freely shared with her. There were even nights when alcohol hadn't commandeered him, when there was a sweet hour, when he was amorous and present and even considerate of her needs. She still had those needs, apparently.

It was taking much longer than it should to consider these factors. Those seven years had somehow tiptoed by like a phantom in the night. When this sunk in, her mind returned to making a plan to leave the marriage, but it was a contemplation that was now more like mental molasses.

It was Gilda who bulldozed into whatever shaky edifice of divorce she was trying to build. On her twenty-fifth birthday, she announced that she would marry her college pin mate Robert Ray Dillingham. This fresh job appeared suddenly—mother of the bride—and it took away any plans of earthly salvation for herself, at least for now.

Gilda's wedding would be an entirely different affair than Gwendolyn's simple wartime ceremony. Her fiancé was the heir to the Dillingham family fortune in Washington State lumber. This obligated them to provide a much different kind of wedding than the one her parents had afforded her. Gwendolyn was okay with that, seeing it as just another one of her duties to perform with competence. What kept her up the night of the announcement was her concern for Gilda. Robert Ray seemed like a good enough match for her, but that wasn't the problem. He planned on entering medical school in the fall at Johns Hopkins, and his family seemed nice, even somewhat down to earth despite their wealth. Still, something felt off.

Around 3 a.m. on the night before everyone from the Dillingham family would arrive to begin the five days of wedding festivities, Gwendolyn woke up and realized what had been niggling at the corners of her mind: Gilda was marrying a man who, just like her father, had two first names and who everyone also referred to by both names, *Robert Ray*. He was going to be a doctor, just like her father. Another easy prey for predatory nurses, too. At least he didn't seem to "like to drink," nor was he prone to Paul Stanley's wild and harried moods. *But still . . .*

As fast as the thoughts came, she shook them off as crazy. Just because these facts had ruled her life, this wouldn't necessarily be the same for Gilda. Nevertheless, it troubled her that Gilda, who had been an outstanding student—valedictorian of her class and president of the Kappa Kappa Gamma Sorority—would squander these accomplishments on the easy benefits of marriage to a wealthy young man. Her creamy blonde looks had matured into a gorgeous woman with an almost perfect figure, devoid of the Bollinger tendency to Germanic squareness. Paul Stanley had joked that Gilda, with that figure and cool personality, was destined to be a rich man's wife. Gwendolyn rued this prediction, which she found to be coarse and demeaning to her shining daughter.

Gilda had gotten a job right out of college as an assistant to the top designer favored by the privileged inhabitants of Chicago's North Shore and had risen steadily in the firm. Gwendolyn feared that a demanding domestic life would sequester these artistic talents. Her new job would no doubt become being the wife of a prince. Gwendolyn had always hoped that both of her girls would find their talents to be useful in the world of business or professions, never wanting them to feel the lack of options that so entrapped her.

She had always dreamed of her daughters' weddings and how they would strengthen their bond. However, she wasn't prepared for the creeping feeling of alienation that she soon experienced as Gilda became more and more intense in her insistence on making what Gwendolyn found to be strange and extravagant choices.

First, there was the church. Gwendolyn had always expected they would marry her daughters in the small brick Episcopal chapel where she and Paul Stanley had been married. She had made that expectation clear to Gilda.

"That is definitely not possible," Gilda informed her mother when it first came up.

Gwendolyn asked her why.

"Let's just say Robert Ray and I will not be having a humble wedding like you and Dad. We're going to need a bigger venue, like the First Baptist Church."

"That monstrosity?" came Gwendolyn's quick response. "We're not even Baptists."

When she found out the Dillinghams weren't either (they were actually Episcopalians), she was doubly mystified. It had to be there, proclaimed Gilda—it was the only venue that could house the wedding she was intent on having. "We'll just say that Robert Ray was raised a Baptist," were Gilda's last words on that subject.

No local florist was good enough, so Mr. Victor, who did all the big society weddings in St. Louis, was employed. Gilda deemed the local country club too shabby for the reception—"I can't even imagine Mrs. Dillingham sitting on one of those awful floral-patterned sofas"—so they chose to hold the party in an elaborate tent brought up from Memphis, complete with chandeliers and a full orchestra, erected on the back lawn of the house on the hill. Mrs. Mabel Lonsbaugh, the German lady who catered everyone's wedding in Cape, would definitely not do, either: "I will not have my new in-laws eating strudel and schnitzel."

She insisted that they fly in the Dillingham's personal chef to oversee the catering, a command that Gwendolyn found embarrassing, both in the snub to Mrs. Lonsbaugh but also because of its grandiosity.

The mother-daughter bonding was not going as expected.

Nevertheless, Gwendolyn remained determined to make this a joyous time. She planned a trip to Chicago, complete with appointments at all the best bridal salons. She was hoping the choosing of the wedding dress would become a special memory.

While having tea together at the Drake after a day of shopping,

Gilda took Gwendolyn by surprise by asking, "Mother, why aren't you happy with Daddy?"

Gwendolyn was breathing in the warm smell of bergamot from her teacup when this question materialized unexpectedly. She looked up at her daughter. "Why do you ask such a question?"

"You just don't seem, well, very alive when you're around him. I can remember when you were different. You used to look at him differently. It just makes me . . . wonder," she faltered.

Gwendolyn could sense the doubt casting her daughter's mind in shadow. "Makes you wonder about?" She already knew.

"Oh, forget it. Your marriage is none of my concern."

Gwendolyn reached out and touched Gilda's hand that was resting on the table. She realized how delicate and finely shaped it was, with her long, tapered fingers, and a vermilion blush to the skin. Her beautiful daughter. "Sweetheart," she said, "don't worry. You and Robert Ray love each other. You're facing a brilliant future . . ." she trailed off, realizing that she was about to get stuck in a spiderweb of platitudes.

Gilda looked up from her teacup. Her eyes were wet with feeling. "But is love enough?"

This gave Gwendolyn pause. She wanted to take another long draught from her teacup, but she kept her gaze steady on her daughter, touched by the solemnity of the question.

"No, darling," she said after a weighted pause. "No, love is not enough. But that only means you have to work at it."

Blessedly, the waiter appeared at that moment and asked if they would like any more tea sandwiches. This seemed to shift the mood for Gilda.

Gwendolyn noticed. "What?"

"To be honest, even I think this wedding might be getting a little, I don't know, conventional. What do you think we could do to make it more memorable?"

"Oh, I don't know. Maybe you could ask Uncle Busby to design the bridesmaid dresses?"

"Oh my god, can you imagine? I know! I'll make Eddie the flower girl."

"First off, he's not a girl, and perhaps more relevant, he's a monkey."

They broke into the relief of shared laughter. The image of Eddie as the flower girl freed them to lighten their hearts for the rest of the trip.

※ ※ ※

Gwendolyn could feel all of the eyes upon her as Oliver, handsome in his groomsman's morning coat, walked her down the aisle. She allowed herself some secret enjoyment about how good she looked in her lavender silk Bill Blass couture gown. Settled into her front row seat, she tried to not focus on the cost of this wedding: over a hundred thousand dollars! Gwendolyn had to admit, the wedding had a sumptuous beauty. The lavish profusion of flowers—blue delphiniums, white roses, clematis, not a sprig of baby's breath—covered every inch of the interior, obscuring the ugly grandeur of the First Baptist Church. At least the cavernous space smelled heavenly.

Gwendolyn glanced over at Robert Ray's mother, Sue, seated across the aisle next to her distinguished husband with a silver mustache. She offered a smile that Sue readily returned. Gwendolyn liked her and saw it as a positive sign for her daughter that her new husband had a gentle mother, unaffected, it seemed, by her immense wealth.

The church atmosphere accelerated with anticipation as twelve groomsmen filed out onto the front of the church. They all looked handsome and young and somewhat hungover in their morning coats and lavender ties. This initiated the procession of the twelve bridesmaids in lavender gowns and gardenias in their hair. Perhaps it was the invariability of it all that untethered Gwendolyn's mind from the moment, allowing it to roam out of bounds . . .

Does Gilda realize she's about to mortgage her life to a man? Gwendolyn flinched. *This isn't what the mother of the bride is supposed to be thinking at her daughter's wedding!*

The increased buzz in the room jolted her from these troubling thoughts, and she turned to see Franny, the maid of honor, walking down the aisle toward her. Dressed like the other bridesmaids except with a tiara of gardenias atop her long, lustrous brunette hair, she was breathtaking. Accustomed to seeing her younger daughter in overalls with more concern for fixing a bird's broken wing than doing her nails, she watched her pass by and take her place on the altar. Her gorgeousness hit Gwendolyn as an unexpected revelation.

The sudden swell of the "Wedding March" brought her to her feet along with everyone else. Gilda, resplendent, walked down the aisle on the arm of her father.

The minister stood in front of them as they arrived at the altar. "Who gives this woman to be wed to this man in holy matrimony?"

"I do," Paul Stanley answered.

As he turned from his delivery of the bride and walked to take his seat beside Gwendolyn, she thought, *Why is Gilda being given away? Is he transferring the burden of the care and feeding of their daughter as if she were some kind of pampered poodle? Gilda is a woman, not a piece of chattel.* She shuddered, trying to rid herself of these intrusive thoughts. What was she trying to do—undermine her daughter's special day? *How is it that I've become so cynical? So unGwendolyn like?*

While the minister droned out a homily, she glanced at Paul Stanley and her cynical thoughts evaporated. He looked handsome in his usual way, his profile especially fine as it showed off his finely-shaped Greek nose and strong, square jaw. His thick auburn hair was combed straight back, reminding her once again of a leading man from a thirties film. He had been looking down but must have noticed her studying him; he glanced over at her with his smile, saucy and innocent at the same time. Unbidden, memories flowed over her like a warm rain on an upturned face...

A crisp October day: They had just moved into their new house on the hill when Paul Stanley showed up early from work. She had been unpacking, her hair tied up in a scarf, no makeup, dust all over her. "You look gorgeous," he had said. "Pack your bags." By midnight, they were in New York City, checking into the Plaza, and the next day he insisted that she go to Saks Fifth Avenue and buy a special dress because that night they were going to the Metropolitan Opera to see *La Traviata*...

The trip to Hawaii with Busby and Dixie: He had disappeared on a fishing trip with Busby, leaving her restless and bored lying on the beach with Dixie, listening to her endlessly assess the quality of the local beach boys. When he returned, she was prepared for him to disappear into the dive tiki bars of Waikiki Beach. Instead, he showered, put on a silly looking Hawaiian shirt, and insisted they go for a drive up to the North Shore, where they landed at a beachside bar and drank daiquiris and ate oysters while the setting sun and balmy breeze made everything exquisite.

Gilda's voice, as she began speaking her vows, jolted Gwendolyn out of her confounding reverie. Her eldest daughter looked so poised, so confident, it gave Gwendolyn pause. *No matter what happens, at least she will always have this moment.*

❖ ❖ ❖

The tent behind their home up on the hill looked spectacular, like a big wedding cake glowing from within. Guests were being shuttled up the hill from where they parked in the front field below the old farmhouse. Everyone appeared dressed as if they were going to a Met Gala, and perhaps this was the closest thing Cape Girardeau would have to such an event. The band from Memphis was playing recognizable Beatles songs as the guests swarmed and the bow-tied waiters circulated with flutes of champagne. Gwendolyn observed it all with awe and a little unease as she stood alone on the back terrace of the house.

Dixie bounded up to her, followed by Busby in a tartan kilt of a dazzling bright plaid that Gwendolyn was pretty sure had nothing to do with Scotland.

"I didn't know you were Scottish, Busby," Gwendolyn said with what anyone would perceive as uncharacteristic dryness.

"I am tonight," he said.

"He's not wearing anything underneath it, if you want to take a peek," said Dixie. Gwendolyn turned her attention to her. On her head perched what Gwendolyn would later learn to be called a fascinator. It wasn't what you normally saw at a wedding in Missouri. And it was black, as was the dress that barely covered her bottom. But the most shocking thing was the cut of her bodice.

"My god, Dixie, I can see your nipples."

"Can you?" she asked coyly as she tugged at her top.

"And you're all in . . . black."

"Well, I'm not the bride pretending to be a virgin. Come on, Gwennie, get with it. Nineteen seventy-two—miniskirts are the style and black is definitely in."

Busby was staring at his wife admiringly. "It takes guts to practically bare your bum at a Bollinger wedding." Then he turned to Gwendolyn with his typical look, always a pastiche of a classic film actor with a pencil mustache, which he was sporting. "You look lovely as always, Gwendolyn my dear. Where is the father of the bride?"

She didn't know, but this prompted her to look around with the sudden realization that they had not seen each other since they left the church.

"Over there," Dixie said, nodding not so discreetly to tables set up around the pool.

Gwendolyn felt a sudden clutch in her gut, yet she followed Dixie's directive nod. There was the father of the bride standing at one of the high-top tables with a pretty, younger woman with long brunette hair and bangs. She recognized her as Maureen, his office nurse. They were leaning into each other. His hand rested on the table, next to hers. Their fingers drew together and barely touched, then they pulled apart suddenly, guiltily it seemed to Gwendolyn. Some would see them and think nothing of it—a doctor talking with his nurse—but some who looked closer would see a frisson of sexual energy. Gwendolyn certainly did.

"The Local Nurse," Dixie said with her familiar, sticky innuendo.

Gwendolyn knew in an instant what she meant. It would have been so obvious, so rude, and unimaginable to the twenty-one-year-old Gwendolyn who married a man—this man!—who would one day in the future act in this way. At their daughter's wedding, no less! She looked at Paul Stanley as if she were seeing a stranger. Someone who was surreal, someone who didn't make real sense.

Though she never permitted it, she always knew it would be Maureen.

Gwendolyn looked at the barely touched VO Press she held in her hand. She could have downed it and ordered another. But she put the drink down. She would not be Dixie; she would not create an uproarious anecdote to amuse future audiences. She would turn around and walk out of her eldest daughter's wedding without incident.

Dixie put a gentle restraining hand on her arm. "You want me to take her out?"

Gwendolyn came out of her head and looked at her friend. "What? Wrestle her to the ground? Put her in a headlock?"

"I can take care of that bitch."

Gwendolyn looked at Busby, who stood nearby. He shrugged noncommittally.

Gwendolyn turned back to Dixie, who was obviously enjoying this little drama. "You're drunk."

"Properly fueled, as I prefer to call it."

Thoughts raced through her mind like stampeding, frightened horses. She wanted to bolt, to leave the scene, but if she did, she would be ceding her ground to that woman, Maureen, from Bollinger County. The Local Nurse.

The obnoxious announcer, imported from St. Louis's top-rated television station, hijacked her quandary by calling the mother of the bride forward for a toast.

She heard the applause, the encouragement that sounded like a demand. She had no choice. She turned and hesitated, but the crowd was using their champagne-fueled enthusiasm to exert an inescapable gravitational pull on her. Without showing her inner panic, she reversed course and, with her best glamorous smile instantly recalled from some old familiar place, turned and walked up to the stage and took the microphone. It felt like she was in a dream. She paused as she looked around. Practically everyone she ever knew stood before her, smiling in a suffocatingly assumptive way.

"Thank you. Thank you all for coming. Paul Stanley and I thank you for celebrating this wonderful marriage of our Gilda and her Robert Ray." She stopped, glancing around. "Has anyone seen Paul Stanley? He should be giving this toast. Isn't it traditional for the father of the bride to do this?" A tense murmur came from the crowd. The St. Louis MC leaned in and whispered that they had searched but couldn't find him.

Gwendolyn looked back at the gathering and fought for composure. Gilda, standing right in front with her arm entwined in Robert Ray's, shifted on her feet and chewed on her upper lip. Gwendolyn took a deep breath. "Well, it seems like he's been called away, probably a medical emergency. You know how they are—doctors I mean." She said this intending to lighten things up, but she was pretty sure it just came off as awkward.

Acutely aware of the focus on her which now seemed searing, she plunged forward. "What can I say? This merger, this event, I mean this wedding, has meant so much to us . . ." she faltered. The ensuing twitters of polite laughter from the audience made her look around and momentarily lose her compass. She smiled her automatic smile and somehow found some grounding. "Life—isn't it beautiful? It brings us to a strange place, don't you agree? Do we ever ask for what we get? I . . . I don't know. I wish we could all figure that one out." She realized she was smiling a lot. Maybe it looked weird and inappropriate. She suspected she wasn't connecting to them or to her own ranging mind. "What was I saying? Oh yes, this strange, beautiful life. We move along some trail that we never expect. Yet we move forward, right? Gilda and Robert Ray could have never known on the moment they met, the moment they first set eyes on each other, that they would end up here, in this little town on the Mississippi, committing themselves to . . . to this." She waved her hand around, without knowing what she was indicating. "It's strange, isn't it? Isn't it? Let's drink to that!" She raised her glass. There was a weighted moment and then everyone, captured by some perplexing wonder, did the same.

Wineglass held aloft, her smile now looking haunted to anyone who was really paying attention, she toasted, "So beautiful, the life we live, this unexpected life that changes all things."

❖ ❖ ❖

It was 2 a.m. and the last guests had left two hours before. It was a moonless night and Gwendolyn was still up, alone and pacing around the silent house.

Rummaging about in the utility room, she found a half-used pack of Romaine's Salem cigarettes. Settling into a wrought-iron chair on the front veranda, she lit up a cigarette and coughed twice, covering her mouth, while the unfamiliar smoke enveloped her in the dark night. She could barely make out a barge with its sweeping pilot light in the Mississippi River. She focused on it, but it didn't calm her.

Perhaps she should pray.

But what would she pray about? She had everything she needed—a beautiful home, a husband who provided, and even a daughter who was entering what most would consider to be a promising marriage.

She closed her eyes . . . *Why?* That was the word that came so purely into her agitated mind.

But no answer to this simple question arrived.

You live with a man for years, you become used to his habits, you learn to live with him in the ways that he never seems willing to change, the soiled underwear dropped on the bathroom floor, the lack of gratitude for the endless meals served. You try your best to repair all the faults he creates in your shared firmament. You get used to his smell, to the point where there's no smell at all. Everything becomes normative as your life slides by. Then you look across the room and you see this man you've lived with for more years than you can count, and you don't recognize him at all.

She stubbed out the cigarette that was making her nauseous, and before she realized it, she was standing in front of Eddie's cage.

"Why?"

The question came again, only this time she said it out loud.

Eddie, who must have been sleeping, emerged from the dark depths and climbed up the wire front of the cage. Without making a sound, he reached through one of the square wire openings as if he were grasping for food.

Before Gwendolyn knew it, she spoke out loud the thoughts that coursed through her mind. "What's it like in there, Eddie? Are you happy in your home? I guess it's really a cage, isn't it? I know you didn't choose this. Funny thing is, I did choose my home, this life. Or I thought I did. I thought this house was what I always wanted, grander than I ever imagined, a dream come true. I doubt this is a dream come true for you, is it, Eddie? Calling this a home is . . . what's the word? A euphemism? It's a damned cage! How do you stand it? Do you hate us for what we've done to you? We feed you, and we make sure you have a comfortable place to live. We care for your needs, but it's still a cage."

She paused, struck again by how quiet he was, just looking at her with his big brown eyes that at times could look soulful. Tonight, they even seemed reverential.

"The world is big. It's wide, beyond what you or I can ever know. I see it on the television, and it makes me see my world as so small, just a sad little slice of the whole pie. Why? Why are we here, Eddie? We all have our jobs, it seems, in this life we've been assigned. We all have our duties. Do we choose them, or does some god assign them to us? How can that be? It makes no sense to me, but why? Why would I have chosen this set of tasks I perform without question? Do they make a difference? To me, to anyone? What if I weren't here? What if I went on strike? What if I didn't get the guest room ready for the Dillinghams? Would the world be different? Would it . . . would it become . . . what? Incomprehensible? Tragic? Did all of this survive all these years because I dreamed it? Paul Stanley? My marriage?"

Gwendolyn realized she was babbling, so she stopped and took a deep breath. In that moment, she felt as if some invisible hand slapped her across the face. She was startled by the sudden realizations that she had been speaking out loud to Eddie. She again noticed Eddie looking at her, only now it seemed more like a stare.

"Oh, Eddie, I'm sorry. I woke you up from your sleep. I hope you'll forgive me. Oh, how silly of me, you don't know about forgiveness or about any of this foolishness I'm saying."

She went into the kitchen and opened the refrigerator, where she found a quarter round of Edam cheese left over from the wedding party. She brought it back to the cage where Eddie was still clinging to the wire as before.

She handed him the cheese. "Please forgive me, Eddie."

16

Party Process

Dixie showed up the day after the wedding, as expected, ready to "party process." That's what they had always called it. Gwendolyn's anticipation wasn't without ambivalence. Dixie encounters could be disturbingly crunchy. And, after last night, she wasn't sure she was in the mood for one.

Dixie arrived around 10 a.m. and wasn't taking any chances. She brought her flask filled with brandy for her *cafe corte*, claiming to have learned about this in Spain—cutting your coffee with a dollop of brandy in the morning as a surefire pick-me-up.

They were alone in the house. Romaine had the day off, and when she had checked on Paul Stanley in their bedroom, he wasn't there. To avoid the crew dismantling the party at the back of the house, they went to the front terrace and there settled in to process the party with coffee and wedding cake.

They quickly dispensed with the fashion review (most of the women in their bridge club should avoid the current fashion trend of miniskirts, except for Dixie, of course, who "had the personality" to pull it off), a critique of the caterer (too fancy for Cape Girardeau), praise for the flowers, boos for the unctuous MC from St. Louis.

"And didn't Gilda look utterly beautiful!" Gwendolyn exclaimed, rising momentarily out of her funk.

"That's a word you're very fond of."

"What's that supposed to mean?"

"Beautiful. Everything is beautiful with you. Your life, your home, most of all your children. You probably even think Eddie is beautiful."

"What on earth are you saying? That they're ugly?"

"Hardly. It's just that you cling to that word like a life raft."

"I have no idea what you're talking about." Gwendolyn was showing her irritation. She was on thin ice as it was.

"A meretricious dame in the woodpile, not so beautiful."

"What? A woman of merit?"

"Meretricious. Otherwise known as a voracious fucking whore."

"Good lord, Dixie, how you talk."

"As you are surely aware, I am well known for my outstanding vocabulary skills."

They eyeballed each other for a dense moment of attempted comprehension.

Dixie broke the moment. "What're we going to do about it?"

"You mean, what am I going to do about Paul Stanley."

"Even better, but I think I know the answer to that one."

"How could you when I don't even know?"

"Let's just say I know things you don't know."

Gwendolyn looked away from the view and to Dixie. She was already pouring her second dose of brandy into her coffee, not seeming to mind that it was now cold.

Dixie looked up at her. "What? You have a problem?"

Gwendolyn looked back at the verdant view that rolled toward the Mississippi River. "I moved into the guest room last night. I locked the door."

"Now that was a bold Gwendolyn move. How did it go over?"

"Not at all well. He didn't get home until around three, and then he banged on the door, yelling, cursing. I thought he was going to break through it. And then he disappeared back into the night."

"How so very *Streetcar Named Desire* of him. He went to see the Local Nurse, no doubt."

Gwendolyn knew this was the truth, but she didn't want to say it out loud to Dixie. It would make it all too real; it could risk one of Dixie's rude censures. She ventured a side glance at her friend and was surprised to see her leaning toward her, her eyes soft with compassion: "Hon, you know this is a choppy time for you, what with Gilda taking off and all."

She realized why she wanted to see Dixie today, on this day that might be the day she was tacking . . . where? Somewhere else? She could always count on her to tell the truth, even if it sounded sometimes ragged and profane.

Gwendolyn looked up at her. "Have you ever done that? Put Busby out, you know, denied him?"

"Good god, it wouldn't do any good. He would just happily go over cross the river to one of his sluts, or at the least, go into the guest room and spank the monkey."

"What are you talking about?"

Dixie snorted out a laugh. "That's what he always said when we had the monkey, that he was going into the bathroom to give him a good spanking. I knew what he meant, but I thought it was funny at the time because, you know, we actually had Monkey."

Gwendolyn didn't laugh. "I'm not sure I need to know all that. And his name is Eddie." Her wan face suddenly infused with color. "I'm serious, Dixie. This was difficult for me, cutting him off like that. I took a pledge to love, honor, and obey."

"Seriously, sister, get a grip. Honor and *obey*?"

"It thrilled me to say those words. You remember how he was—smart, handsome, exciting, and fun—"

"Yes, until the third drink."

Gwendolyn looked away at nothing in particular. "I don't know why he drinks so much. It changes him."

"They all do. It's that damned war," Dixie said, her voice more contemplative than waspish. "Whether they came back heroes or not, it changed them. And they needed the booze to make it all evaporate."

Gwendolyn kept looking away to the dewy view. "I saw him driving down Broadway one spring day, looking so handsome in his uniform. He had the look of, well, a prince. I asked my girlfriend who that was. She said, 'Paul Stanley Bollinger. He's going to be a doctor just like his daddy.'"

"Oh, so that clinched it. A doctor. And a Bollinger doctor at that. Becoming a doctor's wife—I guess that pulls a royal flush around here. You could have fooled me." She flicked her burned-down cigarette over the terrace half wall. "Did your friend also tell you he was an alcoholic?"

"I just thought he was under a lot of pressure. Medical school, having to wait for sex until we got married. He was very impatient. I was a virgin when I married him."

"I'm shocked."

"Well, a technical virgin, actually."

"I don't even want to know what that means." She took a long drag on a newly lit cigarette. "Then there's that mother of his, the one with the dry tit. Yes, I know, so many reasons for him being a drunk with a sexy smile."

"For Pete's sake, it's hard to keep up with you."

"You really don't like being distracted by reality, do you? I saw her at the wedding. It was clear as dawn. Her quiet, remote disapproval of her son, the way she turned away from him with a wince when he tried to go in for a goodbye kiss when she was leaving. Sure, he was sloppy drunk by then, but you could see it all there, his needing his mommy's affection, her inability to give it. It was all pathetic."

"Sometimes I see him like that, a needy little boy who just wants to be loved."

"Therefore, the trap."

"Trap?"

"Come on, girl. You're smarter than this. He's so handsome, so dashing, so masculine. A fucking sexy wild card. He hunts, he fishes, he rides horses. He was a Golden Gloves boxer. Yet he's really just a sweet little boy, so needy for love, so hungry for it he can't keep his dick in his pants."

"Dixie, I don't know. You're always so . . . so rough."

"I'll tell you what I am: someone who faces down the truth. I'd sure as hell rather do that than turn my back on it. That's the way truth sneaks up on you and bites you in the ass."

"Where's this going?"

"You know you're not so special, right?"

"I never said I was."

"Of course, you haven't. You're much too demure for that."

"Is this one of your jokes?"

"No *blague, ma chérie.* Just some hardcore truth."

"You're not making sense, and I don't see what this has to do—"

"Everything, darling. It has to do with everything. Yes, most everyone in this town would think Gwendolyn Bollinger *is* special because—despite her heralded beauty and grace—she is no princess, she never acts like she is privileged, she's downright unassuming. What they don't know is what a secret egotist you are. And why do I make such an incontrovertible claim? Because you think you are special enough to be able to make your wild and woolly husband come to heel, to stop his thirsting, lusting ways, that the love of this good woman can do all that."

Gwendolyn realized she was staring at Dixie, openmouthed. "Let me have one of those," she said, gesturing to her pack of Benson & Hedges lying on the table. Dixie obliged and then lit her cigarette.

"It's hard to see you so confused," Dixie said after a moment. "It makes you weak, and you can't be weak if you're married to a Bollinger. You seriously need to buck the fuck up."

After coughing out the smoke from the cigarette, Gwendolyn said, "I really don't know what to say."

"Gwennie, honey, listen to me. Danger is afoot if you don't get a grip on yourself. You'll end up becoming one big tit for this hungry little boy, but not the sexy kind in a lace bra. That assignment goes to that poor impressionable nurse. You'll become the tit his mother never provided. But that's not the end of the story. Then guess what? You'll start drying up with resentment. And then what? Voila! You're his mother, the bitter, desiccated woman for whom he has to feel tragically ambivalent about. Good work if you can stomach it."

Gwendolyn looked at her for a long penetrating moment. She took a drag on her cigarette and forgot to cough. "You amaze me. How do you know this stuff?"

"I'm from Memphis," she said, matter-of-factly.

"Yes, I know. And a Democrat." After another drag on her cigarette, she said while staring out at the river, "But what about love? Doesn't that—"

"Your naivety never ceases to amaze me. No wonder you believe in fairy-tale princes. Love isn't enough, don't you know that?"

"I said some version of that to Gilda before the wedding. I just wish I had your sureness."

"You want to know my secret with Busby?"

"Making sure he's scared to death of you?"

Dixie honked a laugh. "That's a good one, Gwennie." She poured another shot of brandy into her coffee cup. "Sure you won't join me?"

Gwendolyn nodded in the negative.

"Suit yourself. You know Busby. He's like one of those pesky cats you drive to the other side of town and drop off. Only he beats you back to the house and sometimes you even start to miss him and go hunt him down and bring him back yourself."

"That's your secret?"

"Busby and I are a lousy rhyme, but that's okay because I don't much care for poetry. My secret? Simple. I don't expect much from love, which means I don't expect much from him more than he's capable of giving me. Accepting reality seems like hard work sometimes, but it actually makes life easier."

Tears eddied in Gwendolyn's eyes, and that made Dixie's widen in astonishment. "What is it?" she asked, her voice soft.

Gwendolyn spoke slowly, barely audible. "Last night, at our daughter's wedding, in front of our whole world, the world we had made together, my husband blatantly and without any consideration for me—the mother of that precious daughter who was herself risking her future on marriage to a man—declared himself in lust with his nurse."

Dixie sucked hard on her fiercely lit cigarette and blew it up into the air. "Those Bollinger boys think they can do whatever the fuck they want, like the rules won't apply to them. And they do it right out in the open. That's how arrogant they are. They don't even hide their chicanery."

"Why do they do it, Dixie? Why?"

"Because they can?" She looked at her friend, trying to find some levity in this plunging conversation. It was evident to her that humor wouldn't work. She took in a deep breath, exhaled, then said, "You know what they say. Men have affairs so they can stay in a marriage, and women have an affair to get out of it."

Gwendolyn couldn't look at her. "That doesn't help."

Dixie leaned forward and took her friend's hands in hers. "Gwennie, honey, what're you going to do?"

Gwendolyn paused. "Hope? For the best?" Her voice was weak, unconvincing.

Dixie fixed her hard with her gimlet stare. "Gwendolyn Bollinger, hope is not a strategy. What the hell are you going to *do*?"

17

La Jolla

The night of her arrival, she ordered room service: a Cobb salad and a glass of white wine. It seemed very modern to her to do such a thing: a woman alone in a hotel room in California, ordering room service. And wine! She knew that younger women these days, those who worked, often traveled for their jobs and were likely to do that. She had even heard that they would go to the hotel bar alone. It all sounded very sophisticated—very *Cosmo*—but she definitely wasn't ready for that. The wine made her giddy. She had never heard of it—*Pouilly-Fuissé*. She stared at the printed name on the card that came with the wine and realized she had no idea how to even pronounce it.

Soon, her giddiness slid into a bog of self-doubt. *What the hell am I doing here?* These types of questions had been stalking her mind.

It was so strange sitting in a hotel room at the La Valencia, and not at home in Missouri. Romaine was the only one she had told about her self-declared sabbatical. All her children were out of the house, immersed in their own lives, so there was nothing to be concerned with there. Her only charge now was Eddie, and she was grateful when Romaine, having evidently overcome her aversion to the monkey, agreed to look after him.

"Does the doctor know?" Romaine had asked, alarm registering on her expressive face.

"This isn't about him," Gwendolyn retorted more sharply than she intended. And as soon as she had said it, she knew that was a lie. This trip was all about Paul Stanley. Her entire life was about Paul Stanley. She instructed Romaine to tell him, should he even ask, that she had gone to see her friend, who lived in Scottsdale. He hadn't come home the night before, so it was easy to make her escape without his interference.

She left him a note that said, "I need time to think. Please give me that. This isn't right."

After it was written, she stared at it for a long time, focusing on her handwriting, which was in its distinctive straight-up style, no slant to the right or left. She remembered reading an article on graphology in *Reader's Digest* that described persons with this style of handwriting as always guided by their reason, disinclined to take chances; they seldom acted on impulses and were consistent in mood and manner. That seemed spot-on at the time she had read the article. But as she folded the paper and put it into an envelope with her initials embossed on the back, she thought, *So much for graphology.*

The post-wine fog was gathering a murky confusion in her mind. What was she doing, for Pete's sake? She knew what Dixie would do. Order another glass of wine, keep the party going. But she wasn't Dixie, and she would not get on the slippery road of drinking her mood into a hazy box canyon, although tonight it had its appeal. She decided to go to bed instead and let the actual fog swirling outside the French windows of her room envelop her as she gave in to sleep.

The next day, she called Dixie. It had only been one day, but she needed to check on things.

She got her on the second ring.

"Where the hell have you been, woman?"

"La Jolla. It's in California."

"And what might you be doing in La Jolla, California?"

She hesitated. "I'm on a garden tour?"

"Bullshit. What's his name? And don't you dare say Delphinium."

"There's no name. I just need some time to figure things out."

"Couldn't you have just gone somewhere on your three-hundred-acre estate?"

"It's a farm, not an estate."

"Not the point. Where are you staying?"

Gwendolyn hesitated, unsure of how much to reveal.

Dixie picked up on this. "Okay, Woman of Mystery—not your usual role by the way—don't tell me, but what if something happens here where you might want to be informed, like Franny gets knocked up or your son is caught cross-dressing at Yale?"

"For Pete's sake, Dixie." But she paused. *What if . . . something?* "Okay, if I tell you, promise not to tell anyone?"

"You mean Paul Stanley, of course. Okay, bitches' honor."

"I'm at the La Valencia, you know, in La Jolla."

"Isn't that where your Grandmother Farnsley always spent her summers?"

"Yes. I suppose it had something to do with it. But actually, I drove to St. Louis and went to Lambert and just looked at the departures and chose San Diego without thinking too much about it."

"So not Gwendolyn Farnsley Bollinger."

"Maybe I'm not so predictable after all."

"That could be wonderful for you, sister. Just be safe."

They hung up, with Dixie promising to only contact her on a need-to-know basis. Gwendolyn sat on the edge of her bed, dazed with the truth of what she had done. Talking to Dixie, so much a part of her normal life, shook her into an awkward reality. She wasn't in Missouri, with her husband and her beautiful home on the hill; she was two thousand miles away in a place where the land ended. She was standing on a cliff.

She shook off this troubling rumination, recalling what her Grandmother Farnsley always said: "Pull up your girdle, and get on with your business." She brought no girdle with her, having decided that these modern times didn't require such restrictions. Besides, her figure was holding thanks to her daily Jack LaLanne workouts in front of the television.

The fog had burned off earlier that morning, and the sun was making the Pacific shimmer as she found a place on the beach directly in front of the house her grandmother used to lease for the summer. Just like the moment she directed her car toward the St. Louis airport, she felt she was being guided to every decision point by some unseen force.

The dark shingled house with many gables and a deep porch still looked like it did during her childhood. Gazing at it from the beach, memories rushed her mind: Her family making the long drive down from Los Angeles past miles and miles of orange trees; feeling pretty in a starched, white low-waisted dress with a blue ribbon; the excitement of her tow-headed cousins arriving from Missouri on the train; her Grandmother Farnsley, tiny but intriguingly imperious, holding court on the porch, which always seemed, in retrospect, to be lessons in elocution; the nighttime grunion runs on the beach, the swarm of little fish shimmering like magic in the moonlight. This last memory brought forth her father. She could see him on this very beach: lean, tanned, and handsome in his white onesie bathing suit, chasing after her as she scampered into the receding surf after the grunion, both free with glee. The later realization of his darkening melancholy was far away from that little girl, happy to be in the sunny paradise of La Jolla. She so loved her father, so earnest and quiet in his love for her, he was. With a father like him, why was her destiny thrown to Paul Stanley? It didn't sync up, despite her cousin Helen's theory shared with her in Florida.

This feeling of unreality enveloped her. The breeze coming off the Pacific and the mesmerizing light helped ground her, so deeply familiar. Seated on her beach towel, she started to take off her coverup but paused as she regarded the other women perched nearby. The first thing she noticed was that it was a sea of blond, making her, a brunette, stand out. They also wore bikinis. This presented another contrast. Her two-piece swimsuit consisted of a bottom that had a skirt and the matching top looked like a substantial bra, the kind, it occurred to her, that a big-bosomed matron would wear under a dress. What was she going to do, stay fully clothed on a Southern California beach? She took off her coverup and risked it. After all, that was what this sabbatical was all about, wasn't it? Risking it? Doing it—whatever *it* was—differently?

As she massaged sun cream on her legs, she heard a male voice: "Nice."

She looked up and saw a figure looming over her, blocking the sun. By shading her eyes and squinting, the apparition focused into a tall, muscular man, with shoulder-length, sun-streaked hair, carrying a surfboard under his arm. He smiled, and then he was gone. He had a big white smile and was so expectable as to be a cliché, and yet . . .

She watched him as he ran toward the water and leapt in, then looked down at her legs, which must have elicited the compliment. She had to admit, they were long and shapely, and her naturally olive skin took to the sun.

A shadow fell across her; hours must have passed. She knew it was him before she opened her eyes—the bracing smell of salt and coconut. Looking up, she suddenly felt vulnerable. He squatted down next to her, his thigh and calf muscles bulging.

Gwendolyn sat up. "Yes?"

"Hi, my name's Cody." He said this with his big, easy smile.

Gwendolyn didn't know what to say. She had never been in a situation like this. He seemed younger, but she couldn't really tell his age. Definite lines radiated from his eyes and his forehead crinkled beneath the flop of his sun-streaked hair, but that could just have been because of the hours he spent in the sun.

Recovering, she said, "How was the surf?"

"It's great today. Wanna try it?"

"Oh no, I couldn't. I never have . . ."

He was on his feet, pulling her up alongside him. "Come on, there's always a first time."

It was like in a dream. She ran with him down to the surf line and then, without hesitation, let him pull her right into the invigorating surprise of the chilly water. It felt both dangerous and exhilarating, and she gave herself over to it. She never really got up on the board, and Cody was patient and fun about her awkward attempts. Eventually, she was able to lie on the board and surf that way into the shore.

Back on her towel, she caught her breath and laughed about her surfing calamity with Cody, who sat cross-legged beside her. They talked easily, about surfing, about San Diego, about Nixon (he hated him, the whole Watergate scandal confused her), and about the Vietnam War (he was vehemently against it, she had doubts about the entire thing but struggled with guilt about feeling unpatriotic). They talked about the summers she spent in La Jolla and how much it had changed, about what it was like for him, growing up there. It was the first time since Gilda's wedding that she wasn't tortured by thoughts about Paul Stanley.

The day skated by pleasantly until a sudden chill descended as the evening fog rolled in and the sun began kissing the horizon.

Gwendolyn shivered. "How long have we been here?"

"Why don't you come over to my place for a drink?" he asked.

She blurted, "I'm married."

"I won't hold that against you."

"I'm older than you."

"Maybe not, but it wouldn't matter anyway since I'm not going to ask you to bear my children." He added along with an affable smile, "And I've got lobster."

It was when she was standing on the Mission Beach boardwalk watching Cody locking his Vespa and then unlocking the front door to his cottage that she realized her heart was beating fast and she was having a hard time catching her breath. Cody noticed.

"Are you okay?"

"A little nervous, I guess."

He smiled. "Sometimes you have to be like the blind man—just have to tap and step forward."

She had protested his invitation. She was sticky with saltwater and suntan lotion, and she hadn't showered or redone her makeup and hair; Gwendolyn Bollinger, who never even went to the grocery store without meticulous grooming! Her protests weakened with her insistence that she at least go back to the La Valencia and freshen up. "Do you know the hotel?" she had asked. "I know it well. Been there many times," he answered. The panic tightening her chest increased as she thought about that. *Why would he have gone to the La Valencia many times when he lives nearby? Does this mean he's a gigolo? Is he expecting me to want sex and to pay him?*

Step forward? Blindly? It was something she had never done before.

A group of young people on the other side of the sand-retaining wall grabbed her attention. She imagined they were those long-haired hippies plastered all over the news lately. They were chanting something, and one of them was thumping on a drum. Everyone smiled at her, and two of them held up the index finger and middle finger in what she recognized as a peace sign. Cody noticed her curiosity and explained that they were having a sit-in.

"What are they wanting?"

"Who knows, maybe the right to stand up?"

She laughed as he opened the door for her. "Welcome to my humble abode."

He disarmed her, once again. And she would not make a fool of herself and run shrieking in the opposite direction. So, she entered.

Cody busied himself with host duties, which surprised Gwendolyn as she couldn't imagine any of the men in her life who would bother with such labors.

"What music would you like?" he asked as he extracted a cork from a bottle of wine.

Another surprise. Paul Stanley always insisted on playing his awful, scratched opera records with no consultation from her.

"Maybe something jazzy?"

"Dave Brubeck. Coming right up."

He went over to his phonograph and removed an album sleeve. Taking out the record, he blew dust off and put it on the player, placing the needle like you might imagine a surgeon would. He came over to her with a glass of white wine for each of them and sat down opposite. The driving rhythms and mellow melody of "Take Five" filled the small space. They listened to the song in silence. When it ended, she said, "That was mesmerizing."

He smiled at her as he got up to retrieve a wooden plank filled with cheese, crackers, nuts, and what looked like dried apricots. "Here, have something to eat."

She had read about this, wine and cheese, the hip thing to do. She made a mental note to introduce it to Cape Girardeau at their next cocktail party.

She didn't prethink, so she just said, "Why do you drink?"

He looked at her, his brow crinkling to indicate a question.

"I know," she said quickly, "stupid question."

"Maybe not. Maybe it's part of your discernment process."

What on earth am I discerning here? She felt hot with embarrassment and hoped it didn't show. She took a delicate sip of the wine. "This is good."

"Why do I drink? I suppose I drink just enough to see if life makes sense. When it does, I stop."

"Oh," was all she could say, so novel was this thought.

Cody was looking at her with intention. "Why did you come here?" he asked in his gentle, agreeable voice.

"Here? Maybe I wanted to see how a hippie lives." She was trying to be funny but realized how ridiculous she sounded.

"Is that how you see me? A hippie?"

"Oh, I don't know, I was just . . ." After a pause, she blurted, "Why are you so familiar with the La Valencia? I mean, why would you go there so much if you live here?"

The corners of his eyes scrunched in a way that held Gwendolyn in some assurance that she had not insulted him, that he understood where she was coming from, and that it was all right.

"Gwendolyn," he said without any note of patronization, "I have gone there every Sunday morning as long as I can remember because my grandfather owned the dump, and we were all expected for Sunday brunch. Every damned Sunday."

"Oh," she said, "I see." She knew she must have sounded tense. She could feel her mouth tighten around her teeth. "Do you work?"

"Do you mean do I do something other than surf and chat up beautiful ladies on the beach? Yes, I teach English at an inner-city high school."

"Oh, yes, of course, you said . . ."

Cody got up and went to the kitchen counter and then returned with what looked like a cigarette. He lit it with a match, and it flared up briefly. It had a strange, skunky smell. He took a long drag from it and then held it forward for her.

"Oh no, I can't," she said as she recoiled.

"Have you ever tried it?" He held it forward again. "There's always a first time for everything."

She looked at him while the thought invaded her mind. *He's trying to drug me and then he'll have sex with me, and I won't be able to resist.*

He said, "It won't harm you, and neither will I. Promise."

His expression was so disarming, so the opposite of threatening. Without further thought, she took the joint, took a quick puff, and then started coughing. He handed her a glass of wine. She took a sip, calming her cough. She put the glass down and noticed that he was looking at her closely.

"What?" she asked, already feeling a little floaty. He continued to look at her gently. "Are you trying to get me high?" she said, realizing that she sounded more flirty than suspicious.

He laughed. "No, I'm just trying to help you relax."

She took another sip of her wine. She *was* feeling more relaxed. "We don't drink much wine in Missouri. Oh, don't get me wrong, we drink. Some a lot."

"I don't think you really answered my question."

"What's that?"

"Why did you come here, to La Jolla?"

His gaze was steady on her. It was a little unnerving.

"Oh, my grandmother used to spend her summers here and we would come down from Los Angeles, along with cousins from Missouri who would come by train. I have fond memories." She ended with a little giggle that escaped before she could clamp down on the torrent of giggles she was sure would erupt.

"What is the actual reason?"

"The real reason?"

"Yes, the real reason, not the nostalgic one."

She hesitated but couldn't stop the tears from ambushing her eyes. She quickly wiped them away. Cody's gaze felt like a comforting caress. Moments passed. Then, "I think I lost hope."

He took his time. "Hope can give birth to love." He took her hands in his. "But it can't sustain it."

Gwendolyn looked down at their intertwined hands and then gently removed hers from his. She looked up at him. "But I still love my husband. That's what confuses me."

There it was again: Confusion! I'm so tired of it. His soft gaze steadied her; she could feel the agitation of confusion dissipating as her breathing became deeper. After some moments, he stood up. "Let's have some pasta. Spaghetti and meatballs okay with you? I don't feel like murdering a lobster tonight."

She nodded, still inarticulate as her confusion fluctuated.

He hummed while he stirred the sauce and boiled the pasta. Dave Brubeck continued to play on the stereo. It was all so new to her, this music, this man, a stranger cooking spaghetti and meatballs, being so far away from her children. From Paul Stanley.

Cody lit some candles, and there was a strange smell in the small space. Gwendolyn asked about it and he said it was patchouli, a word she didn't recognize, but it was pleasant in its strangeness. They ate the pasta for a while in silence.

She took another sip from her wineglass that seemed to always be full. *En garde, Gwendolyn!* But again, maybe she was just being too square. Isn't that what those kids outside would call her?

Wiping her mouth off with the paper towel provided, she said without consideration, "Why did you come up to me on the beach today?"

Easily, he answered, "You're unique."

"I hardly think I'm . . . that."

"On that beach you were."

"Oh. You mean because I'm not an eighteen-year-old blonde in a bikini?"

"Exactly."

"No, really."

"I was drawn to you. You looked so alone."

All at once she realized she was having more of a conversation with this stranger than she had ever had with Paul Stanley. The beginning of tears startled her once again. Cody leaned forward and looked directly into her eyes. She was speechless, stunned by the truth of what he had said. Her tears overflowed. This was so not like her; she never cried, at least not in front of anyone else. He waited for her.

She dried her tears with the paper towel. "I don't know if I really have a life I can call my own."

"Did you ever?"

"I suppose I might have. Once."

"Tell me about it."

"Oh, it's silly, really."

"I'd like to hear."

Gwendolyn took a hard look at Cody. Who was this man, this surfer-man, this sexy, maybe-younger man, so foreign to her? "What is it you want from me, Cody?" She couldn't tell how it came out. Accusatory? Flirtatious?

The question didn't dissuade him. He smiled as he said, "Nothing, Gwendolyn. Nothing at all. I'm just enjoying getting to know you. And I believe I have a question on the table."

She stuttered, "I'm not sure I know how to answer."

"Tell me what you were like when you were a little girl. Before you became confused."

She was taken aback by this at first, but then noticing the warmth in his tone and smile, she relaxed some. A long sip of her wine helped. "I grew up in Los Angeles, the first twelve years, before my father went broke during the Depression."

She paused, realizing how loose she was feeling and sounding. Cody nodded his encouragement. "I was always putting on plays in my backyard. Daddy built a stage for me, and Mother sewed costumes. As I think about it, I knew no fear back then. One day I even walked all the way up past Wilshire where the houses were mansions. I somehow knew where Jean Harlow lived, you know the famous actress. I knocked on her front door like I belonged there. An older man, dressed in a tuxedo and wearing white gloves, opened it and nicely asked what I wanted.

"I told him I was there to see Miss Jean Harlow. He asked me what I wanted to see her about while reminding me that she was a very busy movie star. I told him I knew and that's why I was there. I explained that I was putting on a play in my backyard for my friends and was wondering if Miss Harlow had any of her costumes she could donate. He smiled and told me to come into a giant room with a huge chandelier high overhead. I couldn't exactly see her clearly at first. She stood at the top of a long staircase, light from a floor-to-ceiling window behind gave her a glow.

"She walked slowly down the stairs dragging what looked like a dead animal behind her. When she walked up to me in the foyer, I could clearly see it was none other than Jean Harlow, only tinier than she appeared on the screen. She bent down and looked at me closely. 'I understand you're in show business, too,' she said. I nodded; I was mute with awe. She draped a fur stole around my shoulders. 'There you go, honey. You look just like a movie star.' She adjusted the fur. 'It ain't mink but that's no reason you shouldn't follow your dream.'"

"And did you?"

"Sometimes I feel like my life is a dream." After a reflective moment, she said, "Maybe that's why I'm so plagued by confusion."

He replenished their wine glasses. "Did you ever realize the Jean Harlow prophesy?"

"The closest I came was in college. I was an art major, but my real passion was theater. Because I'm tall, I suspect, they always cast me in the leading lady roles. They seemed to have a thing for Ibsen at my college, which is strange when I think about it, because it was only a Missouri state teacher's college. My biggest part was Nora in *A Doll's House*?"

"I can see you in that."

She deepened her voice slightly. "'Our home has been nothing but a playroom. I have been your doll-wife, just as at home I was papa's doll-child; and here the children have been my dolls.'" She laughed, feeling mildly embarrassed.

"Brava. Why didn't you stay with it? Acting, I mean."

"I've been so occupied with taking care of people, things, my house, the yard, three children, a husband who's an important, busy man; a monkey."

"I thought you might have been quoting Nora again, except for the part about the monkey. Seriously? You have a monkey?"

"How come everyone who finds out about Eddie has the same reaction?"

"Probably because one doesn't encounter a monkey mom every day."

"Monkey mom! I hardly think—"

"I actually read an article about it. That's what they called them—monkey moms—and these women were proud of that title and referred to themselves that way. They seemed to see them as 'forever children.'"

"Good lord, that's ridiculous. Who would sign up for a 'forever child' to begin with? And if these women needed such a thing, why would it be a monkey? If they're anything like Eddie, they would be a forever terror."

"I read that they can easily revert to their wild nature, even attack their humans."

"Eddie has done that to everyone in my family except me. He's a rascal."

"So why do you keep him?"

"What am I going to do? I can't exactly take him back to the jungles of South America. He's now mine to keep, it seems. Just another part of my job."

They fell into an easy chat as she helped him wash the dishes. As they were doing so, once again it struck Gwendolyn how different this was. She couldn't even imagine Paul Stanley helping her with cleaning up after dinner; it wouldn't even occur to him to offer. After they dried the dishes and put them away, Cody suggested they go for a walk on the beach. "It's moon-bright out there tonight."

The thought swamped her: *Is this when he slits my throat?* The Manson murders were still fresh in her mind. There was something so dangerous—and thrilling—about all of this. When Cody put a sweatshirt around her shoulders and led her into the luminous night, she went with no more thought.

The sit-in kids had moved on, and the beach before them was

quiet, with only the rhythmic lapping of the waves on the shore. They walked without words across the sand and then, with shoes off, along the surf line.

Gwendolyn broke the silence. "You know a lot of things about me, but I don't know that much about you."

"Well, let's see. I told you I teach English to disadvantaged kids, but I probably didn't tell you what a challenge it is to teach Shakespeare and Ibsen to inner-city kids who're dealing with fear and loss every day. You know that my grandfather built the hotel you're staying in, and you know, surely by now, that I am harmless."

She laughed at this. "But I don't know if you're married, if you have children."

"So now you want to know me by my failures."

They walked on, side by side down the beach, for many minutes in silence.

Finally, Cody spoke. "I've had a blessed life. A golden boy kind of life. Rich family, La Jolla, private schools, summers surfing in Hawaii, all of it. I always knew I wanted to help those less advantaged. I felt secure in that aspiration. Even though my father was a hardcore businessman, he and my mother emotionally supported me in my 'artistic lifestyle,' as he referred to it."

He paused. Gwendolyn side-glanced at him and could see trouble overtaking his face. "So far doesn't sound like failure," she said.

"As they say, there's more to the story." They moved on down the beach for a few silent moments. "Mary was her name. We met at the school where we both taught. She was the PE teacher. Kind of boyish, and I found that attractive. We fell in with each other doing a lot of sport stuff—racquetball, bike riding, and of course, surfing. We drank beer together at dive bars and played pool, and on one of those nights we fell into bed. She was fun there too, but we weren't in love with each other, and you probably can guess the outcome of that one beer-buzzed night."

"A child."

"A precious little girl named Elizabeth. We called her Lizzy. We were only in our mid-twenties, but we were very adult about it. We talked about the options calmly and acknowledged, also without drama, that we didn't want to get married just because of the pregnancy. We agreed that she would have the baby and we would coparent her. And we did. She was a marvel to us both, and she grew up strong and with an unrelenting joy about life. Even though Mary and I went on to other relationships, we always cooperated, guided by what was best for Lizzy. She grew up fast and strong. Like me, she was a water baby, took to it like a tadpole, and it was no time before she was playing in the waves right here on this beach, and then no time longer that she was surfing like she was born to it."

"It sounds like she was."

"It was hard to get her out of the water. I got her a small surfboard fitting for an eight-year-old, but she wanted a 'real one' and she was hard to deny. I was always with her when she surfed, but I got more confident about her ability the more she did. And then one day . . ." He swallowed then stopped and turned to face Gwendolyn, who was already feeling dread. "It was a bright day, so brilliant, the glare on the ocean. It was sometimes hard to see. I was talking to a friend who walked by as I crouched at the surf's edge. When he went on, I squinted into the sun to see where Lizzy was."

Gwendolyn gasped as her hand flew to her mouth. "No."

"I couldn't see her. Anywhere. I ran into the ocean, shouting her name. Nothing came back to me. Just the sound of the surf and a vast nothing. She was found later, farther out at sea, a victim of a vicious riptide."

Gwendolyn searched his face. Even in the moonlight she could see his eyes were clouded, as if he were looking into an abyss. "I can't imagine . . ." she said, trailing off, not really knowing what to say.

"Lizzy always seemed like a dream to me. Losing that dream has trapped me in a well of loneliness."

Gwendolyn took this in. "Yes," she said, barely audible. "I do understand that."

"I know you do. That's why I'm telling you this. I haven't spoken of it in years, to anybody."

"But why me?"

"When I saw you on the beach today, I knew you would understand. I knew you were somehow dealing with loss. I think that's why I was drawn to you."

"I've never experienced a loss like you have. I wouldn't even know how I could."

"We never can compare the pain of our losses. Pain is incomparable."

"I think you overestimate me. I'm not so brave as you."

"Brave?"

"When it comes to loss. Facing it. I don't think I can."

"I don't think you know what you're capable of, Gwendolyn, married-lady-from-Missouri, reluctant monkey mom, woman standing here in the moonlight at the edge of the continent with a perfect stranger."

It was so natural that Gwendolyn had no thoughts in her head. In retrospect, she would understand what all those silly romance novels described, what Scarlett O'Hara must have felt at the bottom of that grand staircase right before she was carried up it, what swoon really meant. The smell of the ocean, the moonlit path out to the horizon, the bracing smell of the salt air, his arms enveloping her, their lips meeting as if drawn by magnetic force—it was something she had never, ever felt before.

He had wanted to take her back to the La Valencia on his Vespa, but she knew that wasn't the right idea and so he called her a taxi. After she arrived at the hotel, she went to her room and busied herself with her nightly toilette. As she bent over the sink, splashing her face twenty-five times, she wondered if on this night she was really engaged in absolutions. When she sat on the edge of her bed, not in her nightgown as usual but in a T-shirt and panties, she rejected that idea.

What was it about Cody, the stranger in the moonlight? What

was it about him that allowed her to forsake all that she had known, abandon herself so unusually? She pictured him, like snapshots in a mental photo album. It was his eyes, how they crinkled at the edges, disarming everything he said. No, it was more. It was how he looked at her with soft eyes, not possessive or hard with greed. Soft.

She smiled to herself and turned out the light. Before she fell asleep, she wondered what Dixie would say about her day. She could only imagine. It was a comfortable decision: She would keep the smile she had for this unusual day to herself.

◈ ◈ ◈

The next morning broke bright, no morning fog. She awoke with the anticipation of a visitation from the maddening ogre of guilt. But none came. Instead, she stretched luxuriously like a cat and anticipated the day ahead. Cody had asked to pick her up around eleven, promising a surprise, something he wanted to share. It amazed her how much she trusted him.

A knock came on the door. She looked at her watch and saw that it was a little past ten. Had she gotten the time wrong? She did a quick brush through her hair and application of her lipstick before opening the door with an expectant smile.

Paul Stanley stood there with a clutch of yellow roses and a small valise.

Gwendolyn's smile dropped. "Paul Stanley! What're you doing here?"

He stepped forward and gave her a kiss that she met awkwardly, turning her head away.

He handed her the flowers. "Here, these are for you. I picked them up at the airport."

She looked at them and then at him. "I wasn't expecting you."

"Dixie told me. We need to talk," he said.

He insisted that they go down to the hotel restaurant and have brunch—a "dry brunch," he clarified when he saw her silent reluctance.

Gwendolyn did her best to quell the panic arising within her. Cody was appointed to arrive in just a short time, but what was she to do? It would be too suspicious if she refused her husband, who had flown two thousand miles to surprise her with yellow roses. She had no way to get ahold of Cody; she didn't even know his phone number.

When they arrived at the restaurant, she asked the receptionist for a seat in the back, explaining to Paul Stanley that she wanted a seat by the window. She also insisted that she take the seat where her back would be to the entrance.

She couldn't concentrate on the unusual small talk Paul Stanley was promoting. She could barely notice his nervousness as hers was overtaking her mind and body.

And suddenly he was there, standing just ten feet away from their table, facing her. He must have come in through a back entrance—of course, his family owned the hotel—and there he was silently looking at her and at the back of Paul Stanley. Apprehension flooded her, and her face flushed. Her head moved slightly side to side. Silently, she said, *No*.

His smile deflated. Time suspended for Gwendolyn. Cody flashed her the peace sign then turned around and walked out the back door.

Paul Stanley must have noticed, as he turned to glance over his shoulder and then, turning back to Gwendolyn, asked, "What was that?"

"I don't know what you mean."

"You looked like you'd seen a ghost."

"Maybe I did."

He reached across the table and put his hand on hers. "I've missed you."

She took her hand away. "Why would I believe that?"

"Because I'm telling you, that's why."

"You certainly seemed to be keeping a lot of company," she said.

"What're you talking about?"

"Oh, don't even. You know exactly what I'm talking about."

He regarded her closely. "You seem different. You sound different."

"I don't know what you mean," she said, even though she did.

"What's gotten into you?"

She did sound different, her tone firmer, not at all beseeching. "Don't turn this on me. I'm talking about her, that nurse, Maureen. How could you, Paul Stanley? How could you!" She pulled up, realizing that she was raising her voice.

Paul Stanley glanced down at the table set for brunch. Moments passed, and then he looked up at her. "That's why I'm here. To tell you . . . to tell you I want to do better."

"Why do you do it?"

Another long moment, looking out the window, then he turned back to her. Quietly, he said, "I don't know."

Gwendolyn remembered the time she had asked Dixie why their husbands persisted in going with other women. Because they can was her reply.

She leaned in, "Why don't you just leave me, if these women are so important to you?"

"They're not. They're not at all."

"Then, why?"

"I know I have the power to either love you or hurt you. It's beyond my comprehension why I misuse that power."

His voice was barely audible; his eyes cast aside. He seemed so lost, which gave Gwendolyn pause. She sat back and waited.

Finally, he looked at her, his eyes full of pain. "I need to stop the booze."

"Yes, you need to, but do you want to? Can you?"

"I need to. It has a lot to do with . . . with why I do . . . those things."

"I suppose you mean your need for sex with those women."

"When I drink too much I lose my judgment and I go . . . there."

It was finally clear to Gwendolyn, without any self-doubt, that this was disrespectful to her. Before this last month she never denied him sex, even when he was drunk. She was a good wife. This realization gave her a curious calm and so she said nothing, just observed him evenly.

"I'm going to give it up," he said.

"It?"

He looked like a confused, scared child. "Her, Maureen. Bourbon, all of it."

She had heard this before, and her mouth set with suspicion.

"I can't do it without you, Wendy," he said, his eyes averted, his upper lip almost quivering.

"Why, Paul Stanley, why do you drink?" She realized that this question, the one she had asked Cody last night without sense, was the one she really wanted her husband to answer.

His head jerked back, as if the question had never occurred to him. "Why? I don't know. I guess because I like it, the way it makes me feel. Because I'm thirsty?"

"I'm in no mood for comedy right now."

Paul Stanley tried to shrug it off, but her unwavering gaze lassoed him into a real consideration of her question. His eyes turned toward the window and the vast Pacific. "Why do I drink? Maybe so I don't have to see myself."

"Dixie thinks it's because of your mother."

"My mother? That's what Dr. Dixie Freud thinks?"

"Yes," she said, bypassing his sarcasm.

His eyes lost their focus, and after a moment, regained it. "I could never bring my dreams to her. She was always so cynical about them. I always ended up feeling humiliated for sharing them."

Gwendolyn could see it on his face, the hotness of his shame. He looked like he might cry. Despite herself, she softened. "You're a good man. Deep down I've always known that, even when you do the things you do. And I know you want to see yourself that way. And I actually believe you when you say you want this marriage to continue. That's why I don't understand why you're always doing things that you know hurt me to my core. It doesn't make sense."

He looked like he had been punched in the stomach. Gwendolyn realized that she was speaking with more assuredness, in a more defined way, than she was used to.

After some moments passed, Paul Stanley leaned forward, putting his hands on the table in front of him. "I'm going to try. I'm going to do my damnedest to make you feel loved, to make this"—he gestured to the space between them—"feel real. I'll do whatever it takes. I know I can do better."

She instinctively started to take his hands in hers, but she hesitated then sat back in her seat and considered his words. "I'm from Missouri," she said. "Show me."

❖ ❖ ❖

They arrived at the Del Mar racetrack during the third race. The grandstands were full, and the Turf Club was vibrant with the quiet merriment of those privileged enough to be sequestered from the others. The sun was shining, and a salty breeze was wafting from the nearby ocean.

Paul Stanley had always wanted to come to Del Mar and had somehow arranged admittance to the Turf Club in advance. When they found their table with a panoramic view of the track, the horses were arriving at the starting gate for the fourth race. Paul Stanley rushed off to place a bet before they closed the gate while Gwendolyn, now feeling more relaxed, ordered them both an iced tea.

Dashing back to the table, he waved his tickets. "I got one for you, too."

She glanced at him as he watched the race through his binoculars. He wore a light-gray suit with a blue tie and pocket square. His hair seemed newly barbered and his profile, she noticed, was admirable as always. She checked herself. Was she being seduced?

The horse Paul Stanley chose didn't even finish, but this wasn't dampening the elevating mood. He picked up his iced tea and toasted her. "Cheers," he said.

He had brought back a second racing form and gave it to her. This had never happened in all the years they had attended the Kentucky Derby. They huddled together as he explained the speed ratings, the past racing history, even the breeding that he claimed was important to consider.

He asked her to pick the horse for the next race. She had always picked her horse based on his recommendation or, when feeling a bit wild, by a name that struck her.

"Scotch and Soda," she said, surprising herself with her own incautiousness. That made them both laugh.

"Justify it from the racing form," he said.

She liked that he was teaching her something and wanting her to make a choice. They looked at the racing form together. She ended up picking Scotch and Soda after all, and he asked her why. She had an answer. "He's by Bold Ruler, and I heard you say his horses have stamina to go this distance." This seemed to please him, but he told her she should make a place bet so that if he came in first or second, she would collect.

He came in third, but the race was thrilling in a way it had never been; she felt more invested. The next race was the feature, the Del Mar Handicap, and she asked him to pick the winner for her. She was feeling lucky, ready to cash a ticket, but she knew he would be the one who could best make her that winner.

Holding two betting tickets aloft, he rushed back to her from the betting window.

"Don't tell me which horse," she said. "Surprise me."

The race went off without a hitch, with the energy of the crowd heightened given the stakes. It felt like thunder when the eight horses bolted from the gate. Paul Stanley was on his feet, leaning forward into his binoculars, his fist clutching the rolled racing form, slapping it on his thigh. Gwendolyn, also on her feet, shifted her eyes from the track and the horses stringing out on the backstretch to Paul Stanley as he intensified his apprehension of the race with tense shouts. It was a moment out of time as she studied him, his passion, his deeply familiar handsomeness.

Her trance was broken by him punching the air above him with the hand clutching the rolled-up racing form and yelling, "We did it!" He turned, swooped her up, and twirled her around. *"Payant!"* he yelled over the roar of the crowd. "Twenty to one!"

She went with him to cash their winnings. They stood in the line together, breathless. He handed her the winning tickets as they stepped up to the betting window. "Stick with me, babe, you'll be a winner," he said.

Doubt passed through her, a momentary feeling like she was one of those loose women who would go with whatever man who was wearing the best cologne. She laid her head on his shoulder. "Thanks," she said.

After a gorgeous surf-n-turf dinner at a Del Mar restaurant overlooking a Pacific Ocean crowned by a lambent night sky, they taxied back to the La Valencia. There, they made love in a way that was long forgotten. Paul Stanley was less insistent; she could feel his tenderness, his need.

And yet . . . even during genuine passion, she thought of him. Coconut. Sea salt. She was helpless. And ashamed.

After, while she was lying awake and he had turned his back to her, she asked quietly, "Paul Stanley, are you sure? Are you sure you want me only?"

She looked over at him, his silent back. She heard his soft snoring.

Sleep was elusive for her that night. Her mind was like a projector stuck on rewind. The flickering images of her night with Cody kept repeating, sometimes like an old stuttering silent movie and at other times like a glorious Technicolor Hollywood musical. One scene kept returning: After their talk about her theatrical triumphs, he had said, "Your husband seems to be the star in your play." She asked him what this meant as it was a comment that put her back on her heels. "It seems you make him the leading man in your story." She made a weak protest: "Isn't that what a good wife is supposed to do?" Then he said—and this was what was sticking the most for her—"You live in his shadow out of some perceived convention, but maybe you want to be the star of your play. Maybe you *are* the star of your play."

The next morning, Paul Stanley left just as the sun was rising. He had a 7 a.m. flight from San Diego. Gwendolyn took her time packing and eating her breakfast as her scheduled flight wasn't until noon.

When she went down to the front desk to check out, the desk clerk handed her an envelope. "A gentleman left this for you late yesterday."

It was from Cody. Her hands trembled slightly as she opened the envelope and read, "As our friend Mr. Ibsen said, no doubt thinking of that innocent, hopeful couple on the brightened beach: 'When I lost you, it was as if all the solid ground dissolved from under my feet. Look at me; I'm a half-drowned man now, hanging onto a wreck,' to which she replied, 'I'm also like a half-drowned woman on a wreck. No one to suffer with; no one to care for.'"

With an instinct guiding her, she turned the piece of paper over and there was something more written. "I will always live in the wonderment: Will we ever meet in another life?"

She folded the note carefully and put it back in the envelope before placing it in the bottom of her yellow leather handbag. As she snapped the purse shut, she knew that she would keep this with her forever.

18

A Different Truth

Things were back to normal at the Bollinger house up on the hill.

Gwendolyn confirmed this by planning for their traditional Christmas holiday—always a festive extravaganza thanks to her decorating flourishes for the season. Out came the boxes of puckish little statues of elves (her favorites), gold-leafed reindeer candleholders, various versions of Santa (always jolly, one clearly inebriated). Then there were the boxes of ornaments, lovingly and carefully wrapped every year as if they were precious heirlooms. She loved to take them out of their paper nests and let each one envelop her in a memory. She particularly loved the ones made by her children when they were young, each one reflecting their emerging personalities. Gilda's, perfectly painted in coordinated colors; Franny's, made of humble materials she had found; and Oliver's, sparkled with glitter and glass shards.

The house would be festooned with greenery—all real and fragrant—plus holly that she collected from the farm. And the tree! It was always perfection. She made certain of this by giving Mr. Blakely at the tree lot a generous tip every year, which encouraged him to hold aside the best ten-foot tree of the season. By far, her favorite ritual was baking her famous Christmas cookies. She had inherited the recipe and the molds from her grandmother. They were just ordinary sugar cookies with a sweet vanilla-infused icing and sugar sprinkles, but everyone said there was something special about them. She had tried to interest her daughters in inheriting this legacy, but they lost interest around the time they discovered boys. It was Oliver who had asked her to send him the recipe so he could make them for his Yale housemates.

Gwendolyn put the angel topper on and stood back to admire this year's tree, a magnificent fraser fir, perfectly symmetrical. She took a moment to savor in delicious anticipation of what was to come. Gilda and Robert Ray were flying in from Baltimore, where Robert Ray was doing his residency at Johns Hopkins, Franny was driving down from Mizzou, where she was finishing up her medical school entrance exams, and Oliver was flying in from Connecticut. It seemed he had a girlfriend and announced that he was bringing her back with him, which was an exciting possibility for Gwendolyn.

In response to this news, Paul Stanley said, "Don't get your hopes up," which she found odd. They had met Oliver's girlfriend once, when they went to Yale for Parents' Weekend. She seemed to be an amiable girl from a nice family and smart but not stylish. She tended to wear jeans and T-shirts without a bra, and she wore her hair in a utilitarian style. It didn't matter, really. Gwendolyn was just glad to see Oliver doing more than endlessly redecorating his room, reading everything F. Scott Fitzgerald ever wrote, and participating in more normative interests. She really did just want the best for her boy.

It was a special pleasure for her to know that her three children were looking forward to being together for this holiday. And the best thing of all: Paul Stanley.

He had remained on the wagon, as he liked to put it, since returning from La Jolla, and the difference in their marriage was practically tasty. He came home most nights when he wasn't on call and ate dinner with her. It was quite strange at first, as his rare appearances at dinnertime before would almost always entail his refusal to eat, as it "killed the buzz" of his endless cocktail hour.

And the lovemaking! He had never been a particularly generous lover, but these past few months he was a different man—tender, almost like a little boy suckling at his mother's breast. She shuddered this thought off immediately; it was too strange. Random and unlikely thoughts constantly invaded her mind ever since she returned from La Jolla.

La Jolla . . .

She jumped up to stem the images that were trickling into her mind before they became a flood that would sweep her away. La Jolla was in the past. She was now back "in her box," preparing for her family to gather, with a husband who was now coming home for dinner. And sober. How he cut it off like that was a mystery to her, and, if she was being honest, a cause for worry. But worry was just a prayer in reverse—she had read that somewhere—and it seemed like an appropriate slap back into reality to remember it.

Besides, there were many things to do, and she had to get on with it.

❖ ❖ ❖

As Gwendolyn bustled around her kitchen, preparing her Christmas morning hash (secret ingredient: house-made Italian sausage from Taveggia's Market), she felt snuggled in the warmth of her family gathered for the traditional opening of the presents beside her beautifully decorated tree. Gilda had arrived the day before without Robert Ray, who had a last-minute emergency in his residency, and Oliver arrived later that night without his promised-for girlfriend, whose absence was vaguely dismissed as a family conflict of some sort. Franny was arriving at any moment, promising a big surprise. Gwendolyn tried not to give much thought to the surprise but did hope it had nothing to do with a boy or the more encroaching consequences of such, as her Franny had a promising future as a physician and therefore a life that wasn't dependent upon a man.

When she arrived in the living room, she saw Franny hugging her brother and sister. Gwendolyn's hand flew to her mouth, stifling a gasp. A bandanna was wrapped around Franny's head and her hair was loosely braided into pigtails; she wore white painter overalls decorated with a peace sign and heart appliqués, no bra, and combat boots. Her gorgeous daughter looked like a hippie!

"It's okay, Mother. I'm just Franny," she said as she went to hug her.

Paul Stanley arrived holding a coffeepot and a bottle of brandy.

"Coffee, everyone?"

"Dad," Gilda said, "what's with the brandy?"

"Relax, daughter. I'm only playing bartender."

All three accepted the brandy and coffee as Gwendolyn looked on from the doorway. *To heck with Dixie*, she thought, *my family is beautiful!*

Franny changed out of her clothes into her pajamas like everyone else, and Gwendolyn went out to the carport to retrieve Eddie. Christmas was one of the rare occasions when Eddie was allowed inside. He always added to the festivities by his joyous havoc with the discarded gift wrappings.

Everyone fell into the ritual of opening the Christmas presents one by one, taking turns. Sweaters were modeled, and they joked about the T-shirt Oliver had made for his father that said, "A Legend in His Own Mind." As soon as Franny opened her present from Gilda—Elton John's *Honky Chateau*—she put it on the stereo, causing everyone, including Eddie, to erupt into a dancing frenzy.

Once they were all seated at the dining room table and eating the Christmas hash, Gwendolyn asked Franny about her big surprise.

She looked at her father as she spoke, "I do have some news." She pulled out a copy of *National Geographic* from her bag and held it up to show a gorilla on the cover. She had everyone's attention. "I'm going to Rwanda."

"In Africa?" Gilda asked.

"Yes, where Dian Fossey is studying mountain gorillas. I've written them, the Karisoke Research Center, and I plan to go volunteer."

Paul Stanley couldn't hide his distress. "You're going to volunteer? What about med school? Your application?"

"I walked out of the exam. It was there I knew I didn't want to be that kind of doctor."

"What other kind of doctor is there?"

"Oh, I don't know. Maybe a vet?"

"Gorillas?" interjected Gilda. "Really?"

Oliver said, "Yeah, Franny, if you've got a thing for that why not volunteer to take on Eddie. I'm sure he could use your help." He looked pleased with himself, but no one was laughing.

Paul Stanley got up and poured himself another coffee from the sideboard. "I knew something was wrong when you showed up dressed like a Polish farmhand."

Tears swelled in Franny's eyes. "Wrong? What's wrong with me wanting to work with endangered animals? It's what I want to do."

Paul Stanley wheeled around, sloshing coffee from his cup. "Wrong? I'll tell you what's wrong." He jabbed his finger at Oliver. "He was going to carry on the Bollinger legacy. He wasn't up to it. When I took him into surgery with me, he fainted straight away with the first incision. It was you who stepped up to the plate. You who figured out Eddie had a fungal infection on his tail and how to cure it. You, my Nurse Fran Fuzzy Wuzzy. You were going to be the next-generation Bollinger doctor—that was your promise."

Gwendolyn, who had been silent up to this point, said, "Franny is under no obligation to carry on some Bollinger legacy." She turned to Franny, who was seated next to her, and put her hand on her cheek. "The gorillas will be very fortunate to have you, sweetheart."

◆ ◆ ◆

The Christmas night open house had been a tradition in the Bollinger home ever since Gilda was in high school. Earlier on, Gwendolyn was careful to provide fizzy, colorful drinks that she intended to be a wily dodge for the high schoolers. Only later did she realize that the vodka bottles in the family room bar would become mysteriously lighter after these festivities. Now that the party had become a reunion gathering of old friends who had returned from college or post-college jobs, she relaxed her prohibitions, which she had realized was a losing battle anyway. Tonight, she was concerned about Paul Stanley. He always loved to party with his children's friends, especially the boyfriends of his daughters, some of whom were fond of calling him "Hoss." When she shared her concerns with him, he assured her he would be fine and was looking forward to seeing everyone.

She left the invites to her kids but knew their casualness about it wasn't really a problem. Like an ancient conch shell, the friends, and even some of their parents, arrived without formal invitation year after year. By 6 p.m., the house was vibrating with mirth and joyous reunion. Wearing a flowing tiger-print hostess gown, she circulated through the crowd passing drinks and appetizers, homemade pigs in a blanket with spicy mustard being everyone's favorite.

"You're looking especially ravishing tonight, Mrs. B," commented Patrick Sommers, one of Franny's high school friends. He had always reminded her of that friend of Beaver Cleaver's. What was his name? Eddie Haskell?

His mother, a short, enthusiastic woman named Brenda, popped up beside him. "Oh, Gwendolyn, I so enjoy coming to these parties. I hope you don't mind me tagging along."

"Of course not, Brenda. Nice to see you again this year."

"Your house is so lovely, as always. And your beautiful family! I always say the Bollingers are the Cape Girardeau version of the Kennedys!"

Gwendolyn never understood why people said that. Everyone surely knew they were Republicans.

Paul Stanley purchased her mind, as he so often did. She hated feeling compelled to check on him. Continuing with her hostess duties, she circulated through the house and finally found him sitting in his chair in the family room, wearing his silly Santa Claus outfit and surrounded by his Hoss Fan Club. She went over to see if he needed anything—and to see if he was behaving himself. As she walked up behind his chair, she could hear him telling some story about when he was at the Midwestern Golden Gloves boxing championships in Peoria back in 1938. She relaxed; all was going as it should.

"Here you go, Hoss."

Gwendolyn looked up and saw Bill Wilson, one of Gilda's classmates and a regular at the Christmas gatherings, handing him a large glass tumbler full of amber liquid, no ice.

Gwendolyn came around in front of the chair. "Everyone having a good time?" she asked, keeping her voice neutral. Then to Paul Stanley directly, she said, "Wouldn't you like to have some appetizers?"

"No thanks, I'm good." He turned back to his story, which was now about to get to the gory part when bone and blood flew.

There was nothing she could do now, so she hoped for the best as she went back into the living room, where most of the guests were gathered. As she rounded the corner, Dixie blocked her, lit up brighter than the Christmas tree. An enormous poinsettia flower emerged from her cleavage; she wore a tight-fitting, satiny-red minidress and black fishnet stockings. She toddled toward Gwendolyn on ridiculously high heels.

"Looking festive, Dixie," Gwendolyn said.

"Feeling festive!" she answered, brandishing a drained martini glass.

"How long have you been here? Where's Busby?"

"Hanging out with the high school cheerleaders, probably. Me? I've been here long enough to make some new friends." She leaned in like she had an important and sensitive piece of information to share. "One college boy, very well built, probably a football player, told me I was his favorite Mrs. Robinson."

"What's that supposed to mean?" Gwendolyn asked, distracted.

"You know, from *The Graduate*, the most fuckable mother in the room."

"Good lord, Dixie!"

Dixie peeled off one of her laughs. "'Good lord, Dixie!' Can't tell you how many times I've heard you say that. Promise you'll put that on my tombstone—'Good lord, Dixie!' And don't forget the exclamation point."

"Don't you think you should slow down a bit?"

"Why? What doesn't kill you makes you popular at parties, that's always been my motto."

Gwendolyn had shifted her focus, her brow crimped with worry. The merriment drained from Dixie's eyes as she observed her friend. "You can lower those eyebrows. Not worth the forehead wrinkles." She leaned in. "You haven't been the same since you returned from California."

"I *am* different. Paul Stanley's different. We're different. Or back to where we were . . . before . . ." She withered under Dixie's merciless stare. "What?"

"You know what they always say? First time a victim, second time a volunteer."

Gwendolyn flushed hot. "That's a fine thing for you to say after what you did! After you betrayed my trust."

Dixie regarded her with unfocused eyes. "Yeah. And when did I do that?"

"For Pete's sake, Dixie, you don't remember, do you? You told Paul Stanley I was in California when I specifically asked you not to." Gwendolyn was aware her voice was tight with anger.

"Looks like I did you a favor, sister. You can thank me later." With that she toddled off.

Attempting to shake off her anger at Dixie and eclipse her

anxieties about Paul Stanley, Gwendolyn resumed her flow through the party, eliciting updates from the friends of her children, offering drinks, and always leading the way with her wide, gracious smile. Every time she was near the Christmas tree, she automatically rearranged any disturbed tinsel back into its proper order. This task was the most calming of all, although Paul Stanley was never far from niggling the edges of her mind.

Paul David, a friend of Oliver's, appeared suddenly by her side with his excited plea for her to come see something that was happening in the kitchen. She rushed there and found Dixie leaning against the doorway, smoking a cigarette. "What's going on?" Gwendolyn asked.

"Your inebriated husband is dancing with an inebriated monkey."

In the kitchen, a crowd surrounded the large kitchen island. "Excuse me, Pat," Gwendolyn said.

"Yes, ma'am," Pat Sommers said, stepping aside. "Sorry, Mrs. B." She had to tap another boy on the shoulder to get to the front of the exhilarated human barrier. Shouts of encouragement filled the room: "Go, Hoss!" "Show him how it's done!" The stereo was blasting the familiar beat of "Wooly Bully."

Then she saw it—Paul Stanley in a half crouch, arms akimbo, weaving from side to side in front of the kitchen island, where Eddie was doing his own agitated version of dancing. His repetitive shrieking made it clear that he wasn't enjoying this.

A high-pitched scream pierced the room, followed by a collective gasp. Everyone looked at Georgina, one of Gilda's best and most polished friends, who stood stunned like a statue in the park with a coronet of bird shit on her head. Only hers was made of monkey shit flung at her by a frenetic Eddie.

Gwendolyn surged forward. "Can't you all see he's terrified?"

Eddie, upon seeing her, leapt onto her back, hugging his arms around her neck. The crowd became silent and parted as she walked toward the back door. As she passed by Paul Stanley, he said, "Come on, Wendy, we're just having some fun." He was securely in his cups and off the wagon. She answered him with a look that surely conveyed her disgust. A husband acting like a monkey in a Santa Claus suit. *Seriously.*

As she tended to Eddie, trying to calm him, she could hear the party breaking up. A moment of guilt lassoed her; she was shirking her hostess duties. Eddie's agitation refocused her attention on his need for calming. It wasn't easy. He vaulted his skinny little body from one corner of the cage to another, making a tension-filled chattering sound. Nothing she could do would soothe him. Suddenly, she had an idea—peanut butter. She remembered when he was younger, back when they lived in town and a Skippy peanut butter jar was always on the counter, she more than once found it opened and half of the peanut butter gone. She figured it was one of her kids sneaking the sweet treat but soon realized it was Eddie who had a peanut butter fetish he indulged whenever he escaped. She placed an unopened jar of peanut butter in front of him and watched as he eagerly unscrewed the lid and started pulling out gobs of the gooey brown butter and shoving it into his mouth.

She walked through the now mostly emptied house, right past all the abandoned drink glasses, plates of mauled food—all the detritus of an enjoyed party—and totally unlike her, she went straight back to her bedroom without cleaning up. If history was any guide, Paul Stanley was off with one of his young fans, probably across the river at the Purple Crackle, keeping the party going by purchasing an endless stream of drinks. She glanced out to the back terrace and saw Gilda and Franny, huddled with a few of their friends. She didn't even stop to say good night. She was done.

❖ ❖ ❖

The alarm clock on her side of the bed read 2:10 a.m. She must have dozed off, but her sleep was fitful. An awkward mixture of concern and anger about Paul Stanley and his spectacular return to drinking overtook her. And where was Oliver? He had also disappeared from the house.

Noise from the family room drifted into her consciousness.

Wrapping her robe around her, she went there to find all the lights on. Paul Stanley had his back to her, fumbling with the record player. He dropped the needle onto the record and it bounced, causing an awful screech and then the scratchy but unmistakable sounds of Caruso singing "I Pagliacci." He was in his happy drunken phase; when it progressed to his manic drunkard phase, he was more likely to be playing Ravel, and when the end of his marathon spree was near and it had turned to the bitter, paranoid phase, it was always Wagner. She was in no mood for any of it, so she turned to go back to the bedroom.

"Wendy!"

She turned back to see Paul Stanley stumbling toward her, his arms outstretched, warbling off pitch along to Caruso. This struck her mute with ambivalence, with part of her wanting to flee and another part feeling pulled toward her needful husband.

"You really should go to bed," she said in her most mollifying tone.

He was now arcing over her. She could smell the alcohol on his breath, and it repelled her. She felt trapped.

"I'm here, aren't I?" he said.

"Yes, so what does that mean?"

"I'm not with her, I'm with you," he said as he lunged toward her.

"Stop it! I'm not in the mood."

"What's the matter with you? We've been good together, haven't we?"

"You're drunk."

Her arm wrenched from his sudden grasp as she moved quickly away. She gasped as she felt his powerful arms grab her from behind and twist her around, forcing his mouth onto hers. With both hands, she shoved him away. He stumbled backward, almost losing his balance. Her hand jerked to her mouth, shocked at what she had just done. His face distorted further into brief confusion then rearranged quickly into rage. He advanced toward her with his left fist raised. "How dare you refuse me!"

She stood frozen. Was he going to hit her? He had never done that. It was all so quick that she couldn't compute what was happening. Paul Stanley suddenly lurched backward, his upraised arm pulled from behind, knocking him off-balance.

Oliver stood next to him, rigid, his face burning with fury.

"Don't ever do that again," Oliver sputtered. Gwendolyn had never seen her son like this.

A taunting smile pervaded Paul Stanley's face. "Don't ever do what?"

Oliver grabbed his father's shirtfront and balled it in his fist. "I mean it."

Gwendolyn watched, tense, as Paul Stanley's smile twisted further into a smirk.

"What're you gonna do about it? Huh? Those are pretty big words coming from you."

Gwendolyn put a hand on Oliver's shoulder. "That's all right, honey. Let's all go to bed."

Eyeball to eyeball, locked into a fierce scrum of wills, Oliver lunged at his father, flailing a fist at his face, grazing his chin. This brought Paul Stanley up. He blinked in surprise and massaged his chin with his right hand. Then he smiled, a different smile, one that looked strangely pleased, even proud. Gwendolyn looked from her husband to her son. Oliver appeared to be in shock.

"That almost landed," Paul Stanley said. "I didn't know you had it in you."

Gwendolyn stared at both of them and then turned without saying a word. She walked back to the guest room, crawled into the bed, and pulled the covers over her head.

❖ ❖ ❖

She awoke from a restless sleep when she heard voices drifting up from the basement. She glanced outside and saw it was dawn. Gathering her robe around her she stepped out into the hallway. That's when she heard billiard balls thwacking and then the muffled sounds of her husband and her son talking along with the occasional clinking of ice cubes in glasses. She crept down the stairs to the finished basement and sat silently on the stairs, out of sight.

"You're not very good at this, are you?" It was Paul Stanley's voice, more composed than she expected.

"Don't worry, Dad. I'm not as good at this as you. Nothing to worry about."

More thwacking of the balls.

Paul Stanley said, "That was a good shot you took at decking me. Guess I taught you well."

"Taught me? You terrified me, trying to make me into a boxer, into a junior Golden Gloves champ or something. You bought those little boxing gloves when—what was I, all of ten? Then you punched at me with your huge boxing gloves. I remember them coming at me like bombs. There was that time you hit me in the face, and I ran off crying."

"I was just trying to teach you how to defend yourself. You were getting bullied at school. I was worried about you, that's all."

The lack of tension was striking to Gwendolyn as she heard Paul Stanley's unmistakable baritone laugh.

"I'm raising you to be better than me."

"Are you? Or is that just what you're supposed to do?"

"You're getting pretty cocky, aren't you?"

"If you say so, Dad." Oliver sounded good-naturedly sarcastic.

"I wouldn't tell your mother about what we talked about."

"Why not?"

This really got Gwendolyn's attention.

"She'll think it's all her fault," Paul Stanley said as the clap of cue on ball could be heard.

"I would think she'd blame you."

"Your mother isn't the blaming type, and don't they say it's all about being too close to the mother?"

"I don't know what they say. I'm confused about the entire thing. How did you know anyway? You really surprised me."

"First off, you didn't show up with your girlfriend, which I expected. Then when you were talking about her and how much you were—how'd you put it?—'into her' I just knew you were lying, almost like you were saying something to please me."

"I've never known how to please you."

"Am I that hard?"

"Not if I could be just like you, which apparently I'm not."

Silence. Gwendolyn felt tense. All she heard were pool balls being hurled at each other.

Then, Oliver's voice: "How long've you known?"

A pause, another pool ball thwack. "I guess I've known ever since you were a toddler."

"What? How?"

"Probably when we were at the beach down in Florida—you were three, I think. I used to hold you up, sitting in my palm, over my head. Most boys would have been shrieking with glee. But you were bawling like a little girl. You weren't like other boys."

Oliver said nothing. Gwendolyn tried to imagine his expression.

Then Paul Stanley said, "Oliver?"

"What?"

"You know, I really admired my father. He was a doctor. He loved horses. I never thought I would be anything but like him. It never occurred to me I could be a different kind of man. But you"—the catch in his voice could be felt around the corner—"you, you're not like me. You hold a different truth. I always knew that, even though I tried not to. It was always hard for me to figure that out or what to do about it." He stumbled to an obviously emotional ending.

"But you did, Dad. You figured out who I am. You said it out loud. It's okay."

Gwendolyn's confusion enveloped her like a dense, dark fog, making it difficult for her to leave her stair seat. It felt like how one might experience a stroke. But she didn't have a stroke, and before she realized it, she was around the corner and standing in front of them.

"Hi, Mom," said Oliver, looking surprised. They were both positioned on opposite sides of the billiard table, leaning on their respective cue sticks.

"Playing pool?" she asked.

"Hey, Wendy," Paul Stanley said, "how about rustling up some eggs and bacon for your men?"

※ ※ ※

The next day around 1 p.m., Oliver showed up in the kitchen, where he found his mother cleaning up and putting groceries away. Gwendolyn eyed him. "You look worse for the wear," she said.

"Do you have any orange juice?" he asked as he rummaged through the refrigerator.

Gwendolyn swept into action. She got out her juicer and plucked two oranges from a wire basket, corralling a dozen Valencias that were delivered to her from California monthly, one of the few indulgences she allowed herself and a welcome reminder of her California origins.

She handed the result of her efforts to Oliver, who was now sitting on a stool at the kitchen island, his head in his hands.

"Thanks, Mom."

Gwendolyn sat down opposite him with her cup of Earl Grey tea. She let him imbibe several droughts of his juice, then she said, "Oliver, we need to talk."

He looked up at her with an expression that didn't register as welcoming.

But she persisted. "Oliver, I overheard your conversation with your father last night."

"You did?"

"I heard about what you told him, about yourself being . . . you know."

"Gay? You can say it, you know." Oliver put his half-consumed glass of orange juice down with a thud, slopping some of the orange liquid onto the island. "Sorry," he said, not looking at her.

When the silence in the room compelled him to look up, he found her staring at him. "What is it, Mother? You're surprised?"

"I can't say I'm surprised, no. But honestly, I prayed you'd find another way."

"You got on your knees and prayed, really?"

"Don't be rude, Oliver. I only want you to be happy, and I worry."

"Like I had a choice," Oliver muttered to his spilled orange juice.

Gwendolyn's mind filled with cotton. She didn't know what to do, so she got up and began cracking eggs into a skillet. The sizzle of the bacon grease broke the uncomfortable silence. Oliver stared at her back, rigid with tension. Without warning, she wheeled around and thrust her greasy spatula at him. "How could you, Oliver?"

"How could I what?"

"How could you do this to your father?"

Oliver's face flushed crimson. "What're you talking about?"

Gwendolyn lowered her thrusting spatula. "You know how your father is. How something like this could cause him to go off."

"Off?"

"You know what I'm talking about. Your father is in a delicate condition. This is the kind of thing that could make him, you know, go off the wagon."

Oliver jumped up, knocking over the stool he was sitting on. "Me? What about Franny ruining his dynasty dreams?"

Gwendolyn's face crumpled. "Oh, this is hard. All of this is so hard."

"Me? Make him drink again? As if he ever needs an excuse. I can't believe this," he said as he turned to flee from the kitchen. "Merry fucking Christmas."

1980

19

"Epithany"

What the hell are you going to do?

Dixie's question still resounded in her head, following her about her daily rituals like a hound dog fierce on the scent. It seemed like a lifetime ago that Dixie had challenged her with this question, and yet it seemed like it was just yesterday, too. La Jolla had long ago become a dream evaporated in the morning light.

What the hell *was* she going to do?

She felt stuck, mired in a confusion that was once unthinkable, but more and more, familiar. Dixie was right—after eight years of not being able to find an answer to that question, it weakened her. It wasn't how she knew herself. She had always had her head down and bum up, as her grandmother used to say. Or maybe that was Dixie.

Sudden realizations that changed everything were rare for Gwendolyn. But she had one, one day in June.

She just knew: It wasn't right to keep Eddie caged. At least she could do something about that. He wasn't happy. That had been obvious for a long time.

When this decision came to her, it arrived with clarity. The kids were all away, living their lives. Franny had her "hippie wedding" to a fellow vet student—Richard, a nice young man who didn't have two names, and apparently wasn't plagued by the demons of the male ego—and they were off somewhere in Africa working for Veterinarians Without Borders. Oliver had received a doctorate from Yale in English literature and was now working a plum job as a professor at an elite New England liberal arts college. Gilda and Robert Ray had moved to Seattle, where he was installed as the head surgeon at the Dillingham Memorial Hospital, and Gilda ran the hospital's medical auxiliary. They still had no children, which concerned Gwendolyn.

And Paul Stanley? More and more he was missing in action, something she was becoming increasingly inured to. She wondered if he even knew Eddie still lived with them. And she wondered if he would remember that today was her birthday. Today, June the seventh, the day she was born sixty years ago.

She considered calling Dixie to discuss her decision about Eddie but decided it was time to take matters into her own hands. Romaine had arrived and was in the utility room already ironing. Gwendolyn breezed by her with her coffee mug and a determined look.

"Romaine," she said without pausing, "can you make sure if the doctor calls you'll let him know I stepped out to run an errand?"

"Yes'm," Romaine replied, looking at her sideways.

Gwendolyn got in her Mercury Colony Park station wagon and wondered why she had said such an inane thing to Romaine. Did she really hope that her husband would think of her on this day? He seemed to be thinking of anything but her these days.

She ground the car into gear and drove down to the old red barn, where Eddie had been housed for the past several years. When she entered the dusty space where bales of hay created crude ochre totems, guilt clutched her. Why on earth did she ever agree to place him in this awful place? It seemed like a good idea at the time. Eddie enthralled young John, a local slow-witted farm boy who wanted the job of feeding the horses so that he could play with him. She thought it could be better for Eddie than being cooped up in the cage in their carport with so little interaction.

The old barn creeped her out. It smelled like history but not a particularly pleasant one. Through the cobwebs and gloom, she could see Eddie staring at her behind the wire gate of his cage. His eyes were vast with . . . what? Wonder? Hope? Recrimination? She could never really tell, although she always tried.

When Gwendolyn approached, he greeted her with a cooing that signaled recognition. She opened the cage, and he lowered his head as she snapped his leash on to his old, frayed collar. Suddenly, he squealed with what sounded like delight and bounded onto her right shoulder. She could feel his tail slapping rhythmically on her back as they walked out of the barn into the daylight.

Once in the car, Eddie started jumping around in his familiar dance. Gwendolyn couldn't figure out if he was agitated or happy. As she drove past the turnoff to her house and continued along the gravel road that led to the back of the farm, she decided Eddie was happy. Who wouldn't be, released from a cage in a musty barn?

She had a destination in mind—the end of the road where the woods began. It was a dark and dense hardwood forest, untouched by any clear cutting for many generations. It backed up to a two-hundred-fifty-acre tract of woods that had remained in its pristine condition per the agreement with the Bollinger family when they donated this acreage to the state for a future park.

Gwendolyn came to a stop when she couldn't go any farther, put the car in park, and turned off the motor. She stared at the woods, suddenly unsure of herself. This was one of those moments that required her to cinch up her metaphorical girdle and stride forward. When she opened the tailgate, Eddie looked at her with apparent curiosity as she unsnapped the leash from his collar. He didn't hesitate, leaping out of the wagon, darting around, not seeming to know where to go. Then, as if propelled by a swift burst of intention, he hurtled himself forward toward the edge of the woods. There, he stopped and turned. He looked right at Gwendolyn—or that's how it impressed her. She realized that this imagined look could bring a tear to her eye.

But she would not allow it.

"Go," she said instead, with a steady voice. "Be free."

He turned and flew into the nearest tree, and then he disappeared into the dense foliage of the woods. Gwendolyn stood there staring at the dark-green wall that confronted her. She thought she could hear Eddie's distinctive voice among the chirping of the jays. She turned and got back into the Mercury.

Good, she said to herself, *this is where he should be, in the forest, with the trees to scamper on, seeds and bugs to feast upon, just like it was meant to be.*

Back at the house, Gwendolyn went directly to the utility room, the one place in the house where she felt at home these days. There was a hamper of dirty laundry and although Romaine was working today, she pushed the soiled sheets and towels into the washing machine, administered the Tide, and turned the machine on.

Romaine found her there. She was staring out of the utility room's leaded-glass window; a stare that focused neither out nor in, revealing to the outside world as little as possible.

"What're you doin', Miz B? I was about to get to that before I go."

Gwendolyn turned to her, a carton of Tide held absently in her hand. "Oh," she said.

"Miz B, is everything fine?" she asked tentatively.

"Yes, Romaine. What can I do for you?"

"I was hopin' I could get the day off tomorrow. I already cleaned the upstairs bedrooms. The only thing left for today is vacuuming."

"Is anything the matter?"

"Oh, no, ma'am! Everything's just fine. My great-grand baby was born this mornin'. A pretty little girl."

"Lord-o-mercy, we're practically the same age and I don't even have one grandchild yet."

Gwendolyn caught herself. She straightened the front of her dress and turned to face Romaine. "That's truly wonderful. What's her name?"

"Epithany."

"That's an interesting name. What does it mean?"

"I don't know exactly, but it's religious."

"Don't you mean Epiphany?"

"No," Romaine said.

"I think the word is Epiphany, with a *ph*," Gwendolyn persisted, "only it's pronounced like an *f*."

Romaine looked at her without expression. Gwendolyn continued, "That's when the Three Wise Men brought their gifts to the baby Jesus, and they beheld the face of God." She paused, suddenly aware that she was sounding like a Sunday school teacher.

"It's Epi*th*any, just like I said it." Romaine raised her head slightly. "And she weighs nine pounds, two ounces."

"Well then, that is a substantial baby, for sure," said Gwendolyn, walking past her. "I think this calls for a celebration. How about a nice glass of champagne?"

Romaine followed her into the kitchen, her eyes large with surprise. Gwendolyn opened the refrigerator and peered inside. "Oops, none in here. Looks like we're going to have to have our champagne over ice." She rushed past Romaine toward the pantry. "How was I to know you would be having a great-grand baby . . . so soon! Now where did I put those bottles? I know I bought several when it was on sale at Kroger last month."

"Have you looked in the broom closet?" Romaine suggested.

"Yes, maybe I did store it there to get it out of the way. I've got so much on my mind these days."

The two women shared a silent understanding that Gwendolyn always hid any alcohol she brought into the house but pretended otherwise. The champagne wasn't in the closet, so Gwendolyn suggested they have a glass of sherry, which she had hidden to ensure it was on hand for her bridge club. Romaine followed her outside into the heavy, fragrant air and sat at the wrought-iron table on the back terrace, which provided a lovely view of the swimming pool and the woods beyond. Romaine took her Salems out of her apron pocket and offered Gwendolyn one.

She hesitated a moment and then accepted a cigarette. "I rarely smoke in the afternoon, unless I'm playing bridge, of course. But what the hay, this is a celebration."

Once Gwendolyn finished pouring the sherry into petite crystal tumblers, Romaine lit them both a cigarette. A hesitant silence filled the humid air where no breeze stirred. It was an unseasonably sultry day for early summer in Southeast Missouri.

"You Black people have such interesting names," Gwendolyn said, feeling an old familiar awkwardness with Romaine, which she tried to manage with a distinct politeness.

"Black? Why would you call me that? Can't you see my skin is colored?"

"I'm so sorry, Romaine. I was just . . . I mean Franny told me that saying colored is not right anymore. The proper thing to say is Black."

Romaine shifted in her chair. "It's okay, Miz B. The world is changing pretty fast, for all of us I 'spect."

"Yes, I find time hard to keep up with more and more."

Romaine held out her glass. "Mind if I have some more of that sweet drink? It tastes mighty fine."

"Of course." She topped off both of their glasses.

Romaine took a sip. "I'm thinking you might just get you a grandbaby yourself soon. Gilda seems ripe."

"I don't think I've been a beneficial influence on my daughter. She smokes, you know. Robert Ray thinks she's quit, but she hasn't. I guess she can't. All my kids smoke—all three of them." She stubbed her barely smoked cigarette out in the ashtray.

Romaine looked at her. "Are you all right, Miz B?"

Gwendolyn straightened herself in her chair and smiled at the other woman in that gracious way that pretty women who have always been pretty do. "Why yes, of course I am Romaine. Why do you ask?"

Romaine shrugged. Both women took a long sip from their glasses of sherry.

Gwendolyn broke the silence. "Romaine. Now that is an interesting name. When did you first realize they named you after a vegetable?" The question just flew out of her mouth, without consideration.

Romaine didn't hesitate. "I always knew it. My momma said I was good enough to eat and good for her and I was as pretty as the word sounds."

"That's lovely, it is. The names we're given are so important, don't you think?"

"Yes'm, I 'spect I do."

"They're the first gift we receive from our parents, and they surely influence who we become."

Gwendolyn took a reflective draw on her sherry as she looked out over the nearby alfalfa field. "I've always hated my name. It's never meant anything to me. And I hate the way people insist upon shortening it—Gwen, Gwennie, Wendy—although I've gotten used to that last one, seeing that's what the doctor has called me ever since we were married. I suppose that's why I named Gilda what I did. People always assume I named her after Golda Meir, you know, the woman who was president of Israel. But that makes little sense since we're not Jewish and they don't even have the same name." She realized she was feeling a little too loose and her chatter showed it. "Sorry, Romaine. I don't even know what I'm talking about."

"Where did you get it?"

"What's that?"

"That name you gave to Gilda?"

"Have you ever seen the movie *Gilda*?"

Romaine shook her head.

"It was Dr. Paul Stanley's favorite. Rita Hayworth played her, kind of a passionflower type. He always said I looked like her, though I'm hardly that type. On a whim, I surprised him by naming her Gilda before he even got to the hospital."

"Well, you named her right. She sure is a pretty girl."

"Yes, she is that. I don't know why I did it when I really think about it. And Gilda—the one in the movie—was really strange, very loose morals. She was always saying she hated her husband then claiming she loved him. Back and forth, all very dramatic, just like they were the same thing, love and hate. It was like a strange virus infected her that she couldn't control." She looked at Romaine. "Have you ever heard of such a thing?"

Romaine shrugged.

"Oh, I'm sorry, Romaine. I'm just not making much sense, am I?" Again, she was aware that she was repeatedly apologizing for her communications with Romaine.

Just then, the telephone rang. Both women started to get up, but this time Gwendolyn was quicker. She looked tense, expectant. "No, you enjoy your drink. It's probably for the doctor."

"May I have some more of that sherry?"

"Why not? We're celebrating, aren't we?"

"I sure like the way it makes this summer heat look all shimmery."

When Gwendolyn returned, she topped off Romaine's glass, poured herself a full one, then sat down.

"Was that Dr. Paul Stanley?" Romaine asked.

"No," Gwendolyn said. "It was decidedly not the doctor."

Romaine shook forth a cigarette from her pack and held it out to Gwendolyn. "Would you like another?"

Gwendolyn downed half her glass of sherry then jumped up from her seat. "Oh, no thank you. It's time to turn on the pool filter."

Gwendolyn marched to the pool house in that way she had when she had something on her mind she had to do; the top half of her body bent forward, as if she were heading into a wind. There, she flipped a switch and the machine whirred into action. The sound competed with the crickets in the field. Romaine watched as she cleared the top of the water with efficient, angry arcs of her pool skimmer.

When Gwendolyn sat back down in her chair opposite Romaine, she took a healthy sip of her drink. "I was just thinking that maybe I shouldn't have named Gilda like I did."

"Why, what a thing to say! I can't imagine Gilda being called anything but. That's what I called her since she was a little baby."

Gwendolyn fell silent. Romaine waited then helped herself to some more sherry. She sat back in her chair. "You know, Miz B, I was also just thinkin' about what a friendly place you got here. I don't believe I ever took the time to just sit and admire it like I'm doin' now. I 'specially like those yellow bushes out over there."

She was referring to the forsythia bushes that made a genteel border, separating the manicured lawn and gardens from the wildness of the alfalfa fields.

"Yes, it is nice here. The doctor has worked very hard to provide all this," Gwendolyn said in a ritualistic monotone.

"Yes'm, of course he has. And that swimmin' pool, I really think that's special."

Gwendolyn downed the rest of her sherry in one gulp. "That damned pool." She reached for the bottle and poured them both another glassful, splashing a little on the table. "I had that thing built with my own money, from the small trust fund my mother left me. I don't know what I was thinking. I guess I thought it would make a difference. Now, I just clean it endlessly and fiddle with it so that the kids can come home from wherever they've gone off to and invite their friends over for pool parties. Once I found a condom caught in the filter. A condom! That's what they think of this pool, like it's a bordello. I said nothing about it. I really don't know what I was thinking."

"Maybe you thought it would look pretty. I like the way the water sparkles in the sun."

"I think I always had this idea that Paul Stanley and I would go skinny-dipping."

"Skinny what?"

"You know, with no clothes."

"Oh. Bare-assed."

A slight blush lifted Gwendolyn's face. "In ten years, we've never done it."

"I 'spose when you build yourself a pool, you gotta swim in it."

Gwendolyn looked at Romaine then laughed suddenly. "Is that like when you make your bed you have to lie in it?"

They were both giggling now, like girls who had gotten drunk for the first time at a slumber party.

"Romaine," Gwendolyn blurted with a flush of excitement, "have you ever played 'hostages'?"

"No, ma'am. What's that?"

"We exchange secrets. You tell me one and I tell you one of mine, and then they'll be safe because we both have the goods on each other."

Romaine hesitated, her brow furrowed. Gwendolyn said, "Come on. It'll be fun."

"All right, Miz B. You go first."

Gwendolyn thought for a few moments. "Okay," she said, taking a deep breath. "I suspect that Dr. Paul Stanley is a satyr."

"A what?"

"You know, one of those men with horse ears and tails, given to lust and drunkenness. I think they were Greek," she said with an eerie mirth.

Romaine sat quietly for a few moments. "You mean he's horny, especially when he's on the liquor."

"I guess you could say it like that, but lately he just doesn't seem to be that interested in being, you know."

"That usually means he's got another woman stashed somewheres."

"Why would you say that?" Gwendolyn asked, but it was more like a demand.

Romaine laughed at this strange conversation. "Oh, that's the way the men are. Guess I'm wondering why you aren't thinkin' that. It only makes sense."

"I don't know what you're talking about."

Romaine looked at her, maybe for the first time, straight on. "Yes you do, Miz B. You're a smart woman. You know they like to have their own traveling circus, the one they're in charge of. You know, like a . . . a . . ."

"Ringmaster."

"Yes, like that."

Gwendolyn started to say something, but it caught in her throat like a gob of snot.

Romaine looked at her. "You must be asking yourself what I'm asking myself about you. Why you put up with it?"

Gwendolyn suddenly stood up, facing the woods beyond the pool. Then, after a moment, she sat back down. "I have a family, three children, a house . . ." She hesitated, then almost inaudible, said, "A life."

Romaine cleared her throat and said nothing.

Gwendolyn shifted in her chair. The wrought-iron legs made a slight spark on the terrace bricks. "You know what the doctor said to me last week?"

"No'm, I surely don't."

"He said I should just wait for him. He's getting older and soon he'll get all of this out of his system and there'll be no more other women. He said that, like I just needed to wait my turn."

"You know how they are," Romaine said, taking a casual puff from her cigarette.

"I'm not sure," she faltered.

"They want you to know them, but only in the way they want you to know them. But we—we ladies—we know them for who they really are. We know what they're scared of in the night. We know what they can't say out loud. We know all of it, the whole shebang."

"You'd think that would be a good thing."

"It makes us dangerous. That's why they go for the young ones who don't know nothin'." Romaine stopped as she noticed Gwendolyn staring at her. "Ma'am?"

"Yes, I've heard that all before. It's their nature or some such. I'm starting to think it's not a good enough reason."

They both fell into silence. Then Gwendolyn said, "Maybe you ought to take your turn now."

When Romaine said nothing, apparently contemplating her hostage, Gwendolyn looked at her, perhaps more closely than she ever had. Romaine's unwrinkled face, normally guarded to scrutiny, twisted painfully.

"What is it, Romaine?" Gwendolyn asked, her voice soft.

"I had another girl besides Delia."

"I didn't know that."

"You wouldn't. I got rid of her."

Gwendolyn stayed in silence.

Romaine flashed her eyes to Gwendolyn. "She wasn't Percy's. She was from a White man, a man who had bright-red hair and spots on his face. If she was born with orange hair and those spots, Percy would know. He's not a man who can deal with that, 'specially a White chile. Her daddy was white as snow, whiter than you. I knew that, so I killed my baby."

"You mean . . ." Gwendolyn hesitated, "you had an abortion?"

Romaine barely nodded her confirmation. "I called her Lawanda."

"You named her."

"Yes'm. I thought it sounded like poetry."

"How come you and Percy didn't have any more children?"

Romaine looked down at her hands that were folded in her lap. "Old Miss Jackson down in Delta, she was the one who did it. She tried her potions. They usually made the baby go straight to heaven, but it didn't work that way on me. She had to use something else. It was metal. I don't know 'cause I passed plum out. It worked, but whatever she done tore me up inside so I could never have no more babies." She glanced over at Gwendolyn, who was pale as a bleached sheet. "Miz B, are you okay? I'm only telling you because we're playing this here game."

Trading the hostage of her own abortion seemed like the right thing to do. She wanted to tell her, to empathize with the pain of making that horrible choice. But the words choked, swallowed back like vomit rising in her mouth. They had both made the same heartbreaking choice, yes, but she knew that this was where the similarities ended and any effort on her part would only come off as a hollow simulation of empathy. She was stormed by the realization that while her procedure was done in the sterile environment of a doctor's office, the Black woman sitting next to her was forced to go to some backwater witch.

"I'm so sorry," she said as she stood up and began clearing the glasses from the table.

Romaine put a hand on her arm. "We ain't done yet," she said.

"What do you mean?"

"You told me a secret about Dr. Paul Stanley, nothin' on you. You still owe me a hostage."

Gwendolyn paused, momentarily lost in the stare. An image, a picture as if in an old scrapbook, appeared in her mind.

"I was not always faithful to my husband." She shifted her look from the empty stare to Romaine. "You may think I had every right to be, given how he is. But I never saw it that way—like marriage was some kind of ledger that needed to be rectified." She returned to the inner space that no one else could see. "There was this man, this man in California. He was kind. He was beautiful in all the right ways. And, to be honest, he wasn't Paul Stanley. For that brief moment with him I forgot all about my husband, I forgot all about my obligations. It all got lost in that night on the beach, in the moonlight, when we kissed." She turned back to Romaine, who remained as before in her benign attention. "Yes, that's all we did. That kiss. That one kiss."

Tears sprang to Gwendolyn's eyes as she turned away. Those damned tears—those damned tears that she had guarded so frugally, now so wanton.

Romaine got up and walked over to her employer and put a hand gently on her shoulder. "I'm sorry, Miz B. Maybe we shouldn't be playing this game." She looked straight into Gwendolyn's tear-filled eyes.

The intensity of that moment felt unique to Gwendolyn. It made her slightly dizzy. She looked up at her. "I set Eddie loose today."

Romaine took a handkerchief from her apron pocket and handed it to her. Gwendolyn accepted it and dabbed at her eyes.

"I'm sure he probably appreciated it, Miz B, him being a monkey and all."

"It's my birthday," she said, barely audible. "I'm sixty. Sixty years old—sixty years!"

"Oh, Miz B, I'm sorry. I didn't know."

"That's all right. You're not expected to know."

Her eyes lost their focus as she stared off into the woods, where Eddie was making his new home. "There's a terrible moment in life when it all slips away. You go to bed one night, a young woman with dreams, and then you wake up an old woman. Oh, I know I'm not exactly old, as in nursing-home old, but you know somehow that you'll never be anything but what you've been. It's like the rest of your life is set by some invisible force, and you just get up out of bed and go about living it for as long as you can."

Gwendolyn walked to the edge of the pool. Romaine hesitated a moment and then followed her. It was twilight, and the fireflies danced above the forsythia bushes.

"Did I tell you I let Eddie go free today?"

"Yes'm, you did."

"I took him out to the woods at the back of the farm, near where the state park begins, and just let him go. I think he was happy about it."

Romaine looked out at the darkening woods that weren't far from the edge of the lawn. "I hope a hawk doesn't swoop down on him and carry him off for dinner."

"Good gracious, I never thought of that."

"I'm sure he'll be all right, Miz B. He's an ornery little cuss."

"Do you have another cigarette?"

Romaine reached into her apron pocket and pulled out the pack of Salems. Gwendolyn took one and waited for Romaine to light it for her.

She inhaled deeply then looked back at the view, the pool, the forsythia bushes with their sparkling diadem of fireflies. "Today I thought to myself something I've never allowed myself to think: *Paul Stanley, you are a selfish bastard.* And I also thought, *I need to say this out loud to someone.* But I can't. I could never do that. It's like a code of honor with me that I never speak ill of him, certainly never curse him. Today I kept thinking to myself, *Paul Stanley, you're a son of a bitch.* But it wasn't enough. I knew I had to say it out loud. I knew I had to say, *Paul Stanley, you're a son of a bitch and I'm sixty years old and you didn't even notice!*"

"Miz B, you just said it."

"What?" She had been sobbing.

"You just said what you had to say. Out loud. To me."

Gwendolyn looked directly at Romaine and, after a timeless moment, smiled. It was a different smile than any Gwendolyn had offered Romaine in the thirty-three years she had worked for her. It was one that could be felt.

"I did, didn't I? I really said it out loud."

She stood with that in a stunned silence. And then, "You know, Romaine, it's my birthday today, and I will finally go skinny-dipping."

With that, she unbuttoned her blouse. Then she unzipped her skirt and stepped out of it. Romaine watched her, frozen in place.

"Come on," Gwendolyn said. "Come with me."

Gwendolyn turned away from her and undid her bra. She flung it into the forsythia bushes, creating a flurry of light as the fireflies erupted. She pulled down her slip and stepped out of it, losing her balance slightly as she did so. Only her panties remained. She hesitated a moment then took them off. Clutching them to her chest like a crumpled corsage, she turned slowly to find Romaine standing, as she was before, only now naked.

Gwendolyn stared frankly at Romaine's body. Realizing she was doing so, a giggle escaped as her hand shot to her mouth. "When I was a girl, I used to wonder if Black women had chocolate milk in their bosoms."

A smile broke across Romaine's face, a big wide grin. "Why, Miz B, what a funny thing to think. Looks to me like we're pretty much the same. Look, you're hangin' heavy as me." Romaine gestured to her nipples then to Gwendolyn's—both were indeed lounging at approximately the same southern latitude. She giggled. "Guess we've been tugged on plenty in our years."

Gwendolyn wasn't thinking at all as she continued to look at the body that had always been covered in a fading flowered shift or a white uniform as it cleaned her house and took care of her children. And Romaine stood calm and magnificent under her gaze.

A sudden eruption from Gwendolyn's increasingly friendly subconscious brooked this moment. "Last one in the pool is a toad!"

Romaine remained where she stood. She had never learned to swim. She gave Gwendolyn a nod of encouragement. This was a day when her assigned chore would not be to iron Miz B's sheets nor was it to be her sudden playmate. She was here to be a witness.

Without waiting for Romaine, Gwendolyn dove into the pool. Her body sliced cleanly through the barely cool water. It was a moment when only the elemental surge of life is experienced, only sensation, primitive and refreshing as an orgasm might have once been. Vanquished was the plaguing awareness that the world was becoming a puzzling and precarious place where her fine manners would offer no real protection. Gone, even, in this moment of rare and pure grace, was the disturbing truth that Gwendolyn Bollinger was this day a sixty-year-old woman with sagging, spent breasts, a daughter with the uncompromising name of Gilda, and a monkey named Eddie that she had just set free in a forest for an unexplored reason and for an unrevealed fate. And that she was now alone, underwater, swimming through the overly chlorinated waters of her goddamned pool.

20

The Wife's Vigil

Romaine left to visit Epithany after making sure to put some food out for Gwendolyn. "Are you sure you'll be okay, Miz B?" Romaine had asked as she stood at the door.

"Of course. Why wouldn't I be?"

She had not heard from Paul Stanley but refused to think about it. Where once she relished in the night's quiet, broken only by the atonal serenade of the crickets, now the familiar silence was deafening. She didn't know what to do with herself. She could pour a proper drink, a VO and water, or even make herself a festive daiquiri. It was, after all, her birthday. But none of it sounded right to her.

The phone rang. She quickly picked it up. It wasn't her husband, but she was grateful to hear Oliver's voice.

"Happy birthday, Mom. Sorry I'm calling so late."

"Hi, dear. It's only seven here. How are you?"

"Oh, I'm fine, I guess."

She could hear the waver in his voice. "What's wrong, Oliver?"

"Never mind. It's your birthday. We should be celebrating. Have you been? Where's Dad?"

"Don't you worry about me. Everything's fine here. But I can tell you're not."

There was silence on his end, then, "Jack left me, says we're too young to be in a monogamous relationship. Hell, I'm thirty-one."

Gwendolyn was surprised but not all that sorry. Oliver had always seemed a little on edge around Jack. As far as she knew, he was his first. He was an ambitious young lawyer but was too sarcastic for her taste. She never voiced this judgment to Oliver and knew better than to do so now. "Oh, honey, thirty-one is young. A lot can happen."

"You were pregnant with me and already a mother by the time you were thirty."

"Things were different then. Besides, our situation was different. We were wanting to make our family, and it was best not to wait."

"Jack and I were planning to start a family," he said.

"How's that possible?"

"We were looking into adoption. In Massachusetts, we can do that."

Gwendolyn didn't know what to say so flummoxed was she by this new possibility.

Oliver breached the silence. "Mom, I don't know what to do. I really miss him."

"Oliver, whatever you do, don't grovel to get him back. Don't embarrass yourself like that." Gwendolyn could hear Oliver's tears through the phone. "Oh, honey," she said.

"I don't know how I'll ever get over this."

"You'll get over it. It may take time. You may never forget it. Heartbreak is unforgettable. And it should be."

"Why do you say that?"

"Forgetting would be a crime against your own humanity."

When she hung up, she was struck by the advice she had so easily given. Where did this unexpected wisdom come from? It was the opposite from how she had been feeling lately. Her thoughts drifted to Cody. That would be like something he would have said. She even thought about trying to find out his phone number and calling him but quickly realized how crazy that would be. She needed to check herself. She had not been acting normal.

The dark enveloped her as she sat mute by the phone. Not realizing how much time had passed, she turned on the table lamp and glanced at her watch. Nine o'clock, normally the time she would be preparing for bed. But darnit, it was her birthday and she should at least celebrate with a nightcap. She poured herself the last bit of sherry into a cut glass tumbler and went into the formal living room, a room that she rarely used these days, to sit on her brocade-covered chair. It faced the view to the Mississippi through a large, leaded-glass window. From here she would be able to see a car approaching from the long drive up the hill. Is this why she chose this rare spot to have her nightcap? So she could keep watch for her husband's return, like the boat captain's widow who paced endlessly on the rooftop of her former house?

These thoughts of a wife's vigil immediately turned her stomach sour. This was getting into waters that were too deep for her on this emotionally exhausting day, so she decided to abandon her vain hope for Paul Stanley's return and try to find some sleep.

As she was turning off the lamp on the sideboard, she picked up a framed photograph of her in 1940. It was the one that Busby once had, and the one Paul Stanley, for some strange reason, insisted that he give him. She stared at it, as if seeing it for the first time. There she was, standing at the top of a staircase, wearing a strapless red gown--that famous red dress. No one that night would have guessed that her mother had sewn the dress out of frugality. But what grabbed her attention was not the humble origin of that memorable gown, not even the gorgeousness of her figure or her perfectly sculpted eyebrows accenting her wide-set green eyes. No, it was her expression as she observed the party she was about to enter. Absent was the dazzling smile she normally flashed whenever she was nervous or about to be photographed. Instead, a look of cool expectancy lifted her chin as she basked in the admiring gaze with confidence. Who was this twenty-year-old woman with such self-assurance? she now wondered. What had the years done to vandalize her youthful aplomb?

She put the photograph back on the table with a silent chuckle, pretty sure she wouldn't be able to fit into that famous red gown today.

The phone rang, startling her from her reverie. What was she doing wasting her time on these improvident thoughts?

She went to pick up the phone.

"Hello, Mother!" came the overly enthused, slurry voice of Gilda, calling from Seattle.

"Hi, honey. How are you?"

"Celebrating your birthday."

"It sounds like it. Don't overdo it on my account. I was just about to go to bed."

"Already? It's only what—ten thirty? Where's Dad?"

"Oh, he's not home yet. Probably some emergency. You know how they are."

"Do I ever."

The sarcasm didn't escape her. "Where is Robert Ray?"

"Oh, you know how they are. Probably some emergency." She laughed a mirthless laugh.

"You're celebrating alone then, it sounds," Gwendolyn said.

"I have to these days if I want to keep up my Bollinger bona fides."

"I'm not so sure that's the best Bollinger quality to emulate."

Gwendolyn could hear the splash of liquid over ice cubes as Gilda rejoined, "Oh, Mother, lighten up! Stop being such a prude."

"I've heard that one before."

The phone call progressed in a vague and unsettling way, leaving Gwendolyn with a now-familiar worry after speaking with Gilda. She often sounded slightly drunk but always exhibited a merriment about her life that didn't sound so merry. Franny seemed to be the only one she didn't worry about. She and Richard were dedicated to their work in Uganda with Veterinarians Without Borders. She had taken her own path in life, which took her farther and farther away from Cape Girardeau. Strange as it seemed, this gave Gwendolyn less disturbance about her younger daughter, who had always seemed more vulnerable to life because of her tender heart. Like most mothers, she always wanted the best for her daughters, but her version of that meant that they would forge a path that wasn't dependent financially on a husband. That was entrapment she prayed they would evade. Then there was Oliver, who was always a worry to her, for no other reason than that she had a difficult time imagining his happiness in life.

She had recently moved back into the guest room. This was improper behavior for a wife, she believed that, but she couldn't stand the late-night interruptions as Paul Stanley stumbled into their bedroom, banging things around as he tore off his clothes. He smelled of Maureen, the cheap perfume Tabu, and she could no longer stomach it.

On many occasions, she had encountered Maureen, who was always polite and deferential to Mrs. Paul Stanley Bollinger. At the annual office party, Gwendolyn greeted her with a tight but still-pleasant smile, asking about the young son she knew she had, and wondered how this younger, naive, and frankly less attractive version of herself could enchant Paul Stanley. The smell of her on him made her sick and think evil thoughts.

Sometimes, when she found herself wandering the aisles of the local Liberty Market in the middle of the afternoon with no actual purpose except to stave off her loneliness, she would stop in front of the canned vegetables and wonder what kind of fool she was to put up with this roller coaster of a marriage. Then there were those times when Paul Stanley shone his love light on her; the feeling of specialness would wash over her, enveloping her in a delicious—if only temporary—amnesia. She really couldn't understand why she fell for it, the tango he would pull her into. For years, her children were why she stayed put. But now, they were all on to their own lives, as they should be. Lately, she had been telling herself it was the grandchildren that she would not want to share with a woman who wore cheap perfume. But there were no grandchildren. What was she afraid of? What was stopping her? She hadn't talked to Dixie about this conundrum in a long time. Both women were becoming more merciless in her reviews of her marriage and, she assumed, fed up with her equivocation.

But then the inevitable turning point of destiny had happened one night.

She had been out at a P.E.O. Christmas party and returned to a darkened house. Paul Stanley's Lincoln was in the carport, which surprised her. She had quietly entered their bedroom and turned on a lamp. As she was taking off her earrings, she heard a stirring and turned around to see Paul Stanley sitting up unsteadily in bed, his eyes unfocused and glazed, a revolver pointed at her. She yelped as she dove to the floor at the foot of the bed. Her only thought was that the revolver was loaded, a fact loudly verified when it discharged its bullet into the wall behind where she had just a second ago stood.

Paul Stanley had rushed to her side, claiming he thought she was an intruder. She had argued with him for years about his paranoid penchant for keeping loaded guns all over the house just in case he had to deal with that marauding band of intruders who never seemed to make it out of the woods and breach the sanctity of his home. He stank of the horrible concoction of whiskey and Tabu. As she stood up, she wondered if Maureen had thrown him out of her apartment and that was why he was home uncommonly early. But what did it matter? The gunshot and near murder of Paul Stanley's wife had been sobering for both of them. She went to sleep in the guest room that night, without any explanation. And there she remained. Quickly, she learned that she needed to double bolt the door, as Paul Stanley didn't take kindly to his wife denying him access.

Gwendolyn walked through the long house, turning out lights but leaving some on that would light the way for Paul Stanley when he returned tonight. If he did.

When she entered her bedroom, she turned on the light and blinked. Something was different; she sensed it immediately. Shrugging off this odd sensation, she walked toward her closet.

That's when she heard it, a sound that seemed to emanate from outside the window by her bed. It was distinctive, familiar. She went to the window and opened it.

Eddie was sitting there on the ledge, shivering, whimpering his sad and lonely song.

She undid the screen and stepped back, expecting him to fly into the room in a fury. Instead, he crept in through the open window, looking unusually tentative. Gwendolyn was at a loss. Had she betrayed her good intentions? Had she traumatized this poor beleaguered creature instead of liberating him?

Eddie looked at her sideways, similar to the way Romaine always looked at her. Then he jumped on her bed and curled up on one of the pillows. He kept looking at her with his large, almost preternaturally human eyes, and she didn't know what to make of it. Was it a look of accusation? Of need? She even wondered *of love?*

Of course not! She shook this silly thought off like a dog ridding itself of the rain. He was a monkey, after all, not a human supposedly capable of such an emotion. She needed to stop all of this attribution of human feelings to Eddie. He was a monkey!

Not sure of what to do with him, she continued with her usual nightly routine. As she slathered cold cream on her face to remove her makeup and then splashed it twenty-five times with lukewarm water, she kept a wary eye on Eddie, half expecting him to rise up in a revengeful fury. Instead, he seemed to watch her with a curious intent, which made her more wary.

She continued with her toilette, which required her to remove her dress, her stockings, and her undergarments. This later task created a sudden unease in her as she felt Eddie's unwavering eyes upon her. In an instinctual act of modesty—strange, she realized—she closed the open door to the bathroom to continue her disrobing unmolested by the monkey's gaze.

When she emerged in her silk pajamas and robe, she found Eddie still curled up on one of her bed pillows. This wouldn't do.

She picked him up, pillow and all, and carried him over to a spot in a corner of the room where she arranged what she hoped would be an acceptable bed. She paused and looked down on him, really looking at him more closely than she probably ever had in the twenty-three years she had cared for him. He looked tired, drained of any wildness, almost docile, like an old dog looking for comfort.

She was utterly weary and would have to figure something out for him tomorrow.

She got into her bed and started to turn out the light, but she felt restive. She picked up a book from her bedside and glanced at it vacantly, lost as she was in her unsettled thoughts. When she focused on it, she noticed it was a book that Dixie had dropped off at her back door a couple of days ago with a note: "A little light reading for the sixty-year-old postmenopausal woman. You're nothing like Anna, but who knows—maybe you are and may learn a thing or two. Or at least find some companionship."

She looked at the cover of the book. It depicted a beautiful woman in a black velvet gown, lounging on a loveseat. *Anna Karenina*. Of course, she had heard of the Tolstoy novel but was always too intimidated by its eight-hundred-plus pages to actually read it.

Oh well, she thought, *perhaps it will help me sleep*. She opened the book to the first page and began to read out loud, as was her preference when she was alone in bed: "'Happy families are all alike; every unhappy family is unhappy in its own way. Everything was in confusion in the Oblonskys' house. The wife had discovered that the husband was carrying on an intrigue with a French girl, who had been a governess in their family, and she had announced to her husband that she could not go on living in the same house with him—'"

Gwendolyn slapped the book shut. "Good lord, Dixie," she said out loud to no one except for Eddie. "This is not restful."

Quickly checking on Eddie to see if he was still on his improvised bed, she reached to turn out the bedside light, muttering to herself, "Tolstoy—what does he know anyway?"

Closing her eyes, she tried to calm her mind. But an unusual thought foiled her: *Maybe Eddie had returned knowing that she was alone on her sixtieth birthday and needed company.* Thoughts about such things as synchronicity and provisions from the universe never found purchase in her mind. Normally, she would chase such a thought away as frivolous and unnecessary. Tonight, she was just too damned tired. Maybe she was just too damned tired to be doing anything in her usual way.

Sleep came, but it was fraught. At some unknown hour, her eyes fluttered open and she knew that sleep was now lost to her. She turned on the light and picked up the Tolstoy book.

Instead of continuing from where she stopped before, she opened the book to the middle and began reading:

"She felt as though everything were beginning to be double in her soul, just as objects sometimes appear double to overtired eyes. She hardly knew at times what it was she feared, and what she hoped for. Whether she feared or desired what had happened, or what was going to happen, and exactly what she longed for, she could not have said. 'Ah, what am I doing!' she said to herself, feeling a sudden thrill of pain in both sides of her head. When she came to herself, she saw that she was holding her hair in both hands, each side of her temples, and pulling it. She jumped up, and began walking about."

Gwendolyn put the book down on her lap. She felt oddly peaceful. It were as if Anna Karenina *was* her companion, like they understood each other. She, at least on this dark night, didn't feel so alone. And at last, this gave her the blessing of sleep, on this night, the night of her sixtieth birthday.

21

Amends

Something awakened her. She blinked and looked out at the alfalfa field. It undulated in the wind coming up from the south. The sky was gray in the predawn, not fully awake itself.

Then she saw him. She bolted upright. Eddie was curled up at the base of her bed, not asleep but watching her. This would not do; she was never one for animals in the bed and certainly not a wild one. But after a moment, she fell back on her pillow with resignation. She wouldn't shelter Eddie in the house, but she was just too tired to do anything about it now.

If she had any doubts, all became apparent to her later that morning, after she left him in her bedroom while she ran errands. When she returned, her always orderly room had been turned into a literal shitstorm. She had always eschewed such a vulgar term, but there was really no other way to describe it. Eddie had flung his feces around the room, dismantled the bedding, and emptied her chest of drawers of her bras and panties. In fact, when Gwendolyn had opened her door, Eddie greeted her wearing the left cup of a brassiere on top of his head. It looked like one of those Chinese peasant hats.

"For Pete's sake," was all Gwendolyn could say as she began cleaning up the mess. It was enough to sober Eddie, who retreated to a corner and observed her.

New arrangements would have to be made. She couldn't imagine returning him to the dark, dusty barn, and he had obviously rejected the woods. There was old Mr. Meister farther out on County Road. He owned the Capaha Wild Animal Park, where he charged two dollars a head to schoolchildren and the occasional tourist who wanted to see his raggedy collection of "exotic" animals—not a zebra or a lion in sight, mostly snakes from the region, a boa constrictor from somewhere else, and a few other animals of some sort.

Gwendolyn took Eddie out to meet him, thinking this might be an acceptable alternative to the woods. At least there he could cavort with other wild animals who might fool Eddie into believing he was back in the jungles of South America.

The trip did not go well. Eddie took an immediate dislike to old Mr. Meister. He screeched in his most ferocious tone and lunged at him when the old man tried to approach. He became very agitated, almost frenzied, when introduced to the farm's resident donkey, who brayed at him in what seemed like his own panic.

"He's too wild for this park," was old Mr. Meister's observation.

"Really?" said Gwendolyn. "I thought this was a place for wild animals."

"Too wild," he concluded.

As she drove away with Eddie, Gwendolyn thought that perhaps Eddie had lived too long around humans to be comfortable with wild things. She smiled when she also decided that her monkey was a discerning creature. Old Mr. Meister did have a most off-putting odor to him.

Returning him to the hay barn was a heartbreaking option for Gwendolyn to consider, but there seemed to be no other alternative. She drove up the walnut-treed lane that would take them there and slowed as she passed the old farmhouse to her left and, without thinking, pulled over and parked.

She knocked on the door, feeling tentative about her visit. She knew why when Opaldine answered the door. From afar, she could see

Duke sitting in the rocker on the side porch, "studying," as he liked to say, what he could accomplish for the day if he were to ever to get off that rocker. Gwendolyn always liked Duke. How could she not, this big broad-faced man with a ready smile, wearing his signature denim overalls, always cleaned and starched by his attentive wife. But she disapproved of his work ethic that, as far as she could see, didn't exist. She had gotten used to him and Paul Stanley's fondness for keeping characters from Bollinger County like him around on the payroll for his own amusement. His job description was to oversee the operation of the farm, which he mainly did just as he was doing now—from the porch. Duke's one real usefulness, according to Gwendolyn, was to drive Paul Stanley around when he had been drinking and keep him in a pleasant mood with his unfailing up-country humor.

Rarely had Gwendolyn come down to the old farmhouse since the couple had lived there, and so Opaldine had telegraphed her surprise when she opened the door to see Gwendolyn standing on the porch in her pretty skirt and blouse, polished leather loafers with gold bridle bits across the top, and Eddie staring at her from atop her left shoulder.

"May I come in, Opaldine?" Gwendolyn asked.

"Oh yes, ma'am, surely!" Opaldine had recovered from her surprise and now beamed her delight. "Would you like a nice cuppa tea?" she asked.

"That would be lovely. Thank you."

The two women and Eddie moved to the back of the house, to the large kitchen. Opaldine busied herself with the preparations as Gwendolyn looked around. Not only was this the scene of so many Bollinger family Sunday dinners when Miss Belle and Doc Ollie lived here—mostly happy memories—but it was also fragrant with flashbacks to the days when her young family camped out here for the two years it took to build the big house on the hill.

A loud command issued from the porch. "Opaldine, fix me a platter! I'm hungry."

Gwendolyn observed that Opaldine immediately started doing as she was instructed. "Excuse me, Mrs. Gwendolyn. I'll fix the tea directly."

As Gwendolyn watched, it reminded her of Paul Stanley, who had more than once joked that he would willingly trade her in for an Opaldine—some good, solid woman from Bollinger County, one who knew the value of hard work and less talk. She wondered if Paul Stanley wouldn't have strayed if she had been more like Opaldine throughout their marriage. What a ludicrous thought. None of her husband's affairs in any way resembled the stout woman with the florid complexion on her apple cheeks that stood before her arranging food on a platter. It occurred to her that Maureen might be capable of hitting that mark, but in a more attractive package.

She asked Opaldine if she could look around. Opaldine paused and considered her with curiosity but gave her assent without a question.

Climbing up the narrow stairway to the upper level, a strange blush of emotions overwhelmed Gwendolyn. She always remembered the two years spent in this old two-story house made of brick, with the steeply gabled hip roof and the wide wraparound porch, as a hopeful and happy time. They had begun the construction on what would be their ultimate dream home, high on the hill above. That site was exquisite, ringed by woods, with a commanding view of the rolling countryside all the way to the Mississippi River. Equally splendid was the Frank Lloyd Wright-inspired home, rising like her castle in the kingdom of her enchanted life. As she topped the stairs, she was struck by the silence, or perhaps it was the sound of foreboding. She knew that all of that was a creative reconstruction of her life; the material facts existed but the embellishments were suspect.

She looked into the open doorway of what had been the bedroom she shared with Paul Stanley during this interlude. Now, it was spartan, with a perfectly made double bed covered with a crocheted coverlet.

A memory commandeered her . . . It is after midnight on the Fourth of July, fifteen years ago, the sound of gravel crunching from a distance, getting louder until it stops and a car door slams shut. The frogs flirt with each other in the pond, not too far away from her open window. *Haven't I been a good wife? Don't I always make myself available to you? Do I ever deny you?*

Paul Stanley did give up the French Nurse, but she was easily replaced by Maureen, the Local Nurse, as Dixie had named her. He had grown bolder with her, spending nights at her apartment in town, taking her on weekend trips to New Orleans and the racetrack, blatantly ignoring the public shame it brought to his wife. After that, Gwendolyn's world changed irretrievably.

She snapped her attention back to the humble bed before her. She wondered how two such large people could sleep comfortably in such a small space. With a silent gasp, she realized this was the exact same double bed she and Paul Stanley had shared when they lived here. And the thoughts rushed her mind before she could consider them: *This is all I ever wanted. This narrow bed. This modest comforter. To be held closely in this bed, securely, free from all fears of displacement.*

She became aware that Eddie, perched on her shoulder, had started picking through her coiffed hair as if he were looking for bugs or perhaps grooming her. "Stop that, Eddie," she said with a firm yank on his leash as she dabbed at her moistened eyes.

Back downstairs, she found Duke sitting at the kitchen table, devouring a platter of fried chicken, mashed potatoes, and corn on the cob. Opaldine sat next to him, passing him a bowl of gravy. Duke looked up, grease dripping down his chin. A big smile broke across his broad face. "Gwen!" He always called her that. She hated it, but never corrected him. "We're proud to see you. Opal told me you were hereabouts. And look at that little feller there. Ain't he a caution?"

Gwendolyn smiled to herself. Paul Stanley had always said Duke was a walking, talking embodiment of Bollinger County.

She understood the importance of that sentiment for him. Duke and Opaldine, who were most likely related and from the same English peasant stock, were a fond reminder of the place where Paul Stanley's family's proud history originated.

Opaldine got up when she saw Gwendolyn and scurried over to the stove, where she had a teapot at the ready.

"Opaldine, please don't bother yourself," Gwendolyn said as she walked over to the kitchen window. It looked out over the field in the back.

"No bother at all, Missus."

Gwendolyn was looking for the chicken coop that Duke had built when they first moved down from Bollinger County. It was still there, but there were no chickens.

She turned back to see Opaldine setting up her humble tea service on the table. Taking a seat, she removed Eddie from her shoulder, letting him root around under the table. "Duke, it seems like Opaldine takes wonderful care of you," she said as she took a sip of her tea. It was Lipton, which she never liked, but it felt somehow comforting to her today.

"Yes, she surely does," he said, reaching over and squeezing her pudgy hand.

"How long have you two been married?"

Duke considered this. "Maybe all my life I can remember?"

A blush bloomed on Opaldine's face. "He took me when I was fifteen and raised me."

"Sometimes I think I done good marryin' her, and sometimes I think I didn't do so good." He said this with his famous verbal twinkle, and she blushed with pleasure. "At least I didn't have to go too far to find her, living in the next holler, she was." This display moved Gwendolyn into complex feelings. She was seeing something she deemed genuine and enduring, which made her happy. So, from where was this sadness invading her?

Duke studied her. "Gwen, we're mighty proud you to come

visiting. Everything okay?"

"Did you know that I tried to set Eddie free into the woods? Of course, you wouldn't know that. The little guy beat me back to the house."

"You don't say? Maybe he's just gotten used to living in a cage and getting his dinner delivered to him," observed Duke.

This idea made Gwendolyn sad. "Yes, I suppose we've done that to him."

"I haven't seen Doc around lately. He's doing some good, I'm a 'specting." It was a question more than a statement.

"Oh yes, he's busy as usual. But why I'm here is that I have a favor to ask."

Opaldine put down the dishrag and said, "What is it, Missus? Anything we can do?"

"Well, perhaps. I need a new home for Eddie."

Opaldine came over and sat back down next to Duke. "Eddie?"

"Yes, I know it's a lot to ask. You see, he just can't stay in that dusty old barn, all alone with the rats. It's just not right. And old Mr. Meister wouldn't take him out at his animal park. Besides, Eddie didn't like it there, that was obvious. I thought of you because you have that empty chicken coop out back and he's used to Opaldine, who's fed him occasionally. It's in such a lovely spot, under the big pecan tree and with a pleasant view across the lower field."

"Are you sure about this, Gwen?" Duke asked.

"Why yes, I think so. Why? Is it too much to ask? I'd understand—"

Duke leaned forward. "You two seemed to have a need for each other."

Gwendolyn stuttered, "I don't understand. He's a monkey."

"Maybe he's more than that."

"I really don't understand what you're saying, Duke," she said, her voice barely audible. Gwendolyn wanted to run out of the room, this house with all its memories, this table with Duke and Opaldine studying her.

"I had a pig once. I named him Roger. Don't know where I got that name, but it was my first mistake, naming him. I was raising him for eating. But the little guy became something else before I knew it. What, I can't exactly say. Creatures are like that. We have them to suit our purpose—to eat, hunt, take us over land—but then we name them, and they take on a different meaning."

Gwendolyn knew Duke was trying to make a point, like a country preacher telling a parable from the Bible, but her mind resisted it. "Did you eat the pig?" she asked vaguely.

"Lord no!" replied Opaldine. "How could we eat a pig named Roger?"

Duke sat back in his chair. "What about building another cage like that up near your house?" Duke asked.

"Yes, that would make sense, but . . ." Gwendolyn trailed off, her mind going soft.

Opaldine retrieved a little ironed linen handkerchief tucked in her sleeve and handed it to Gwendolyn. "Here," she said gently.

"What?" Gwendolyn asked, looking up at her. Then she felt the sensation of tears flowing down her cheeks, plopping on her hands that were folded in front of her on the table like a prayer.

"Gwen," Duke said, waiting for her to look at him, "Opaldine will take care of the little feller. She's good with animals."

Opaldine looked squarely at Gwendolyn. "Surely I will. He's an ornery rascal, but I'm used to them," she said, offering a secret smile to Duke.

Then Gwendolyn looked at Eddie, who was staring at her, it seemed, in wonderment. She picked him up and nestled him in her lap. She saw the gray on his muzzle, the round dark-brown orbs of his eyes; he looked old and sad to her. Was he really old? She didn't really know how old he was.

She put Eddie down and gave the leash to Opaldine. "Thank you," she said. "I can't thank you both enough."

And then, without looking at Eddie, she turned and walked out of the house.

She sat in her car for what seemed like a long time, staring at the old farmhouse. It would be Eddie's new home. Had she done the right thing? Would he be happy living in a chicken coop? Perhaps Duke was right—he might prefer the cage and its negotiated security. Creatures do get used to things, especially when those things provide comfort in the form of food.

"Well, that's that," she said to herself, and then, as if to make sure she reminded herself, she said out loud, "Hesitation is a waste of time."

Putting the car into gear, she backed out into the road. Slowly, she drove up the long winding hill to her house. As she crested the top, she paused, surveying the beautiful view. It was a cloudless day where you could see clearly the Mississippi River. She remembered the first day she took in this view. Paul Stanley brought her here when they were still courting. There was no road then; they could only get to this spot by horseback. She remembered feeling like Barbara Stanwyck in an old Hollywood movie as she galloped on her horse behind the dauntless young Paul Stanley, and when arriving at the top of the hill, he pulled her off her horse and enveloped her in his arms. "This," he said, with a broad sweep of his arm, "this is where we will someday build our home, where we will raise our babies, all ten of them."

"Ten?" she remembered protesting coquettishly.

"A whole gaggle of little no-neck monsters," he said, quoting his favorite, Tennessee Williams. "What do you think of it, Wendy?"

"It's so beautiful here," she said, almost breathless with the magnificence of the moment, forgetting to correct him about calling her Wendy.

The promised home was built. The children were produced. They were all young in their lives—or at least it seemed that way from this vantage point—when they moved to this hilltop home. Now, no one was young anymore. All three of her children were launched into their futures. Eddie was safe now in his new home.

Paul Stanley. And then there was Paul Stanley. Her life's work.

She was tired.

Romaine was right—she knew too much.

Her work was done. She had only one more thing left to do.

22

The Wildness Within

She arrived home at twilight and set about preparing what she thought would be the perfect meal, something she knew Paul Stanley would appreciate: prime rib with her special horseradish sauce, twice-baked potatoes, and roasted cauliflower. She only prepared this meal on special occasions. Surely, he would notice.

This qualified as a special occasion. It would be their last supper.

She did have her moment of doubt, bordering on dread. That's when she decided she needed to talk with Dixie. They had grown apart in recent years. It started with the breach over the La Jolla betrayal, but mostly the distance was due to Dixie's increased submersion in alcohol. But she did miss her willing company, her askew wisdom, and this was one of those times she needed her. She picked up the phone and called the house. Busby answered, which surprised her. When she asked what he was doing home in the middle of the day, he explained that he needed to come back to feed the dogs.

"Where's Dixie?" she asked. "I'd like to speak with her."

An unusual moment of silence passed. "I guess Paul Stanley didn't tell you."

"Tell me what? What's happened?"

"My darlin' girl finally made it to closing time."

"You're unsettling me. May I please speak to her?"

"Betty Ford won't let you."

"Oh, I see. When did this happen?"

"Last week. I flew her out to California and said goodbye. It was harder than I realized."

"Was this her decision?"

"I don't think she felt like she had a choice. We haven't seen you in a while, but let's just say things have gotten a little scary around here."

"I'm so sorry. I should have stayed in better touch. My god, I'm sorry."

"Interesting about the diagnosis."

"Sort of obvious."

"They assigned her a dual diagnosis, all the rage lately in psychiatry it seems."

"I can guess the first one."

"Yes, that doesn't require much inquiry. But the second one, that was interesting—sex addiction. I'm not crazy about them curing that, but I'm going to assume it's all for the best."

After she hung up, she realized she didn't require Dixie's counsel to know what she needed to do, so she made an appointment with Hal Spaulding, their family lawyer. He had gone to high school with both of them and had always handled their affairs. Surprising to Gwendolyn, her questions hadn't put him off stride at all. It almost seemed like he had been expecting them, which was strangely reassuring to her. But then he asked her, "Do you really think you'll be able to live in Cape, separate from Paul Stanley?"

She knew what he was asking, and the question gripped her. She remembered Paul Stanley's reaction to when she had moved out of their bedroom, how her denial of him resulted in his rapacious rage. She thought of all the loaded guns he had around the house, how his alcohol abuse had increased his paranoia. How could she ever have a peaceful, separate life in Cape Girardeau? But still, she had made up her mind. And when this came back to her, calm enveloped her like a warm quilt on a chilly morning. And this time she would not do it in a panic, fleeing from the scene as she had done eight years before. This time she would feed her husband well and tell him that she had made up her mind.

She set the table with her usual care and put on one of Paul Stanley's classical records. She didn't bother to see what it was, just something that sounded soothing. She expected that he would be home by seven, having called his office and checked on his schedule. Based on that, she left a message requesting he get home by six for dinner. She made sure his receptionist knew this was of great importance.

She finished her preparations for the meal in a timely manner and decided to take the final step before he arrived. There was no room for hesitancy; she needed to keep moving.

She went into her bedroom, where she had already laid out a large suitcase. Carefully, she chose only the most essential items; her finest undergarments, three casual skirts with six coordinating blouses, a tailored suit, her pearls, several pairs of earrings, two shorts and halter tops, a swimsuit, a pair of sandals, two flats. At the last minute, she put the heels she had chosen back in her closet. She wouldn't need them where she was going—California. A hotel had been booked in St. Louis near the airport as well as a flight to San Diego the next morning. She didn't allow herself to think much beyond that, only to know that she would need to get far away from Paul Stanley after she broke the news to him at dinner.

Before she closed her suitcase, she looked over at her chest of drawers. Compelled, she walked over to it and retrieved a key from an enameled box sitting on top. Thrown off by a swelter of inchoate feelings, she paused then exhaled a clutched breath and opened the drawer. This was where she sequestered her trove of Paul Stanley's love letters from their courtship years as well as other significant memorabilia. Like an archeologist who knew what she was looking for, she dug down to the bottom of the box. There, she pulled out a small piece of paper, folded over. When she unfolded it, she was first struck by the blue line drawing of a Spanish señorita, the logo of the La Valencia Hotel. She clenched her eyes closed then opened them and read silently until she got to the last few lines, then read aloud: "I'm also like a half-drowned woman on a wreck. No one to suffer with; no one to care for.' I will always live in the wonderment: will we ever meet in another life?"

Is this why she was going to California? In some unconscious—but no doubt vain—attempt to recapture that moment of future possibility? It was absurd! Cody was surely ensconced in his own life with a woman he loved, perhaps more children. She had lived so long in the dream of one man that it would be foolish for her to sacrifice any more of this precious life to another fantasy. She tore up the note and put the pieces back into the drawer, locking it and replacing the key in the enameled box.

It was 7:30 p.m., and there was no crunch of the gravel driveway, no fan of light as his car crested the hill. She thought about calling the office back but decided not to. Instead, she built a fire in the fireplace and sat down on the couch nearby. She closed her eyes and let an insistent parade of images move across the inner screen of her mind . . . *Gwendolyn at ten*, wearing a short, loose-waisted, lacy dress and a bobbed hairdo, looking like a fetching junior flapper, curtsying on the beach in Santa Monica, a gaudy Ferris wheel behind her . . . *Gilda, Oliver, and Franny*, all young and full of radiant innocence, standing in the middle of Miss Belle's daylily garden in full bloom, Eddie on a leash at their feet . . . *Oliver*, a boy of three, on the beach in Florida, being held aloft on the palm of Paul Stanley; father smiling and rippling with the power of his masculinity, son screaming in terror . . . *Gwendolyn and Paul Stanley*, cheek to cheek on the dance floor, smiling gorgeously at an anonymous photographer, in midglide around a dance floor in Havana . . . Their 1941 wedding portrait, she in a simple gray suit with a lace collar, he in a US Army uniform, both looking directly at the camera, the neutrality of their gaze showing off their almost perfect features but leaving an observer perhaps wondering: Is this couple looking into a future where the world is at war and their outcome uncertain? . . . And then a remembered picture, this one finally, strangely, bringing a tear to her eye: Eddie, in rare repose, sunning himself on a lounge chair on the porch of the old farmhouse.

Gwendolyn shook her head, shaking off these mental pictures, wondering, *Are these even real? Are these just photographs that enshrine memories, making them seem more real, and like photographs on black paper, restrained by little photo corners, curated to only entail happy memories where everyone is healthy and happy and all the pain and ugliness is banished to a trash can?* Is memory from the vantage point of sixty just a way of rewriting a life to make it tolerable?

The phone rang, waking her up. She had fallen asleep in her chair in the family room. Glancing at the clock over the fireplace mantel, she could see that it was 10:30 p.m.

"Hello, Dr. Bollinger's residence," she said.

"It's Paul Stanley." She recognized Busby's voice; it was without his usual teasing lilt.

"What is it, Busby? What's wrong?"

"There's been an incident. You need to come down here, to Southeast, immediately." He hung up.

She arrived at Southeast Missouri Hospital at 10:45 p.m., rushing into the lobby and up to the front desk. The receptionist must have recognized her as she immediately got on the PA system. "Paging Dr. Busby, Dr. Busby Bollinger. Front reception."

Gwendolyn stood in front of the emergency room door. She fingered her pearl necklace nervously. The door swung open, and Busby stepped forward, dressed in surgical scrubs, then paused.

"Clutching your pearls, I see."

"Is he . . . is he . . ."

"He's alive, Gwennie, but just barely. A massive stroke, as best we can tell. We've put him into a coma."

She could barely breathe. "May I see him?"

He came up to her and put a comforting hand on her arm, guiding her forward.

A storm of emotions greeted her as she walked through the door to his hospital room. He was pale, comatose, and hooked up to machines by tubes that looked like writhing snakes. She was so stunned that it took her by surprise when she noticed Maureen standing by the bedside. Both women looked at each other for a frozen moment. Then Maureen, with head bowed, walked swiftly out of the room.

Gwendolyn glanced at Busby. He shrugged. "It is her boss. She cares."

"I'm sure she does," she said dryly as she walked to the place by the bed where Maureen had just vacated. Paul Stanley looked gray but peaceful. She turned to Busby. "How did this happen?'

"He just fell to the ground and convulsed."

"Who found him?"

"Maureen."

"Maureen?"

Busby offered his familiar shrug, a noncommittal yes.

"It doesn't matter," she said. She put her hand on Paul Stanley's chest then pulled it away suddenly. "He's so cold," she said, her voice barely registering.

Busby was checking the monitor. "We've induced a coma. Everything's stable for now. He's on a ventilator, and his blood pressure is fairly steady. Better take advantage of it—it's probably the only time you'll see him under control."

"What does this mean, Busby? What does this really mean?"

He got serious. They had just done a CT scan of his brain—a technology that was newly available at the hospital. The results would reveal if it was a hemorrhagic stroke, a brain bleed caused by a broken blood vessel, which he suspected it was.

"What causes that?" she asked even though she was already overloaded with information.

"You know what we say about my cousin, how he epitomizes that old saying 'Rode hard and put up wet'?" He looked over at him. "Poor guy. I guess he rode too hard and finally reached a bridge too far."

Gwendolyn joined him in looking at Paul Stanley, quiet and supine with only the gurgling of the snakes erupting from his body. "I suppose this shouldn't be a shock, but I never thought it could be so, that he could be . . . like this."

She suddenly felt lost without an anchor. She missed Dixie.

Busby came around the bed and put his arm around her. "Why don't you get a coffee or a bite to eat? We won't know anything for at least another hour or two."

When Gwendolyn arrived in the visitors' lounge, she went to the hospitality counter and fixed herself a tea with sugar. As she turned around, she saw Maureen, sitting at a table, looking down at her coffee.

Maureen must have sensed Gwendolyn's arrival. Her eyes lifted from their downcast gaze and met Gwendolyn's. Maureen offered a faint smile. As if impelled by an unknown force, Gwendolyn walked over and sat down at her table. Cradling her teacup with her eyes and her hands, she eventually looked at the woman who had been in the middle of her marriage for what—a decade? More? It occurred to her that in all that time she had never confronted her, this woman who had violated the sanctity of her marriage.

Maureen looked at her with shy, curious eyes. Gwendolyn could see that she was pretty, with round, plump, rosy cheeks highlighting a perfectly oval face framed by brown, lustrous hair cut in bangs and punctuated by long eyelashes. She wore no makeup. She was young. In a flash, Gwendolyn knew she was not to blame.

"How old are you, Maureen?"

"Thirty-nine."

"You've been working for the doctor for a long time, haven't you?"

"Yes, ma'am, since right after I graduated from nursing school."

Gwendolyn could recognize a suggestion of an up-country accent. "You're from Bollinger County, aren't you?"

"Marble Hill, yes."

"I suppose the Bollinger doctors are very special to you."

"Yes, ma'am. It was always my dream to work for one of them. Dr. Ollie was our family doctor. He delivered me."

Too much, Gwendolyn thought. "You're the one who found him, weren't you?"

Maureen looked down. "Yes, ma'am."

"At your apartment?"

She hesitated. "Yes, ma'am."

"You're in love with him, aren't you?"

Tears swamped Maureen's eyes.

A wild, unfamiliar infusion of feeling welled up in Gwendolyn. "Aren't you?" she demanded.

"Yes, ma'am," Maureen said, barely audible.

"Stop calling me ma'am. You've been screwing my husband all this time, for Pete's sake."

Her voice had risen. They both glanced around. An older couple seated at a table in the corner was trying not to look at them.

Gwendolyn looked back at her, lowering her voice. "You obviously don't respect me."

"I . . . I don't know what to say."

"I'm sure you don't."

"I really don't understand it. I wasn't brought up that way. I just don't know . . ."

Gwendolyn looked at her floundering and softened. "Look, Maureen, I get it. My husband can be very charming."

"It's not that, no, not that; yes he is, but it's not that," she said, casting her eyes about, searching. Then, looking up, her eyes now pleading, she said, "Don't you know? He's so needy, like a little boy who needs love."

"I see you've fallen into that trap." It surprised Gwendolyn at how hard she sounded.

"He's sensitive. It puzzled me when I first saw that. He could be so masterful in the OR, and then he would come to my place after, needing comfort—"

"You mean sex."

She blushed and then continued, "He was almost in awe of what he could do in surgery, almost like he didn't really believe he could really pull it off. Sometimes, I'd think he was too sensitive for this world, and that's why he—"

"Was a lush?" As soon as she said this, she realized that Paul Stanley must have trusted this woman with his most vulnerable feelings in a way he had never done with her.

"You sound so cynical, Mrs. Bollinger."

"Do I? I never thought of myself that way." She took a reflective sip of her tea. *Good lord,* Gwendolyn thought, *this young woman feels about Paul Stanley the way I did in the beginning: a handsome hero, a redeemer, a lifeguard.*

She realized that she had been staring at Maureen, which she could see made her squirm. "We're probably not that different. We're both women with limited options." This sat in silence between them before she said, "You might as well call me Gwendolyn."

The door to the patient lounge opened and an orderly stood there. "Mrs. Bollinger?" he said, looking at both women with uncertainty.

Gwendolyn stood up. "I guess that would still be me." She followed the orderly out of the room.

In the hospital room, she found Paul Stanley as before—except there were three men in scrubs, one of them Busby, waiting for her.

"Mrs. Bollinger," said one of the doctors, who stepped forward holding out his hand.

She recognized him as Dr. Norris, head of surgery, someone who had been at odds with Paul Stanley in the past, reporting him for sanctions when he had shown up in the operating room with alcohol on his breath. This resulted in his privileges being suspended for a year at the hospital that his father had founded, something Paul Stanley never got over.

Gwendolyn was wary. Why was he here? Why were they all looking at her?

She looked at Busby. "What's this about?"

Paul Stanley appeared greyer than when she had seen him before. She could barely look at him. "Tell me, Busby."

"It's bad, Gwennie. We've confirmed he's had a massive stroke."

"How did this happen?" she implored, looking at all three of them.

The third doctor—the name embroidered on his white coat identified him as Dr. Blain—spoke up. "We've determined that a weakened blood vessel burst, leaking blood inside his brain."

"It's like a hemorrhage in the brain," Busby added.

This wasn't helpful. Again, she asked, "How did this happen? What caused it?"

"As you know, your husband had an alcohol problem," said Dr. Norris.

"Yes, I'm well aware of your diagnosis of my husband—"

"It's relevant, Mrs. Bollinger. Alcohol thins the blood, and that may be helpful for some medical situations but not a hemorrhagic stroke."

Dr. Blain asked, "Did your husband ever get treatment for his high blood pressure?"

Gwendolyn looked at Busby, who answered her with his usual shrug. She turned back to the nameless doctor. "I wouldn't know. He never talked about anything to do with his own medical condition."

Dr. Norris muttered, "Figures."

"Pardon me?" Gwendolyn said.

Busby stepped in, putting his hands on her shoulders, which calmed her; she realized she was trembling with emotion. "Gwennie, we don't think he's going to make it."

"Make it?"

Dr. Blain said, "His stroke is such that he will either stay in a coma until he dies or if he comes out of it, he will be in a permanent vegetative state, worst case, or best case, some debilitating state of brain and physical impairment."

Gwendolyn looked around, beseechingly. "Isn't there anything that you can do?"

Dr. Blain answered her. "We've ruled out a blood drain to relieve pressure on the brain due to his condition."

"His condition?" She looked at Busby, the wildness in her tone obvious.

Busby stepped forward in front of her. "I'll take it from here. Thanks for the consultation."

Dr. Norris walked out without a word. Dr. Blain paused as he passed Gwendolyn. "He was a fine doctor. His patients loved him."

They left Busby and Gwendolyn standing on each side of the bed, looking at each other across the comatose Paul Stanley. "You have a tough decision to make," he said.

She went over to a chair in the corner. "I need to sit down."

"Gwennie, let's face the truth. He can either die or live in some state that's not really alive."

"Is there a choice?"

"Yes."

"What?" She looked at Busby, hard. "How can that be?"

He came over and squatted down before her. "There is a choice. But only you can choose."

"I'm not sure I understand."

He got up and walked over to the machine, the one that was now Paul Stanley's lifeline.

"You see this?" He put his finger on a switch vividly marked in red. "All you have to do is turn this off. Or not. And a choice has been made."

"Oh my god, Busby. Isn't that—"

"It's a choice, that's what it is. Your father-in-law founded this hospital, and he's still the major stakeholder. Trust me, it's a choice. And only you can make it."

He walked to the door and turned to face her. "I don't envy you, my darlin' Gwennie, but know that you will always have my blessing." Then he left, closing the door.

She didn't know how long she sat there in the dark by her husband's side. It was the deepest part of the night, and it was just her, Paul Stanley, and gurgling hospital sounds. She looked at her watch—4 a.m. It must have been at least an hour or more since Busby left her. Her mind hadn't quieted. It wouldn't come to a point of clarity, however ragged that point would be.

What was she going to do? She tried to think of what Paul Stanley would want. She knew well that he wasn't a believer. His claim of being an atheist had always bothered her, but he had never wavered. He could make no religious objection to—what did they call it—a mercy killing? She looked at him. He seemed so peaceful, his body and face in repose. Everything was fuller, more fleshed out, but his face was still handsome. He had always professed a love of life. Everything was "the best ever." His favorite saying was, "When you have a colt in the field there is always hope." He always had a colt in the field.

Did he have a colt in the field now? The dour look on the doctors' faces said no.

The irony of her situation did not escape her. She might have even laughed out loud if it weren't for the fact that she was staring at an inescapable tragedy. She put her hand on his chest—she could feel its rhythmic rising and falling. This was the man who she thought, at sixty, she would be taking walks with through the woods behind their house on the hill, the one with whom she would share grandchildren. This was the man she once dreamed of, the man who incited those dreams when he showed up in her life, the man who had shattered so many of them. This was the man who she had finally found the courage to leave.

Out of the darkness came a memory. Paul Stanley had gone on a fishing trip with Busby, flying into a remote lake somewhere in

Canada's wilderness. When Busby returned, he was without Paul Stanley and shrugged off any inquiry about his whereabouts. "You know my cousin. I caught the biggest fish and that meant he had to go somewhere to lick his wounds."

When he did show up, a few days later, she naturally wanted to know where he had been. "I ran off with an Indian squaw, but I saw it wasn't going to work out, so I came home." Gwendolyn was pretty sure he was joking, but with Paul Stanley she couldn't always be sure. She must have thrown him a look because he said, "I learned something."

She paused while setting the table and turned to him. His expression was unusually solemn. "What's that?" she asked.

"My salvation was revealed in the wildness."

Gwendolyn cocked her head, "Don't you mean the wilderness?"

That's when he said something that she didn't understand: "Wandering in the wilderness, you can get lost. Discovering the wildness within, you can get found."

"Is that so?" She wasn't sure she succeeded in keeping the sarcasm out of her voice.

"The challenge is to then make peace with that wildness within."

She stared at him as he turned and left the room, claiming he was exhausted. He was often unfathomable to her but never so cryptic. Was this some life-changing epiphany? She couldn't figure out what he was talking about, but she never forgot it.

She sat with this in the darkness of the hospital room. From somewhere in the distance a tortured wail rended the quiet.

Wildness.

She had always associated that word with her husband, never with herself. She had come to this town as a young girl, from a disenfranchised family, and she had figured out how to groom her natural assets, figured out the territory and the rules of the game. She followed them beautifully and won the game.

But now, looking at the dormant figure of the man who had dominated her emotional life for some forty years, she felt it.

Wildness.

How did this happen? How did that perfect dream that bloomed so beautifully within her when she first saw Paul Stanley driving down Broadway, looking so dashing in his Army uniform, how did it come to this? Was she such a fool to believe in her own invincibility that she only had to be the perfect wife, the perfect mother, and the dream would come true? How did it come to this moment when she was actually facing the possibility of killing her husband?

She walked over to the ventilator and put her right index finger on the red switch. She felt the wildness within her, but it was a strange, unnatural feeling, so unexpected, so grotesque, she didn't know what to do with it. The choice was hers. With that realization, a sense of solitude overwhelmed her.

2016

23

La Commedia è Finita

Her eyes fluttered open. A momentary terror. *Where am I?* At first she thought it was a dream but quickly realized that she hadn't been dreaming—or at least remembering them—for years. All was darkness. *Am I dead? Is this what it's like? Nothing?*

Light flooded into the room, briefly blinding her. A nurse had pulled back the curtains, revealing a bright spring day. She walked over and held Gwendolyn's slackened wrist to take her pulse.

"How are you today, Mrs. Bollinger?" she asked, smiling.

Oh yes. Here I am. In a hospital. And, irony of ironies, still at the mercy of nurses.

She chuckled at the thought. "As my doctor said, for my age I'm doing pretty darn good."

She liked this one—Nancy?—and all of the ones that had cared for her, actually. Maybe they were turning out a less voracious class of nurses these days. Or probably, more like it, she had been wrong in the bias she had developed over the years.

"I've got a surprise for you," Nancy said as she plumped up her pillow.

"Don't you know it's dangerous to surprise a ninety-six-year-old woman?"

Nancy revealed that Oliver had flown in from the East Coast, which prompted Gwendolyn to insist on a "complete makeover."

"Sorry, Mrs. Bollinger, you've got a fractured hip. There's only so much we can do."

"Well, do your best. At least some lipstick and hairspray. I don't want to scare my son. He's quite sensitive."

When Oliver opened the door, he was greeted with the sight of Dixie sitting next to his mother's bed, holding her hand. She immediately jumped up, surprisingly agile for a woman of ninety, tottered over on her high heels, and gave him a big hug.

"You look great, Aunt Dixie," he said.

"I should. It's cost me a small fortune."

"I was sorry to hear about Uncle Busby."

"Oh, that's okay. For an old fool, he had a good run. And now, I get to play the role I've waited all my life for."

"What's that?"

"The merry widow!" She snapped her fingers over her head like a flamenco dancer then leaned in and spoke intimately, "I'm so glad you're here, darling. You're who she needs. There's only so much these doctors can do at this point. Come by and see your old auntie before you take off, promise?"

"Of course, I will."

"We'll have tea and cookies. Sorry, no booze. Dixie's still riding the wagon." She turned to leave then leaned into Oliver. "Be sure and ask her about Eddie. She needs to talk." Then she swept back to Gwendolyn and blew a kiss. "Last two bitches standing!"

"If you can call this standing," Gwendolyn retorted.

Dixie left the room as Oliver walked over to the bed. He was holding a bouquet of mauve peonies.

"Those look familiar," she said after he settled into a chair beside her bed.

"I stopped by your garden and cut them."

"Those damned peonies," she said, but without any real malice.

"Why would you say such a thing? They were your prizes."

"And they damn near killed me. Probably will."

"I'll need some more color on that."

"I was in the garden weeding around the peonies when I stood up from my bench, maybe too fast, felt lightheaded, then fell. I rolled down a swale. I couldn't get up. The groundskeepers from the assisted living home found me. Turns out I broke my hip." She looked at Oliver. "You know what that means, don't you?"

"The beginning of the end?"

"I always suspected you were the smartest one. So, you obviously know what happens when an old woman breaks a hip. It means she'd better get her affairs in order and confess her lifetime of sin."

"You look very much alive to me."

"It's no good, honey. I looked in the mirror this morning and said out loud, 'This can't be accurate.'"

"You're funny. I never knew you were."

"I was never a cheap date. Never one to give it up too easily."

She chuckled in recognition of her newfound wit then fell into a silence, her eyes closing. "You know, nothing's working anymore except my mind, but that's feeling more and more like a curse."

"Oh, Mother," he said, choking emotion

"Come on, Oliver, you know you can't repair an old doll that's broken."

"You don't look broken to me."

"I put lipstick on for you, but don't let that fool you. Doctors are pretty clear. It's not just the hip but something about a blow to the kidneys—never my strong point—causing them to fail. They must be right. Everything's fading, getting muddled, receding."

"Are you sure? How do you know this is . . . this is . . ."

"Trail's end? You can say it, honey. It's okay." She shut her eyes for a long inward moment. "Oh, I don't know how I know, I just know. I always loved movies, loved to read. Novels, historical fiction, biographies. I liked getting carried away into other people's lives, imagining how mine might have been, you know, if circumstances were different. But now, lately, I have no energy for any of that, no interest. These days I spend my time in memories, one memory from childhood bumping gently into another from college, to another from living on the farm. They all intertwine easily, creating a nest of memory, a comfortable place to burrow."

A few moments passed, then a smile broke across her face. It was not the brilliant smile of her younger years but one that showed a gentle melancholy. "I no longer dream, I only remember."

Oliver looked away, obviously fighting with himself.

"Never mind all that," Gwendolyn said. "There're a couple of things I want you to know before I go."

"Where're you going?"

"Don't be a smart-ass, Oliver."

"Language, please!" Oliver exclaimed in mock horror. They both laughed at the shared reference to Miss Belle.

"Being so careful to not curse all of my life was a mistake. A lot of good it did me."

Oliver moved closer and put his hand on her mottled hand. "What is it you want to tell me?"

"What's that?"

"You said you had some things you wanted to tell me."

"Oh. I did, didn't I? Let me get my thoughts together." She closed her eyes where tears eddied at the corners.

"Mother, I never realized you indulged in crying," he said.

She blinked at her tears. "What do you mean?"

"In sixty-seven years on this planet, I've only seen you cry once."

"And when was that, pray tell?"

"I was probably eight and we were living in that old house in town. You were in the kitchen, standing at the sink, cutting onions. I saw your back lurch and your body stiffen, then I heard a mere whimper. I rushed over and saw you clenching your hand. It was gushing a fountain of blood. Tears were silently gliding down your cheeks."

"For Pete's sake, I was cutting onions."

"What was most shocking to me wasn't the blood but that you were crying and not making a sound—and the odd fact that you were wearing pearls in the kitchen."

"Oh, there have been tears. I know I had a reputation, but there have been plenty of tears. I always thought it best to keep them to myself."

"Suffering in silence—definitely your thing. Sometimes, I hate Dad for all the heartache he caused you."

"Oliver, your father was a complicated man; everyone said so." She looked away as if she was studying the dogwood tree smothered in tousled pink blossoms outside her window. It was spring, dogwood season, always her favorite time of year. She looked back at him. "I know you always had your troubles with your father."

"I was a disappointment to him. I know he really wanted another son, one who actually liked to shoot ducks and wasn't afraid of a football being hurled at his face."

Without looking at him and without hesitation, she said, "I had an abortion."

Oliver's head jerked back. "What did you say?"

"I was going to leave him. I'd had it with his ways, his greedy need for other women. He got me pregnant, and I knew it was his way of owning me like one of his broodmares."

"Or getting that son he always wanted?"

"Probably that, too, in truth. And don't think I haven't wondered about it, who that little boy would have been."

"An all-state quarterback, no doubt."

She looked at him, his cloudy face distorted as it tried to manage all of the feelings she knew must be crashing into each other. "Oh, honey, please, your dad loved you. He just never knew how to show it. You were confusing to him, but you should know you fascinated him. You gave him the challenge he relished. He called you his prodigal son."

"Right. The one who really never came back, the one who drove him back to drink."

"Oh dear." She grimaced.

"What is it, Mother, what's wrong?"

"You've stumbled into one of my biggest regrets. Saying that to you that Christmas, the part about you causing your father to drink by coming out. That was an awful, selfish thing for me to say. How could I ever not want you to be you?"

"It's okay. I survived."

"I've had to adjust to a lot of changes in my life, and I haven't always been good at it."

"But you tried, Mother. I always respected you for that."

A smile broke across her face, so genuine, so easily felt. "I'm so happy for you, Oliver, so glad you found someone to share your life with. Keith is a lovely man, and you make a beautiful family. I'm grateful I got to know him. But why the hell did you name your twins Paul and Stanley?"

"Just to piss you off, maybe?"

She chuckled then fell into a woeful momentary silence. "I was so ruled by fear. I think I always was, especially, when it came to your father."

He gave her the space and then asked, "Why didn't you leave him?"

She looked out toward what seemed like an abyss, her eyes becoming cloudy, watery, like a sky before a rainstorm.

"I never understood it," Oliver persisted. "Your sacrifice was a benefit to us. It kept us together in a kind of dreamscape, but still . . . what about you?"

"What about me?" Her eyes flashed in defiance.

"Didn't you ever want anything different for yourself? A chance at a different life?"

She looked off into the haze of the flowering dogwoods. "It was so different in my time. You couldn't possibly understand."

"So that's your excuse? You were entrapped by some silly social convention?"

She considered responding to Oliver's angry sarcasm, making an argument of how so many women of her era, no matter their privilege, were hobbled by their lack of options. She took a deep breath, realizing Oliver's emotional response came from not understanding why she had made the choices she did regarding her marriage.

"My life became about your father," she said. "Everything became about him. Most of my life I thought, *I didn't choose this!* But I know, I now know that was a lie. I chose it. It was my life, and I had to live it. He was capable of doing some terrible things. But there were other times. Life with Paul Stanley Bollinger was never dull."

She paused, looking back into a history that was hers alone. "All I ever wanted to be was a good wife."

Oliver started to say something but stopped when he saw her expression. Her eyes were blinking rapidly, her upper lip was twitching.

Gwendolyn spoke, her voice barely perceptible. "Your father was always in pain, always, 'till the end, in emotional pain. He never could escape it, not even with alcohol; he couldn't even name it. I once had a chance to end his pain, to end it for him once and for all." She stopped and saw Oliver gaping at her in astonishment. "Yes, I could have—how do you say it—pulled the plug. I could have done that in the hospital after his massive stroke. But I didn't. I don't know why, but I couldn't do it."

Oliver took this in. "It was hard seeing him at the end. That feeding tube. Eight years after the stroke, he had no life. And neither did you."

"It was awful. He hated that thing and then one day, he found the strength from somewhere to rip it out."

"Oh my god, I didn't know."

"He did that. Five days before he died. Right in front of me. His eyes were glaring. I had the thought, *He's furious at me for not flipping the switch that night in the hospital. So he's going to do what I couldn't."*

"You can't take that on, Mother. You can't."

Gwendolyn came back into focus as some private amusement lifted her face. "You know what his last words were? On that last day, he was drifting in and out of a coma. He hadn't said anything for days and then he looked at me and he said, *'La commedia è finita.'*"

"I remember that one. The comedy is finished. From that opera he used to sing late at night like a drunken tenor, howling at the moon."

She nodded in remembrance and then fell back into silence.

"There's more," Gwendolyn finally said with solemnity.

"Another confession? You know I'm not a priest, don't you?"

"Very funny." Another silence, gathering strength. "It's about Eddie."

"What about Eddie?"

She closed her eyes and turned away from him. "I might as well say it. I'm responsible for Eddie's death."

"What does that mean?"

"I murdered the little fucker."

They both stared at each other for a dense moment and then in unison, burst out laughing.

"I'm glad to see you aren't exactly devastated by this revelation," she said, her laughter now sputtering into a hacking cough.

"Maybe I would've been if you'd told me differently. I suppose I'm most upset we'll have to stop speculating about how Eddie died. What will we talk about at Christmas dinner?"

"Oh, you can still do that. I prefer you not speak of this. Even if you do, do you really think anyone will believe that Gwendolyn Bollinger would be capable of murdering a monkey in cold blood?"

"Why did you do it?"

"We had a complicated relationship."

"You seem to have a thing for those."

"I already told you—"

"I know, don't be a smart-ass."

"What I'm about to tell you is serious."

Her expression, composed and far-seeing, conveyed that this was so. Oliver nodded.

"You knew him. He was mean and sneaky and smelled awful. But none of that mattered to me in the end. He trusted me. I was the only one he did. He was all alone in the world, except for me. I think I must have grown to see him like some hindered child who wouldn't survive without me."

She faltered, taken by thoughts that weren't shared.

Oliver waited a moment and then said, "Tell me what happened."

"After Duke died and Opaldine needed to move back up-country to be with her children, I was faced with what to do with him. By this time, he was so old, so feeble . . ." Her words desiccated into silence.

"Go on, Mother."

"I smothered him with a pillow." Her eyes flashed. "I did that." And then, "He was old and weak and barely protested. At the end, before I did it, he looked up at me with those sad, almost human eyes, and that's when I finally understood. He had been my friend, and strange as it sounds, even my confidant, and I knew he deserved to be freed from this caged life that he had never asked for. He didn't put up any struggle. After I pulled the pillow away, I looked at his small, frail body. He was so still. It was so unlike the Eddie we all knew." Her eyes squeezed shut, like she was trying to hold back the flood. "I finally did it. He was free."

Oliver looked at his mother, wetness pooling in the deep wrinkles around her clenched eyes.

Then tears, undeclared and sudden, swamped him, and he said, "I've always connected with you through your pain."

He waited.

Her eyes blinked open. "Goodness, Oliver, you know that's no way to live, don't you?"

He couldn't answer her, although he knew she had said something true.

After a minute, he took in a big gulp of breath and then slowly released it with a smile of his own. "You know, when Gilda and Franny and I are together, we end up talking about our childhood. We mostly laugh. I'm sure none of us have forgotten it—the manic, all-night alcohol binges; the scratchy opera records keeping us up at night; being awakened in the dawn with gunshots at the trees at the edge of the lawn as Dad was protecting us from the zombie invaders that his bourbon-soaked mind had conjured."

Gwendolyn softly chuckled. "Oh, yes, there was that."

"But the weird thing is we never talk about any of those things. We talk about the horses, the Sunday rides to the back of the farm, how privileged we felt living up on the top of the hill with a swimming pool in the backyard. We laugh about Eddie. We laugh a lot about Eddie. We talk about what a character Dad was, how smart he was, how tenderhearted he could be at times even though he had a hard time showing it."

"Well, it seems like you all found a way to survive the trauma of all that." She said it with a knowing smile.

"Despite it all, I think we felt special in our own small world."

Gwendolyn looked at him, softly. "Oh, Oliver, don't you know? There was nothing really special about our family. The only thing special was that we had a monkey and we named him Eddie."

She closed her eyes. Oliver felt somehow deeply comforted by accepting the simple truth of that statement. He put his hand over her hand that looked ancient with its prominent blue veins.

They remained like that, in a numinous silence for uncharted time.

Her eyes remained closed and eventually, a smile, a lovely smile, softened the wrinkles of her face.

She was watching Eddie in her garden dancing, full of madcap joy. Like a capuchin pied piper, he began dancing toward the dense woods nearby. When he arrived at the veil of the inscrutable woods, he turned to her and, in a gesture that could only be found in a dream, waved for her to follow him.

Acknowledgments

Writing a novel is an act of faith (some may say hubris) as the author is spending uncounted hours spinning words, diving into characters who were once strangers, then deeply known. And all of this effort is made without any assurance that it would find a willing audience.

Since you've gotten to this point, at least I know you've agreed to share this journey with the Bollinger family, and hopefully it hasn't squandered your precious time. I am most grateful.

My journey to publication has been a long one and I haven't done it alone. I must first thank my original editors, Kara Kelley and Nicholas Fuhrmann, who helped me to first shape my ramblings into something coherent as well as adding much needed encouragement to sally forth.

Next came my battalion of beta readers, the all-important first eyes on the story. I'm so grateful to Valerie Friedman, Ann Brown, Richard Dent, Betsy Johnsmiller, Ann Brode, Rendy Freedman, Barry Miller, Joni Tickel, Jennifer Freed, Mary Kay Place, Georgeanne Syler, and Madeline Warren. I extend a special thanks to Neil Koenigsberg, whose incisive review and early encouragement was generative; as well as to Marianne Partridge, whose editorial feedback improved the story significantly.

I'm very thankful to the pros at Koehler Books who have facilitated the birth of *Gwendolyn and Eddie*. My initial thanks goes to Greg Fields, the acquisitions editor, who plucked my humble novel out of the pile. Joe Coccaro's editing and Lauren Sheldon's design work made everything shine. And cheers to the boss, John Koehler, whose innovative model of publishing regards the writer.

I give a special shout out to my stellar siblings—Christy Montgomery, Jan Seabaugh, and William Seabaugh—who gave me the grace to write this book so close to home.

And finally, my gratitude overflows for Michael Morgan and George, the Schnauzer. My life is made rich and fruitful by their faithful love and support.

◈ ◈ ◈

Book Clubs can receive a discount. The author may be available for Zoom-ins for club meetings. A discussion guide is available. To learn more, visit: michaelseabaughbooks.com/book-club/

www.ingramcontent.com/pod-product-compliance
Lightning Source LLC
LaVergne TN
LVHW041906070526
838199LV00051BA/2521